McAllister and His Double

Arthur Cheney Train

McAllister and His Double

ISBN: 978-1-64799-009-1

CONTENTS

MCALLISTER'S CHRISTMAS

I

McAllister was out of sorts. All the afternoon he had sat in the club window and watched the Christmas shoppers hurrying by with their bundles. He thanked God he had no brats to buy moo-cows and bow-wows for. The very nonchalance of these victims of a fate that had given them families irritated him. McAllister was a clubman, pure and simple; that is to say though neither simple nor pure, he was a clubman and nothing more. He had occupied the same seat by the same window during the greater part of his earthly existence, and they were the same seat and window that his father had filled before him. His select and exclusive circle called him "Chubby," and his five-and-forty years of terrapin and cocktails had given him a graceful rotundity of person that did not belie the name. They had also endowed him with a cheerful though somewhat florid countenance, and a permanent sense of well-being.

As the afternoon wore on and the pedestrians became fewer, McAllister sank deeper and deeper into gloom. The club was deserted. Everybody had gone out of town to spend Christmas with someone else, and the Winthrops, on whom he had counted for a certainty, had failed for some reason to invite him. He had waited confidently until the last minute, and now he was stranded, alone.

It began to snow softly, gently. McAllister threw himself disconsolately into a leathern armchair by the smouldering logs on the six-foot hearth. A servant in livery entered, pulled down the shades, and after touching a button that threw a subdued radiance over the room, withdrew noiselessly.

"Come back here, Peter!" growled McAllister. "Anybody in the club?"

"Only Mr. Tomlinson, sir."

McAllister swore under his breath.

"Yes, sir," replied Peter.

McAllister shot a quick glance at him.

"I didn't say anything. You may go."

This time Peter got almost to the door.

"Er—Peter; ask Mr. Tomlinson if he will dine with me."

Peter presently returned with the intelligence that Mr. Tomlinson would be delighted.

1

"Of course," grumbled McAllister to himself. "No one ever knew Tomlinson to refuse anything."

He ordered dinner, and then took up an evening paper in which an effort had been made to conceal the absence of news by summarizing the achievements of the past year. Staring head-lines invited his notice to

A YEAR OF PROGRESS

What the Tenement-House Commission Has Accomplished

FURTHER NEED OF PRISON REFORM

He threw down the paper in disgust. This reform made him sick. Tenements and prisons! Why were the papers always talking about tenements and prisons? They were a great deal better than the people who lived in them deserved. He recalled Wilkins, his valet, who had stolen his black pearl scarf-pin. It increased his ill-humor. Hang Wilkins! The thief was probably out by this time and wearing the pin. It had been a matter of jest among his friends that the servant had looked not unlike his master. McAllister winced at the thought.

"Dinner is served," said Peter.

An hour and a half later, Tomlinson and McAllister, having finished a sumptuous repast, stared stupidly at each other across their liqueurs. They were stuffed and bored. Tomlinson was a thin man who knew everything positively. McAllister hated him. He always felt when in his company like the woman who invariably answered her husband's remarks by "'Tain't so! It's just the opposite!" Tomlinson was trying to make conversation by repeating assertively what he had read in the evening press.

"Now, our prisons," he announced authoritatively. "Why, it is outrageous! The people are crowded in like cattle; the food is loathsome. It's a disgrace to a civilized city!"

This was the last straw to McAllister.

"Look here," he snapped back at Tomlinson, who shrank behind his cigar at the vehemence of the attack, "what do you know about it? I tell you it's all rot! It's all politics! Our tenements are all right, and so are our prisons. The law of supply and demand regulates the tenements; and who pays for the prisons, I'd like to know? We pay for 'em, and the scamps that rob us live in 'em for nothing. The Tombs is a great deal better than most second-class hotels on the Continent. I know! I had a valet once that— Oh, what's the use! I'd be glad to spend Christmas in no worse place. Reform! Stuff! Don't tell me!" He sank back purple in the face.

2

"Oh, of course—if you know!" Tomlinson hesitated politely, remembering that McAllister had signed for the dinner.

"Well, I do know," affirmed McAllister.

II

"No-el! No-el! No-el! No-el!" rang out the bells, as McAllister left the club at twelve o'clock and started down the avenue.

"No-el! No-el!" hummed McAllister. "Pretty old air!" he thought. He had almost forgotten that it was Christmas morning. As he felt his way gingerly over the stone sidewalks, the bells were ringing all around him. First one chime, then another. "No-el! No-el! No-el! No-el!" They ceased, leaving the melody floating on the moist night air.

The snow began to fall irregularly in patchy flakes, then gradually turned to rain. First a soft, wet mist, that dimmed the electric lights and shrouded the hotel windows; then a fine sprinkle; at last the chill rain of a winter's night. McAllister turned up his coat-collar and looked about for a cab. It was too late. He hurried hastily down the avenue. Soon a welcome sight met his eye—a coupé, a night-hawk, crawling slowly down the block, on the lookout, no doubt, for belated Christmas revellers. Without superfluous introduction McAllister made a dive for the door, shouted his address, and jumped inside. The driver, but half-roused from his lethargy, muttered something unintelligible and pulled in his horse. At the same moment the dark figure of a man swiftly emerged from a side street, ran up to the cab, opened the door, threw in a heavy object upon McAllister's feet, and followed it with himself.

"Let her go!" he cried, slamming the door. The driver, without hesitation, lashed his horse and started at a furious gallop down the slippery avenue.

Then for the first time the stranger perceived McAllister. There was a muttered curse, a gleam of steel as they flashed by a street-lamp, and the clubman felt the cold muzzle of a revolver against his cheek.

"Speak, and I'll blow yer head off!"

The cab swayed and swerved in all directions, and the driver retained his seat with difficulty. McAllister, clinging to the sides of the rocking vehicle, expected every moment to be either shot or thrown out and killed.

3

"Don't move!" hissed his companion.

McAllister tried with difficulty not to move.

Suddenly there came a shrill whistle, followed by the clatter of hoofs. A figure on horseback dashed by. The driver, endeavoring to rein in his now maddened beast, lost his balance and pitched overboard. There was a confusion of shouts, a blue flash, a loud report. The horse sprang into the air and fell, kicking, upon the pavement; the cab crashed upon its side; amid a shower of glass the door parted company with its hinges, and the stranger, placing his heel on McAllister's stomach, leaped quickly into the darkness. A moment later, having recovered a part of his scattered senses, our hero, thrusting himself through the shattered framework of the cab, staggered to his feet. He remembered dimly afterward having expected to create a mild sensation among the spectators by announcing, in response to their polite inquiries as to his safety, that he was "quite uninjured." Instead, however, the glare of a policeman's lantern was turned upon his dishevelled countenance, and a hoarse voice shouted:

"Throw up your hands!"

He threw them up. Like the Phœnix rising from its ashes, McAllister emerged from the débris which surrounded him. On either side of the cab he beheld a policeman with a levelled revolver. A mounted officer stood sentinel beside the smoking body of the horse.

"No tricks, now!" continued the voice. "Pull your feet out of that mess, and keep your hands up! Slip on the nippers, Tom. Better go through him here. They always manage to lose somethin' goin' over."

McAllister wondered where "Over" was. Before he could protest, he was unceremoniously seated upon the body of the dead horse and the officers were going rapidly through his clothes.

"Thought so!" muttered Tom, as he drew out of McAllister's coat-pocket a revolver and a jimmy. "Just as well to unballast 'em at the start." A black calico mask and a small bottle filled with a colorless liquid followed.

Tom drew a quick breath.

"So you're one of those, are ye?" he added with an oath.

The victim of this astounding adventure had not yet spoken. Now he stammered:

"Look here! Who do you think I am? This is all a mistake."

Tom did not deign to reply.

The officer on horseback had dismounted and was poking among the pieces of cab.

"What's this here?" he inquired, as he dragged a large bundle

4

covered with black cloth into the circle of light, and, untying a bit of cord, poured its contents upon the pavement. A glittering silver service rolled out upon the asphalt and reflected the glow of the lanterns.

"Gee! look at all the swag!" cried Tom. "I wonder where he melts it up."

Faintly at first, then nearer and nearer, came the harsh clanging of the "hurry up" wagon.

"Get up!" directed Tom, punctuating his order with mild kicks. Then, as the driver reined up the panting horses alongside, the officer grabbed his prisoner by the coat-collar and yanked him to his feet.

"Jump in," he said roughly.

"My God!" exclaimed our friend half-aloud, "where are they going to take me?"

"To the Tombs—for Christmas!" answered Tom.

III

McAllister, hatless, stumbled into the wagon and was thrust forcibly into a corner. Above the steady drum of the rain upon the waterproof cover he could hear the officers outside packing up the silverware and discussing their capture.

The hot japanned tin of the wagon-lamps smelled abominably. The heavy breathing of the horses, together with the sickening odor of rubber and damp straw, told him that this was no dream, but a frightful reality.

"He's a bad un!" came Tom's voice in tones of caution. "You can see his lay is the gentleman racket. Wait till he gets to the precinct and hear the steer he'll give the sergeant. He's a wise un, and don't you forget it!"

As the wagon started, the officers swung on to the steps behind. McAllister, crouching in the straw by the driver's seat, tried to understand what had happened. Apart from a few bruises and a cut on his forehead he had escaped injury, and, while considerably shaken up, was physically little the worse for his adventure. His head, however, ached badly. What he suffered from most was a new and strange sensation of helplessness. It was as if he had stepped into another world, in which he—McAllister, of the Colophon Club— did not belong and the language of which he did not speak. The ignominy of his position crushed him. Never again, should this disgrace become known, could he bring himself to enter the portals of the club. To be the hero of an exciting adventure with a burglar in a runaway cab was one matter, but to be arrested, haled to prison and locked up, was quite another. Once before the proper authorities, it would be simple enough to explain who and what he was, but the question that troubled him was how to avoid publicity. He remembered the bills in his pocket. Fortunately they were still there. In spite of the handcuffs, he wormed them out and surreptitiously held up the roll. The guard started visibly, and, turning away his head, allowed McAllister to thrust the wad into his hand.

"Can't I square this, somehow?" whispered our hero, hesitatingly.

The guard broke into a loud guffaw. "Get on to him!" he laughed. "He's at it already, Tom. Look at the dough he took out of his pants! You're right about his lay." He turned fiercely upon McAllister, who, dazed by this sudden turn of affairs, once more retreated into his corner.

The three officers counted the money ostentatiously by the light of a lantern.

"Eighty plunks! Thought we was cheap, didn't he?" remarked the guard scornfully. "No; eighty plunks won't square this job for you! It'll take nearer eight years. No more monkey business, now! You've struck the wrong combine!"

McAllister saw that he had been guilty of a terrible faux pas. Any explanation to these officers was clearly impossible. With an official it would be different. He had once met a police commissioner at dinner, and remembered that he had seemed really almost like a gentleman.

The wagon drew up at a police station, and presently McAllister found himself in a small room, at one end of which iron bars ran from floor to ceiling. A kerosene lamp cast a dim light over a weather-beaten desk, behind which, half-asleep, reclined an officer on night duty. A single other chair and four large octagonal stone receptacles were the only remaining furniture.

The man behind the desk opened his eyes, yawned, and stared stupidly at the officers. A clock directly overhead struck "one" with harsh, vibrant clang.

"Wot yer got?" inquired the sergeant.

"A second-story man," answered the guard.

"He took to a cab," explained Tom, "and him and his partner give us a fierce chase down the avenoo. O'Halloran shot the horse, and the cab was all knocked to hell. The other fellow clawed out before we could nab him. But we got this one all right."

6

"Hi, there, McCarthy!" shouted the sergeant to someone in the dim vast beyond. "Come and open up." He examined McAllister with a degree of interest. "Quite a swell guy!" he commented. "Them dress clothes must have been real pretty onc't."

McAllister stood with soaked and rumpled hair, hatless and collarless, his coat torn and splashed, and his shirt-bosom bloody and covered with mud. He wanted to cry, for the first time in thirty-five years.

"Wot's yer name?" asked the sergeant.

The prisoner remained stiffly mute. He would have suffered anything rather than disclose himself.

"Where do yer live?"

Still no answer. The sergeant gave vent to a grim laugh.

"Mum, eh?" He scribbled something in the blotter upon the desk before him. Then he raised his eyes and scrutinized McAllister's face. Suddenly he jumped to his feet.

"Well, of all the luck!" he exclaimed. "Do you know who you've caught? It's Fatty Welch!"

IV

How he had managed to live through the night that followed McAllister could never afterward understand. Locked in a cell, alone, to be sure, but with no light, he took off his dripping coat and threw himself on the wooden seat that served for a bed. It was about six inches too short. He lay there for a few moments, then got wearily to his feet and began to pace up and down the narrow cell. His legs and abdomen, which had been the recipients of so much attention, pained him severely. The occupant of the next apartment, awakened by our friend's arrival, began to show irritation. He ordered McAllister in no gentle language to abstain from exercise and go to sleep. A woman farther down the corridor commenced to moan drearily to herself. Evidently sleep had made her forget her sorrow, but now in the middle of the night it came back to her with redoubled force. Her groans racked McAllister's heart. A stir ran all along the cells—sounds of people tossing restlessly, curses, all the nameless noises of the jail. McAllister, fearful of bringing some new calamity upon his head, sat down. He had been shivering when he came in; now he reeked with perspiration. The air was fetid. The only ventilation came through the gratings of the door, and a huge stove just beyond his cell rendered the temperature almost unbearable. He began to throw off his garments one by one. Again he drew his knees to his chest and tried to sleep, but sleep was impossible. Never had McAllister in all his life known such wretchedness of body, such abject physical suffering. But his agony of mind was even more unbearable. Vague apprehensions of infectious disease floating in the nauseous air, or of possible pneumonia, unnerved and tortured him. Stretched on the floor he fell at length into a coma of exhaustion, in which he fancied that he was lying in a warm bath in the porcelain tub at home. In the room beyond he could see Frazier, his valet, laying out his pajamas and dressing-gown. There was a delicious odor of that violet perfume he always used. In a minute he would jump into bed. Then the valet suddenly came into the bath-room and began to pound his master on the back of the neck. For some reason he did not resent this. It seemed quite natural and proper. He merely put up his hand to ward off the blows, and found the keeper standing over him.

"Here's some breakfast," remarked that official. "Tom sent out and got it for ye. The city don't supply no aller carty." McAllister vaguely rubbed his eyes. The keeper shut and locked the door, leaving behind him on the seat a tin mug of scalding hot coffee and a half loaf of sour bread.

McAllister arose and felt his clothes. They were entirely dry, but had shrunk perceptibly. He was surprised to find that, save for the dizziness in his head, he felt not unlike himself. Moreover, he was most abominably hungry. He knelt down and smelt of the contents of the tin cup. It did not smell like coffee at all. It tasted like a combination of hot water, tea, and molasses. He waited until it had cooled, and drank it. The bread was not so bad. McAllister ate it all.

There was a good deal of noise in the cells now, and outside he could hear many feet coming and going. Occasionally a draught of cold air would flow in, and an officer would tramp down the corridor and remove one of the occupants of the row. His watch showed that it was already eight o'clock. He fumbled in his waistcoat-pocket and found a very warped and wrinkled cigar. His match-box supplied the necessary light, and "Chubby" McAllister began to smoke his after-breakfast Havana with appreciation.

"No smoking in the cells!" came the rough voice of the keeper. "Give us that cigar, Welch!"

McAllister started to his feet.

"Hand it over, now! Quick!"

The clubman passed his cherished comforter through the

bars, and the keeper, thrusting it, still lighted, into his own mouth, grinned at him, winked, and walked away.

"Merry Christmas, Fatty!" he remarked genially over his shoulder.

V

Half an hour later Tom and his "side partner" came to the cell-door. They were flushed with victory. Already the morning papers contained accounts of the pursuit and startling arrest of "Fatty Welch," the well-known crook, who was wanted in Pennsylvania and elsewhere on various charges. Altogether the officers were in a very genial frame of mind.

"Come along, Fatty," said Tom, helping the clubman into his bedraggled overcoat. "We're almost late for roll-call, as it is."

They left the cells and entered the station-house proper, where several officers with their prisoners were waiting.

"We'll take you down to Headquarters and make sure we've got you right," he continued. "I guess Sheridan'll know you fast enough when he sees you. Come on, boys!" He opened the door and led the way across the sidewalk to the patrol wagon, which stood backed against the curb.

It was a glorious winter's day. The sharp, frosty air stimulated the clubman's jaded senses and gave him new hope; he felt sure that at headquarters he would find some person to whom he could safely confide the secret of his identity. In about ten minutes the wagon stopped in a narrow street, before an inhospitable-looking building.

"Here's the old place," remarked one of the load cheerfully. "Looks just the same as ever. Mott Street's not a mite different. And to think I ain't been here in fifteen years!"

All clambered out, and each officer, selecting his prisoners, convoyed them down a flight of steps, through a door, several feet below the level of the sidewalk, and into a small, stuffy chamber full of men smoking and lounging. Most of these seemed to take a friendly interest in the clubman, a few accosting him by his now familiar alias.

Tom hurried McAllister along a dark corridor, out into a cold court-yard, across the cobblestones into another door, through a hall lighted only by a dim gas-jet, and then up a flight of winding stairs. McAllister's head whirled. Then quickly they were at the top, and in a huge, high-ceiled room crowded with men in civilian dress.

9

On one side, upon a platform, stood a nondescript row of prisoners, at whom the throng upon the floor gazed in silence. Above the heads of this file of motley individuals could be read the gold lettering upon the cabinet behind them—Rogues' Gallery. On the other side of the room, likewise upon a platform and behind a long desk, stood two officers in uniform, one of them an inspector, engaged in studying with the keenest attention the human exhibition opposite.

"Get up there, Fatty!"

Before he realized what had happened, McAllister was pushed upon the platform at the end of the line. His appearance created a little wave of excitement, which increased when his comrades of the wagon joined him. It was a peculiar scene. Twenty men standing up for inspection, some gazing unconcernedly before them, some glaring defiantly at their observers, and others grinning recognition at familiar faces. McAllister grew cold with fright. Several of the detectives pointed at him and nodded. Out of the silence the Inspector's voice came with the shock of thunder:

"Hey, there, you, Sanders, hold up your hand!"

A short man near the head of the line lifted his arm.

"Take off your hat."

The prisoner removed his head-gear with his other hand. The Inspector raised his voice and addressed the crowd of detectives, who turned with one accord to examine the subject of his discourse.

"That's Biff Sanders, con man and all-round thief. Served two terms up the river for grand larceny—last time an eight-year bit; that was nine years ago. Take a good look at him. I want you to remember his face. Put your hat on."

Sanders resumed his original position, his face expressing the most complete indifference.

A slight, good-looking young man now joined the Inspector and directed his attention to the prisoner next the clubman, the same being he who had remarked upon the familiar appearance of Mott Street.

"Hold up your hand!" ordered the Inspector. "You're Muggins, aren't you? Haven't been here in fifteen years, have you?"

The man smiled.

"You're right, Inspector," he said. "The last time was in '89."

"That's Muggins, burglar and sneak; served four terms here, and then got settled for life in Louisville for murder. Pardoned after he'd served four years. Look at him."

Thus the curious proceeding continued, each man in the line being inspected, recognized, and his record and character described by the Inspector to the assembled bureau of detectives. No other voice was heard save the harsh tones of some prisoner in reply.

Then the Inspector looked at McAllister.

"Welch, hold up your hand."

McAllister shuddered. If he refused, he knew not what might happen to him. He had heard of the horrors of the "Third Degree," and associated it with starvation, the rack, and all kinds of brutality. They might set upon him in a body. He might be mobbed, beaten, strangled. And yet, if he obeyed, would it not be a public admission that he was the mysterious and elusive Welch? Would it not bind the chains more firmly about him and render explanation all the more difficult?

"Do you hear? Hold up your hand, and be quick about it!"

His hand went up of its own accord.

The Inspector cleared his throat and rapped upon the railing.

"Take a good look at this man. He's Fatty Welch, one of the cleverest thieves in the country. Does a little of everything. Began as a valet to a clubman in this city. He got settled for stealing a valuable pin about three years ago, and served a short term up the river. Since then he's been all over. His game is to secure employment in fashionable houses as butler or servant and then get away with the jewelry. He's wanted for a big job down in Pennsylvania. Take a good look at him. When he gets out we don't want him around these parts. I'd like you precinct-men to remember him."

The detectives crowded near to get a close view of the interesting criminal. One or two of them made notes in memorandum books. The slender man had a hasty conference with the Inspector.

"The officer who has Welch, take him up to the gallery and then bring him down to the record room," directed the Inspector.

"Get down, Fatty!" commanded Tom. McAllister, stupefied with horror, embarrassment, and apprehension of the possibilities in store for him, stepped down and followed like a somnambulist. As they made their way to the elevator he could hear the strident voice of the Inspector beginning again:

"This is Pat Hogan, otherwise known as 'Paddy the Sneak,' and his side partner, Jim Hawkins, who goes under the name of James Hawkinson. His pals call him 'Supple Jim.' Two of the cleverest sneaks in the country. They branch out into strong arm work occasionally."

The elevator began to ascend.

"You seem kinder down," commented Tom. "I suppose you expect to get settled for quite a bit down to Philadelphia, eh? Well, don't talk unless you feel like it. Here we are!"

They got out upon an upper floor and crossed the hall. On

their left a matron was arranging rows of tiny chairs in a small school-room or nursery. At any other time the Lost Children's Room might have aroused a flicker of interest in McAllister, but he felt none whatever in it now. Tom opened a door and pushed the clubman gently into a small, low-ceiled chamber. Charts and diagrams of the human cranium hung on one wall, while a score of painted eyes, each of a different color, and each bearing a technical appellation and a number, stared from the other. Upon a small square platform, about eight inches in height, stood a half-clad Italian congealed with terror and expecting momentarily to receive a shock of electricity. The slender young man was rapidly measuring his hands and feet and calling out the various dimensions to an assistant, who recorded them upon a card. This accomplished, he ordered his victim down from the block, seated him unceremoniously in a chair, and with a pair of shining instruments gauged the depth of his skull from front to rear, its width between the cheekbones, and the length of the ears, describing all the while the other features in brief terms to his associate.

"Now off with you!" he ejaculated. "Here, lug this Greaser in and mug him."

The officer in the case haled the Italian, shrieking, into another room.

"Ah, Fatty!" remarked the slender man. "I trust you won't object to these little formalities? Take off that left shoe, if you please."

McAllister's soul had shrivelled within him. His powers of thought had been annihilated. Mechanically he removed the shoe in question and placed his foot upon the block. The young man quickly measured it.

"Now get up there and rest your hand on the board."

McAllister observed that the table bore the painted outline of a human hand. He did as he was told unquestioningly. The other measured his forefinger and the length of his forearm.

"All right. Now sit down and let me tickle your head for a moment."

The operator took the silver calipers which had just been used upon the Italian and ran them thoughtfully forward and back above the clubman's organs of hearing.

"By George, you've got a big head!" remarked the measurer. "Prominent, Roman nose. No. 4 eyes. Thank you. Just step into the next room, will you, and be mugged?"

McAllister drew on his shoe and followed Tom into the adjoining chamber of horrors.

"No tricks, now!" commented the officer in charge of the instrument.

Snap! went the camera.

"Turn sideways."

Snap!

"That's all."

The clubman staggered to his feet. He entirely failed to appreciate the extent of the indignity which had been practised upon him. It was hours before he realized that he had actually been measured and photographed as a criminal, and that, to his dying hour and beyond, these insignia of his shame would remain locked in the custody of the police.

"Where now?" he asked.

"Time to go over to court," answered Tom. "The wagon'll be waitin' for us. But first we'll drop in on Sheridan—record-room man, you know."

"Isn't there some way I can see the Commissioner?" inquired McAllister.

Tom burst into a roar of laughter.

"You have got a gall!" he commented, thumping his prisoner good-naturedly in the middle of the back. "The Commissioner! Ho-ho! That's a good one! I guess we'll have to make it the Warden. Come on, now, and quit yer joshin'."

Once more they entered the main room, where the detectives were congregated. The Inspector was still at it. There had been a big haul the night before. He intended running all the crooks out of town by New Year's Day. Tom shoved McAllister through the crush, across an adjoining room and finally into a tiny office. A young man with a genial countenance was sitting at a desk by the single window. He looked up as they crossed the threshold.

"Hello, Welch! How goes it? Let's see, how long is it since you were here?"

Somehow this quiet, gentlemanly fellow with his confident method of address, telling you just who you were, irritated McAllister to the explosive point.

"I'm not Welch!" he cried indignantly.

"Ha-ha!" laughed Mr. Sheridan. "Pray who are you?"

"You'll find out soon enough!" answered McAllister sullenly.

"Look here," remarked the other, "don't imagine you can bluff us. If you think you are not Welch, perhaps I can persuade you to change your mind."

He turned to an officer who stood in the doorway of a large vault.

"Bring 2,208, if you please."

The officer pulled out a drawer, removed a long linen envelope, and spread out its contents upon the desk. These were fifteen or twenty newspaper clippings, at least one of which was embellished with an evil-looking wood-cut.

"Let's see," continued Mr. Sheridan. "You began with a year up the river. Took a pearl pin from a man named McAllister. Then you turned several tricks in Chicago, St. Louis, Buffalo and Philadelphia, and got away with it every time. Have we got you right?"

McAllister ground his teeth.

"You have not!" said he.

"Look at yourself," continued the other. "There's your face. You can't deny it. I wonder the Inspector didn't have you measured and photographed the first time you were settled. Still, the picture's enough."

He handed the clubman a newspaper clipping containing a visage which undeniably resembled the features which the latter saw daily in his mirror. McAllister wearily shook his head.

"Well," said the expert, "of course you don't have to tell us anything unless you want to. We've got you right—that's enough."

He pushed the clippings back into the envelope, handed it to the officer, and turned away.

"Come on!" ordered Tom.

Once more McAllister and his mentor availed themselves of the only free transportation offered by the city government, that of the patrol wagon, and were soon deposited at the side entrance of the Jefferson Market police court. A group of curious idlers watched their descent and disappearance into what must have at all times seemed to them a concrete and ever-present temporal Avernus. The why and wherefore of these erratic trips were, of course, unknown to McAllister. Presumably he must be some rara avis of crime whose feet had been caught inadvertently in the limed twig set by the official fowler for more homely poultry. Fatty Welch, whoever he might be, apparently enjoyed the respect incident to success in any line of human endeavor. It seemed likewise that his presence was much desired in the sister city of Philadelphia, in which direction the clubman had a vague fear of being unwillingly transported. He did not, of course, realize that he was held primarily as a violator of the law of his own State, and hence must answer to the charge in the magistrate's court nearest the locus of his supposed offence.

Inside the station house Tom held a few moments' converse with one of its grizzled guardians, and then led our hero along a passage and opened a door. But here McAllister shrank back. It was his first sight of that great cosmopolitan institution, the police court.

14

Before him lay the scene of which he had so often read in the newspapers. The big room with its Gothic windows was filled to overflowing with every variety of the human species, who not only taxed the seating capacity of the benches to the utmost, but near the doors were packed into a solid, impenetrable mass. Upon a platform behind a desk a square-jawed man with chin-whiskers disposed rapidly of the file of defendants brought before him.

A long line of officers, each with one or more prisoners, stood upon the judge's left, and as fast as the business of one was concluded the next pushed forward. McAllister perceived that at best only a few moments could elapse before he was brought to face the charge against him, and that he must make up his mind quickly what course of action to pursue. As he stepped down from the doorway there was a perceptible flutter among the spectators. Several hungry-looking men with note-books opened them and poised their pencils expectantly.

Tom, having handed over McAllister to the temporary care of a brother officer, lost no time in locating his complainant, that is to say, the gentleman whose house our hero was charged with having burglariously entered. The two then sought out the clerk, who seemed to be holding a sort of little preliminary court of his own, and who, under the officer's instruction, drew up some formal document to which the complainant signed his name. McAllister was now brought before this official and briefly informed that anything he might say would be used against him at his trial. He was then interrogated, as before, in regard to his name, age, residence, and occupation, but with the same result. Indeed, no answers seemed to be expected under the circumstances, and the clerk, having written something upon the paper, waved them aside. Nothing, however, of these proceedings had been lost to the reporters, who escorted Tom and McAllister to the end of the line of officers, worrying the former for information as to his prisoner's origin and past performances. But Tom motioned them off with the papers which he held in his hand, bidding them await the final action of the magistrate. Nobody seemed particularly unfriendly; in fact, an air of general good-fellowship pervaded the entire routine going on around them. What impressed the clubman most was the persistence and omnipresence of the reporters.

"I must get time!" thought McAllister. "I must get time!"

One after another the victims of the varied delights of too much Christmas jubilation were disposed of. Fatty Welch was the only real "gun" that had been taken. He had the arena practically to himself. Now only one case intervened. He braced himself and tried to steady his nerves.

15

"Next! What's this?"

McAllister was thrust down below the bridge facing the bench, and Tom began hastily to describe the circumstances of the arrest.

"Fatty Welch?" interrupted the magistrate. "Oh, yes! I read about it in the morning papers. Chased off in a cab, didn't he? You shot the horse, and his partner got away? Wanted in Pennsylvania and Illinois, you say? That's enough." Then looking down at McAllister, who stood before him in bespattered dress suit and fragmentary linen, he inquired:

"Have you counsel?"

McAllister made no answer. If he proclaimed who he was and demanded an immediate hearing, the harpies of the press would fill the papers with full accounts of his episode. His incognito must be preserved at any cost. Whatever action he might decide to take, this was not the time and place; a better opportunity would undoubtedly present itself later in the day.

"You are charged with the crime of burglary," continued the Judge, "and it is further alleged that you are a fugitive from justice in two other States. What have you to say for yourself?"

McAllister sought the Judge's eye in vain.

"I have nothing to say," he replied faintly. There was a renewed scratching of pens.

The Judge conferred with the clerk for a moment.

"Any question of the prisoner's identity?" he asked.

"Oh, no," replied Tom conclusively. "The fact is, yer onner, we took him by accident, as you may say. We laid a plant for a feller doin' second-story work on the avenoo, and when we nabbed him, who should it be but Welch! Ye see, they wired on his description from Philadelphia a couple of weeks ago, but we couldn't find hide or hair of him in the city, and had about give up lookin'. Then, quite unexpected, we scoops him in. Here's his indentity," handing the Judge a soiled telegraph blank. "It's him, all right," he added with a grin.

The magistrate glanced at the form and at McAllister.

"Seems to fit," he commented. "Have you looked for the scar?"

Tom laughed.

"Sure! I seen it when he was gettin' his measurements took, down to headquarters."

"Turn around, Welch, and let's see your back," directed the magistrate.

The clubman turned around and displayed his collarless neck.

"There it is!" exclaimed Tom.

McAllister mechanically put his hand to his neck and turned

16

faint. He had had in his childhood an almost forgotten fall, and the scar was still there. He experienced a genuine thrill of horror.

"Well," continued the magistrate, "the prisoner is entitled to counsel, and, besides, I am sure that the complainant, Mr. Brown, has no desire to be delayed here on Christmas Day. I will set the hearing for ten o'clock to-morrow morning, at the Tombs police court. I shall be sitting there for Judge Mason the rest of the week, beginning to-morrow, and will take the case along with me. You might suggest to the Warden that it would be more convenient to send the prisoner down to the Tombs, so that there need be no delay."

The complainant bowed, and the officer at the bridge slapped McAllister not unkindly upon the back.

"You'll need a pretty good lawyer," he remarked with a wink.

"Next!" ordered the Judge.

In the patrol wagon McAllister had ample time for reflection. A motley collection of tramps, "disorderlies," and petty law-breakers filled the seats and crowded the aisle. They all talked and joked, swinging from side to side and clutching at one another for support with harsh outbursts of profanity, as they rattled down the deserted streets toward New York's Bastile. Staggering for a foot-hold, between four women of the town, McAllister was forced to breathe the fumes of alcohol, the odor of musk, and the aroma of foul linen. He no longer felt innocent. The sense of guilt was upon him. He seemed part and parcel of this load of miserable humanity.

The wagon clattered over the cobblestones of Elm Street, and whirling round, backed up to the door of the Tombs. The low, massive Egyptian structure, surrounded by a high stone wall, seemed like a gigantic mortuary vault waiting to receive the "civilly dead." Warden and keepers were ready for the prisoners, who were now unceremoniously bundled out and hustled inside. McAllister stood with the others in a small anteroom leading directly into the lowest tier. He could hear the ceaseless shuffling of feet and the subdued murmur of voices, rising and falling, but continuous, like the twittering of a multitude of birds, while through the bars came the fetid prison smell, with a new and disagreeable element—the odor of prison food.

"Keepin' your mouth shut?" remarked the deputy to McAllister, as he entered the words "Prisoner refuses to answer," and blotted them.

"We're rather crowded just now," he added apologetically. "I guess I'll send you to Murderer's Row. Holloa, there!" he called to someone above, "one for the first tier!"

17

A keeper seized the clubman by the arm, opened a door in the steel grating, and pushed him through. "Go 'long up!" he ordered.

McAllister started wearily up the stairs. At the top of the flight he came to another door, behind which stood another keeper. In the background marched in ceaseless procession an irregular file of men. In the gloom they looked like ghosts. Aimlessly they walked on, one behind the other, most of them with eyes downcast, wordless, taking that exercise of the body which the law prescribed.

McAllister entered The Den of Beasts.

"All right, Jimmy!" yelled the keeper to the deputy warden below. Then, turning to McAllister. "I'm goin' to put you in with Davidson. He's quiet, and won't bother you if you let him alone. Better give him whichever berth he feels like. Them double-decker cots is just as good on top as they is below."

McAllister followed the keeper down the narrow gangway that ran around the prison. In the stone corridor below a great iron stove glowed red-hot, and its fumes rose and mingled with the tainted air that floated out from every cell. Above him rose tier on tier, illuminated only by the gray light which filtered through a grimy window at one end of the prison. The arrangement of cells, the "bridges" that joined the tiers, and the murky atmosphere, heightened the resemblance to the "'tween decks" of an enormous slaver, bearing them all away to some distant port of servitude.

"Get up there, Jake! Here's a bunkie for you."

McAllister bent his head and entered. He was standing beside a two-story cot bed, in a compartment about six by eight feet square. A faint light came from a narrow, horizontal slit in the rear wall. A faucet with tin basin completed the contents of the room. On the top bunk lay a man's soiled coat and waistcoat, the feet of the owner being discernible below.

The keeper locked the door and departed, while the occupant of the berth, rolling lazily over, peered up at the new-comer; then he sprang from the cot.

"Mr. McAllister!" he whispered hoarsely.

It was Wilkins—the old Wilkins, in spite of a new light-brown beard.

For a few moments neither spoke.

"Sorry to see you 'ere, sir," said Wilkins at length, in his old respectful tones. "Won't you sit down, sir?"

McAllister seated himself upon the bed automatically.

"You here, Wilkins?" he managed to say.

Wilkins laughed rather bitterly.

"I've been in stir a good part of the time since I left you, sir; an' two weeks ago I pleaded guilty to larceny and was sentenced to

18

one year more. But I'm glad to see you lookin' so well, if you'll pardon me, sir."

"I'm sorry for you, Wilkins," the master managed to reply. "I hope my severity in that matter of the pin did not bring you to this!"

Wilkins hesitated for a moment.

"It ain't your fault, sir. I was born crooked, I fancy, sir. It's all right. You've got troubles of your own. Only—you'll excuse me, sir—I never suspected anything when I was in your service."

McAllister did not grasp the meaning of this remark; he only felt relief that Wilkins apparently bore him no ill-will. Very few of his friends would have followed up a theft of that sort. They expected their men to steal their pins.

"Mebbe I might 'elp you. Wot's the charge, sir?"

With his former valet as a sympathetic listener, McAllister poured out his whole story, omitting nothing, and, as he finished, leaned forward, searching eagerly the other's face.

"Now, what shall I do? What shall I do, Wilkins?"

The latter coughed deprecatingly.

"You'll pardon me, but that'll never go, sir! You'll have to get somethin' better than that, sir. The jury will never believe it."

McAllister sprang to his feet, in so doing knocking his head against the iron support of the upper cot.

"How dare you, Wilkins! What do you mean?"

"There, there, sir!" exclaimed the other. "Don't take on so. Of course I didn't mean you wouldn't tell the truth, sir. But don't you see, sir, hit isn't I as am goin' to listen to it? Shall I fetch you some water to wash your face, sir?" He turned on the faucet.

The clubman, yielding to the force of ancient habit, allowed Wilkins to let it run for him, and having washed his face and combed his hair, felt somewhat refreshed.

"That feels good," he remarked, rubbing his hands together.

It was obvious that so long as he remained in prison he would be either "Fatty Welch" or someone else equally depraved; and since he could not make anyone understand, it seemed his best plan to accept for the time, with equanimity, the personality that fate had thrust upon him.

"Well, Wilkins, we're in a tight place. But we'll do what we can to assist each other. If I get out first I'll help you, and vice versa. Now, what's the first thing to be done? You see, I've never been here before."

"That's the talk, sir," answered Wilkins. "Now, first, who's your lawyer?"

"Haven't any, yet."

"All depends on the lawyer," returned the valet judicially.

19

"Now, there's Carter, and Herlihy, and Kemp, all sharp fellows, but they're always after you for money, and then they're so clever that the jury is apt to distrust 'em. The best thing, I find, is to get the most respectable old solicitor you can—kind of genteel, 'family' variety, with the goodness just stickin' hout all hover 'im. 'E creates a hatmosphere of hinnocence, and that's wot you need. One as 'as white 'air and can talk about 'this boy 'ere' and can lay 'is 'and on yer shoulder and weep. That's the go, sir."

"I understand," said McAllister.

Under the guidance of his valet our hero secured writing materials and indicted a pitiful appeal to his family lawyer.

A gong rang; the squad of prisoners who had been exercising went back to their cells, and the keeper came and unlocked the door.

McAllister stepped out and fell into line. His tight clothes proved very uncomfortable as he strode round the tiers, and the absence of a collar—yes, that was really the most unpleasant feature. His neck was not much to boast of, therefore he always wore his shirts low and his collars high. Now, as he stumbled along, he was the object of considerable attention from his fellows.

At the end of an hour another gong sounded. In a moment the tiers were empty; fifty doors clanged to.

"Well, Wilkins?"

"Being as this is Sunday, sir, we 'ave a few hours' service. Church of England first, then City Mission. We're not hallowed to talk, but if you don't mind the 'owlin' you can snatch a wink o' sleep. Christmas dinner at twelve. Old Burridge, the trusty, was a-tellin' me as 'ow it's hexcellent, sir!"

McAllister looked at his watch in despair. It was only a quarter past ten. He had not been to church for fifteen years, but evidently he was in for it now. Following his former valet's example, he took off his shoes and stretched himself upon the cot.

On and on in never-varying tones dragged the service. The preacher held the key to the situation. His congregation could not escape; he had a full house, and he was bent on making the most of it.

The hands of McAllister's watch crept slowly round to five minutes before eleven.

When at last the preacher stopped, carefully folded his manuscript, and pronounced the benediction, a prolonged sigh of relief eddied through the Tombs. Men were waking on all sides; cots creaked; there was a general and contagious yawn.

Again the gong rang, and with it the smell of food floated up along the tiers. McAllister realized that he was hungry—not mildly, as he was at the club, but ravenous, as he had never been before. Presently the longed-for food came, borne by a "trusty" in new white uniform. Wilkins, who had been making a meagre toilet at the faucet, took in the dinner through the door—two tin plates piled high with turkey and chicken, flanked by heaps of potato and carrots, and one whole apple pie!

"Ha!" thought McAllister, "I was not so far wrong about this part of it!" The chicken was perhaps not of the variety known as "spring"; but neither master nor man noticed it as they feasted, sitting side by side upon the cot.

"Carrots!" philosophized McAllister, looking regretfully at his empty tin plate. "Now, I thought only horses ate carrots; and really, they're not bad at all. I should like some more. Er—Wilkins! Can we get some more carrots?"

Wilkins shook his head mournfully.

"Message for 34! Message for 34!"

A letter was thrust through the bars.

McAllister tore it open with feverish haste, and recognized the crabbed hand of old Mr. Potter.

2 East Seventy-First Street.

F. Welch, Esq.

Sir: The remarkable letter just delivered to me, signed by a name which you request me not to use in my reply, has received careful consideration. I telephoned to Mr. Mc——'s rooms, and was informed by his valet that that gentleman had gone to the country to visit friends over Christmas. I have therefore directed the messenger to collect from yourself his fee for delivering this answer. Yours, etc.,

Ebenezer Potter.

"That fool Frazier!" groaned McAllister. "How the devil could he have thought I had gone away?" Then he remembered that he had directed the valet to pack his bags and send them to the station, in anticipation of the Winthrops' invitation.

He was at his wits' end.

"How do you get bail, Wilkins?"

"You 'ave to find someone as owns real estate in the city, sir, to go on your bond. 'Ow much is it?"

"Five thousand dollars," replied McAllister.

"'Oly Moses!" ejaculated the valet. He regarded his former master with renewed interest.

21

But the dinner had wrought a change in that hitherto subdued individual. With a valet and running water he was beginning to feel his oats a little. He checked off mentally the names of his acquaintances. There was not one left in town.

He repressed a yawn, and looked at his watch. One o'clock. Just then the gong rang again.

"What in thunder is this, now?"

"Afternoon service, sir. City Mission from one to two-thirty."

"Ye gods!" ejaculated McAllister.

A band of young girls came and stood with their hymn-books along the opposite tier, while a Presbyterian clergyman took the place on the bridge recently vacated by his Episcopal brother. Prayers alternated with hymns until the sermon, which lasted sixty-five minutes.

McAllister, almost desperate, fretted and fumed until half past two, when the choir and missionary finally departed.

"Only a 'arf 'our, sir, an' we can get some more hexercise," said Wilkins encouragingly.

But McAllister did not want exercise. He swung to his feet, and peering disconsolately through the bars was suddenly confronted by an anæmic young woman holding an armful of flowers. Before he could efface himself she smiled sweetly at him.

"My poor man," she began confidently, "how sorry I am for you this beautiful Christmas Day! Please take some of these; they will brighten up your cell wonderfully; and they are so fragrant." She pushed a dozen carnations and asters through the bars.

McAllister, utterly dumfounded, took them.

"What is your name?" continued the maiden.

"Welch!" blurted out our bewildered friend.

There was a stifled snort from the bunk behind.

"Good-by, Welch. I know you are not really bad. Won't you shake hands with me?"

She thrust her hand through the bars, and McAllister gave it a perfunctory shake.

"Good-by," she murmured, and passed on.

"Lawd!" exploded Wilkins, rolling from side to side upon his cot. "O Lawd! O Lawd! O—" and he held his sides while McAllister stuck the carnations into the wash-basin.

The gong again, and once more that endless tramp along the hot tiers. The prison grew darker. Gas-jets were lighted here and there, and the air became more and more oppressive. With five o'clock came supper; then the long, weary night.

Next morning the valet seemed nervous and excited, eating little breakfast, and smiling from time to time vaguely to himself.

22

Having fumbled in his pocket, he at last pulled out a dirty pawn-ticket, which he held toward his master.

"'Ere, sir," he said with averted head. "It's for the pin. I'm sorry I took it."

McAllister's eyes were a little blurred as he mechanically received the card-board.

"Shake hands, Wilkins," was all he said.

A keeper came walking along the tier rattling the doors and telling those who were wanted in court to get ready.

"Good-by," said McAllister. "I'm sorry you felt obliged to plead guilty. I might have helped you if I'd only known. Why didn't you stand your trial?"

"I 'ad my reasons," replied the valet. "I wanted to get my case disposed of as quick as possible. You see, I'd been livin' in Philadelphia, and 'ad just come to New York when I was harrested. I didn't want 'em to find out who I was or where I come from, so I just gives the name of Davidson, and takes my dose."

"Well," said McAllister, "you're taking your own dose; I'm taking somebody else's. That hardly seems a fair deal—now does it, Wilkins? But, of course, you don't know but that I am Welch."

"Oh, yes, I do, sir!" returned the valet. "You won't never be punished for what he done."

"How do you know?" exclaimed McAllister, visions of a speedy release crowding into his mind. "And if you knew, why didn't you say so before? Why, you might have got me out. How do you know?" he repeated.

Wilkins looked around cautiously. The keeper was at the other end of the tier. Then he came close to McAllister and whispered:

"Because I'm Fatty Welch myself!"

VI

Downstairs, across the sunlit prison yard, past the spot where the hangings had taken place in the old days, up an enclosed staircase, a half turn, and the clubman was marched across the Bridge of Sighs. Most of the prisoners with him seemed in good spirits, but McAllister, who was oppressed with the foreboding of imminent peril, felt that he could no longer take any chances. His fatal resemblance to Fatty Welch, alias Wilkins, his former valet, the circumstances of his arrest, the scar on his neck, would seem to make conviction certain unless he followed one of two alternatives—

either that of disclosing Welch's identity or his own. He dismissed the former instantly. Now that he knew something of the real sufferings of men, his own life seemed contemptible. What mattered the laughter of his friends, or sarcastic paragraphs in the society columns of the papers? What did the fellows at the club know of the game of life and death going on around them? of the misery and vice to which they contributed? of the hopelessness of those wretched souls who had been crushed down by fate into the gutters of life? Determined to declare himself, he entered the court-room and tramped with the others to the rail.

There, to his amazement, sat old Mr. Potter beside the Judge. Tom and his partner stood at one side.

"Welch, step up here."

Mr. Potter nodded very slightly, and McAllister, taking the hint, stepped forward.

"Is this your prisoner, officer?"

"Shure, that's him, right enough," answered Tom.

"Discharged," said the magistrate.

Mr. Potter shook hands with his honor, who smiled good-humoredly and winked at McAllister.

"Now, Welch, try and behave yourself. I'll let you off this time, but if it happens again I won't answer for the consequences. Go home."

Mr. Potter whispered something to the baffled officers, who grinned sheepishly, and then, seizing McAllister's arm, led our astonished friend out of the court-room.

As they whirled uptown in the closed automobile which had been waiting for them around the corner, Mr. Potter explained that after sending the letter he had felt far from satisfied, and had bethought him of calling up Mrs. Winthrop on the telephone. Her polite surprise at the lawyer's inquiries had fully convinced him of his error, and after evading her questions with his usual caution, he had taken immediate steps for his client's release—steps which, by reason of the lateness of the hour, he could not communicate to the unhappy McAllister.

"What has become of the fugitive Welch," he ended, "remains a mystery. The police cannot imagine where he has hidden himself."

"I wonder," said McAllister dreamily.

It was just seven o'clock when McAllister, arrayed, as usual, in immaculate evening dress, sauntered into the club. Most of the men were back from their Christmas outing; half a dozen of them were engaged in ordering dinner.

"Hello, Chubby!" shouted someone. "Come and have a drink.

24

Had a pleasant Christmas? You were at the Winthrops', weren't you?"

"No," answered McAllister; "had to stay right in New York. Couldn't get away. Yes, I'll take a dry Martini—er, waiter, make that two Martinis. I want you all to have dinner with me. How would terrapin and canvas-back do? Fill it out to suit yourselves, while I just take a look at the Post."

He picked up a paper, glanced at the head-lines, threw it down with a sigh of relief, and lighted a cigarette. At the same moment two policemen in civilian dress were leaving McAllister's apartments, each having received at the hands of the impassive Frazier a bundle containing a silver-mounted revolver and a large bottle full of an unknown brown fluid.

McAllister's dinner was a great success. The boys all said afterward that they had never seen Chubby in such good form. Only one incident marred the serenity of the occasion, and that was a mere trifle. Charlie Bush had been staying over Christmas with an ex-Chairman of the Prison Reform Association, and being in a communicative mood insisted on talking about it.

"Only fancy," he remarked, as he took a gulp of champagne, "he says the prisons of the city are in an abominable condition—that they're a disgrace to a civilized community."

Tomlinson paused in lifting his glass. He remembered his host's opinion, expressed two nights before and desired to show his appreciation of an excellent meal.

"That's all rot!" he interrupted a little thickly. "'S all politics. The Tombs is a lot better than most second-class hotels on the Continent. Our prisons are all right, I tell you!" His eyes swept the circle militantly.

"Look here, Tomlinson," remarked McAllister sternly, "don't be so sure. What do you know about it?"

25

THE EXTRAORDINARY ADVENTURE OF
THE BARON DE VILLE

I

"I want you," said Barney Conville, tapping Mr. McAllister lightly upon the shoulder.

The gentleman addressed turned sharply, letting fall his monocle. He certainly had never seen the man before in his life—was sure of it, even during that unfortunate experience the year before, which he had so far successfully concealed from his friends. No, it was simply a case of mistaken identity; and yet the fellow—confound him!—didn't look like a chap that often was mistaken.

"Come, come, Fatty; no use balkin'. Come along quiet," continued Barney, with his most persuasive smile. He was a smartly built fellow with a black mustache and an unswerving eye, about two-thirds the size of McAllister, whom he had addressed so familiarly.

"Fatty!" McAllister, bon vivant, clubman, prince of good fellows, started at the word and stared tensely. What infernal luck! That same regrettable resemblance that had landed him in the Tombs over Christmas was again bobbing up to render him miserable. He wished, as he had wished a thousand times, that Wilkins had been sentenced to twenty years instead of one. He had evidently been discharged from prison and was at his old tricks again, with the result that once more his employer was playing the part of Dromio. McAllister had succeeded by judicious bribery and the greatest care in preserving inviolate the history of his incarceration. Had this not been the case one word now to the determined individual with the icy eye would have set the matter straight, but he could not bear to divulge the secret of those horrible thirty-six hours which he, under the name of his burglarious valet, had spent locked in a cell. Maybe he could show the detective he was mistaken without going into that lamentable history. But of course McAllister proceeded by exactly the wrong method.

"Oh," he laughed nonchalantly, "there it is again! You've got me confused with Fatty Welch. We do look alike, to be sure." He put up his monocle and smiled reassuringly, as if his simple statement would entirely settle the matter.

But Barney only winked sarcastically.

26

"You show yourself quite familiar with the name of the gentleman I'm lookin' for."

McAllister saw that he had made a mistake.

"No more foolin', now," continued Barney. "Will you come as you are, or with the nippers?"

The clubman bit his lip with annoyance.

"Look here, hang you!" he exclaimed angrily, dropping his valise, "I'm Mr. McAllister of the Colophon Club. I'm on my way to dine with friends in the country. I've got to take this train. Listen! they're shouting 'All aboard' now. I know who you're after. You've got us mixed. Your man's a professional crook. I can prove my identity to you inside of five minutes, only I haven't time here. Just jump on the train with me, and if you're not convinced by the time we reach 125th Street I'll get off and come back with you."

"My, but you're gamer than ever, Fatty," retorted Barney with admiration. Thoughts of picking up hitherto unsuspected clews flitted through his mind. He had his man "pinched," why not play him awhile? It seemed not a half bad idea to the Central Office man.

"Well, I'll humor you this once. Step aboard. No funny business, now. I've got my smoke wagon right here. Remember, you're under arrest."

They swung aboard just as the train started. As McAllister sank into his seat in the parlor car with Barney beside him he recognized Joe Wainwright directly opposite. Here was an easy chance to prove his identity, and he was just about to lean over and pour forth his sorrows to his friend when he realized with fresh humiliation that should he seize this opportunity to explain the present situation, the whole wretched story of his Christmas in the Tombs would probably be divulged. He would be the laughing-stock of the club, and the fellows would never let him hear the last of it. He hesitated, but Wainwright took the initiative.

"How d'y', Chubby?" said he, getting up and coming over. "On your way to Blair's?"

"Yes. Almost missed the confounded train," replied McAllister, struggling for small talk.

"Who's your friend?" continued the irrepressible Wainwright. "Kind o' think I know him. Foreigner, ain't he? Think he was at Newport last summer."

"Er—ye—es. Baron de Ville. Picked him up at the club—friend of Pierrepont's. Takin' him out to Blair's—so hospitable, don'cher know." He stammered horribly, for he found himself sinking deeper and deeper.

"Like to meet him," remarked Wainwright. "Like all these foreign fellers."

McAllister groaned. He certainly was in for it now. The 125th Street idea would have to be abandoned.

"Er—Baron"—he strangled over the name—"Baron, I want to present Mr. Joseph Wainwright. He thinks he's met you in Paris." Our friend accompanied this with a pronounced wink.

"Glad to meet you, Baron," said Wainwright, grasping the detective's hand with effusion. "Newport, I think it was."

The "Baron" bowed. This was a new complication, but it was all in the day's work. Of course, the whole thing was plain enough. Fatty Welch was "working" some swell guys who thought he was a real high-roller. Maybe he was going to pull off some kind of a job that very evening. Perhaps this big chap in the swagger flannels was one of the gang. Barney was thinking hard. Well, he'd take the tip and play the hand out.

"It ees a peutifool efening," said the Baron.

The train plunged into the tunnel.

"Look here," hissed McAllister in Barney's ear. "You've got to stick this thing out, now, or I'll be the butt of the town. Remember, we're going to the Blairs at Scarsdale. You're the particular friend of a man named Pierrepont—fellow with a glass eye who owns a castle somewhere in France. . . . Are you satisfied yet?" he added indignantly.

"I'm satisfied you're Fatty Welch," Barney replied. "I ain't on to your game, I admit. Still, I can do the Baron act awhile if it amuses you any."

The train emerged from the tunnel, and McAllister observed that there were other friends of his on the car, bound evidently for the same destination. Well, anything was better than having that confounded story about the Tombs get around. He had often thought that if it ever did he would go abroad to live. He couldn't stand ridicule. His dignity was his chief asset. Nothing so effectually, as McAllister well knew, conceals the absence of brains. But could he ever in the wide, wide world work off the detective as a baron? Well, if he failed, he could explain the situation on the basis of a practical joke and save his face in that way. Just at present the Baron was getting along famously with Wainwright. McAllister hoped he wouldn't overdo it. One thing, thank Heaven, he remembered—Wainwright had flunked his French disgracefully at college and probably wouldn't dare venture it under the circumstances. There was still a chance that he might convince his captor of his mistake before they reached Scarsdale, and on the strength of this he proposed a cigar. But Wainwright had frozen hard to his Baron and accepted for himself with alacrity, even suggesting a drink on his own account. McAllister's heart failed him

28

as he thought of having to present the detective to Mrs. Blair and her fashionable guests and—by George, the fellow hadn't got a dress-suit! They never could get over that. It was bad enough to lug in a stranger—a "copper"—and palm him off as the distinguished friend of a friend, but a feller without any evening clothes— impossible! McAllister wanted to shoot him. Was ever a chap so tied up? And now if the feller wasn't talking about Paris! Paris! He'd make some awful break, and then— Oh, curse the luck, anyway!

Then it was that McAllister resolved to do something desperate.

II

"I'm perfectly delighted to have the Baron. Why didn't you bring Pierrepont, too? How d'y' do, Baron? Let me present you to my husband. Gordon—Baron de Ville. I'll put you and Mr. McAllister together. We're just a little crowded. You've hardly time to dress—dinner in just nineteen minutes."

"Zank you! It ees so vera hospitable!" said the Baron, bowing low, and twirling his mustache in the most approved fashion.

"Come on, de Ville." McAllister slapped his Old-Man-of-the-Sea upon the back good-naturedly. "You can give Mrs. Blair all the risque Paris gossip at dinner." They followed the second man upstairs. Although an old friend of both Mrs. Blair and her husband, McAllister had never been at the Scarsdale house before. It was new, and massively built. They were debating whether or not to call it Castle Blair. The second man showed them to a room at the extreme end of a wing, and as the servant laid out the clothes McAllister thought the man eyed him rather curiously. Well, confound it, he was getting used to it. Barney lit a cigarette and measured the distance from the window to the ground with a discriminating eye.

"Well," said the clubman, after the second man had finally retired, "are you satisfied? And what the deuce is going to happen now?"

Barney sank into a Morris chair and thrust his feet comfortably on to the fender.

"Fatty," said he, as he blew a multitude of tiny rings toward the blaze, "you're a wizard! Never seen such nerve in my life—and you only out two months! You've got the clothes, and, what's more, you've got the real chappie lingo. It's great! I'm sorry to have to pull

29

in such an artist. I am, honest. An' now you've got to go behind prison bars! It's sad—positively sad!"

"Look here!" demanded McAllister. "Do you mean to tell me you're such a bloomin' ass as to think that I'm a crook, a professional burglar, who's got an introduction into society—a what-do-you-call-him? Oh, yes—Raffles?"

Barney grinned at his victim, who was just getting into his dress-coat.

"Don't throw such a chest, Fatty!" he said genially. "I think you've got Raffles whipped to a standstill. But you can't fool me, and you can't lose me. By the way, what am I goin' to do for evenin' clothes?"

"Dunno. Have to stay up here, I guess. You can't come to dinner in those togs. It would queer everything."

"I'm goin', just the same. Not once do I lose sight of you, old chappie, until you're safely in the cooler at headquarters. Then your swell friends can bail you out!"

It was time for dinner. The little Dresden china clock on the mantel struck the hour softly, politely. McAllister glanced toward the door. The room was the largest of a suite. A small hall intervened between them and the main corridor. His hand trembled as he lit a Philip Morris.

"Come on, then," he muttered over his shoulder to Barney, and led the way to the door leading into the bath-room, which was next the door into the hall and identical with it in appearance. He held it politely ajar for the detective, with a smile of resignation.

"Apres vous, mon cher Baron!" he murmured.

The Baron acknowledged the courtesy with an appreciative grin and passed in front of McAllister, but had no sooner done so than he received a violent push into the darkness. McAllister quickly pulled and locked the heavy walnut door, then paused, breathless, listening for some sound. He hoped the feller hadn't fallen and cut his head against the tub. There was a muffled report, and a bullet sang past and buried itself in the enamelled bedstead. Bang! Another whizzed into the china on the washstand.

McAllister dashed for the corridor, closing both the outer and inner means of egress. At the head of the stairs he met Wainwright.

"What the devil are you fellers tryin' to do, anyway?" asked the latter. "Sounds as if you were throwin' dumb-bells at each other."

McAllister lighted another cigarette.

"Oh, the Baron was showing me how they do 'savate,' that kind of boxing with their feet, don'cher know!"

Chubby was entirely himself again. An unusual color suffused his ordinarily pink countenance as he joined the guests waiting for dinner. He explained ruefully that the Baron had been suddenly taken with a sharp pain in his head. It was an old trouble, he informed them, and would soon pass off. The nobleman would join the others presently—as soon as he felt able to do so.

There were murmurs of regret from all sides, since Mrs. Blair had lost no time in spreading the knowledge of the distinguished foreigner's presence at the house.

"Who's missing besides the Baron?" inquired Blair, counting heads. "Oh, yes, Miss Benson!"

"Oh, we won't wait for Mildred! It would make her feel so awkward," responded his wife. "She and the Baron can come in together. Mr. McAllister, I believe I'm to have the pleasure of being taken in by you!"

"Er—ye—es!" muttered Chubby vaguely, for at the moment he was calculating how long it would have taken that other Baron, the famous Trenk, to dig his way out of a porcelain bath-tub. "Too beastly bad about de Ville, but these French fellows, they don't have the advantage of our athletic sports to keep 'em in condition. Do you know, I hardly ever get off my peck? All due to taking regular exercise."

The party made their way to the dining-room and were distributed in their various places. As McAllister was pushing in the chair of his hostess his eye fell upon a servant who was performing the same office for a lady opposite. Could it be? He adjusted his monocle. There was no doubt about it. It was Wilkins. And now the detective was locked in the bath-room, and the burglar, his own double, would probably pass him the soup.

"What a jolly mess!" ejaculated the bewildered guest under his breath, sinking into his chair and mechanically bolting a caviare hors-d'œuvre. He drained his sherry and tried to grasp the whole significance of the situation.

"I do hope the Baron is feeling better by this time," he heard Mrs. Blair remark. He was about to make an appropriately sympathetic reply when Miss Benson came hurriedly into the room, paused at the foot of the table and grasped the back of a chair for support. She had lost all her color, and her hands and voice trembled with excitement.

"It's gone!" she gasped. "Stolen! My mother's pearl necklace! I had it on the bureau just before tea! Oh, what shall I do!" She burst into hysterical sobs.

Two or three women gave little shrieks and pushed back their chairs.

"My tiara!" exclaimed one.

31

"And my diamond sun-burst! I left it right on a book on the dressing-table!" cried another.

There was a general move from the table.

"O Gordon! Do you think there are burglars in the house?" called Mrs. Blair to her husband.

"Heaven knows!" he replied. "There may be. But don't let's get excited. Miss Benson may possibly be mistaken, or she may have mislaid the necklace. What do you suggest, McAllister?"

"Well," replied our hero, keeping a careful eye upon Wilkins, "the first thing is to learn how much is missing. Why don't these ladies go right upstairs and see if they've lost anything? Meanwhile, we'd all better sit down and finish our soup."

"Good idea!" returned Blair. "I'll go with them."

The three hurriedly left the room, and the rest of the guests, with the exception of Miss Benson, seated themselves once more.

Everybody began to talk at once. By George! The Benson pearls stolen! Why, they were worth twenty thousand dollars thirty years ago in Rome. You couldn't buy them now for love or money. Well, she had better sit down and eat something, anyway—a glass of wine, just to revive her spirits. Miss Benson was finally persuaded by her anxious hostess to sit down and "eat something." Mrs. Blair was very much upset. How awkward to have such a thing happen at one's first house party.

The searchers presently returned with the word that apparently nothing else had been taken. This had a beneficial effect on the general appetite.

Meanwhile McAllister had been watching Wilkins. Wilkins had been watching McAllister. Since that Christmas in the Tombs they had not seen each other. The valet was unchanged, save, of course, that his beard was gone. He moved silently from place to place, nothing betraying the agitation he must have felt at the realization that he was discovered. People were all shouting encouragement to Miss Benson. There was a great chatter and confusion. The tearful and hysterical Mildred was making pitiful little dabs at the viands forced upon her. Meanwhile the dinner went on. McAllister's seat commanded the door, and he could see, through the swinging screen, that there was no exit to the kitchen from the pantry.

Wilkins approached with the fish. As the valet bent forward and passed the dish to his former master McAllister whispered sharply in his ear:

"You're caught unless you give up that necklace. There's a Central Office man outside. I brought him. Pass me the jewels. It's your only chance!"

"Very good, sir," replied Wilkins without moving a muscle.

The guests were still discussing excitedly Miss Benson's loss. McAllister's thoughts flew back to the time when, locked in the same cell, he and Wilkins had eaten their frugal meal together. He could never bring himself now to give him up to that detective fellow—that ubiquitous and omniscient ass! But Wilkins was approaching with the entrée. As he passed the vol au vent he unostentatiously slipped something in a handkerchief into McAllister's lap.

"May I go now, sir?" he asked almost inaudibly.

"Have you taken anything else?" inquired his master.

"Nothing."

"On your honor as a gentleman——'s gentleman?"

Wilkins smiled tremulously.

"Hon my onor, Mr. McAllister."

"Then, go!—You seem to have a penchant for pearls," McAllister added half to himself, as he clasped in his hand the famous necklace. Common humanity to Miss Benson demanded his instant declaration of its possession, but the thought of Wilkins, who had slipped unobtrusively through the door, gave him pause. Let the poor chap have all the time he could get. He'd probably be caught, anyway. Just a question of a few days at most. And what a chance to get even on the Baron!

But meanwhile the service had halted. The butler, a sedate person with white mutton-chops, after waiting nervously a few minutes, started to pass the roast himself.

Miss Benson had been prevailed upon to finish her meal, and after dinner they were all going to have a grand hunt, everywhere. Afterward, if the necklace was not discovered, they would send for a detective from New York.

Suddenly two pistol shots rang out just beside the window. Men's voices were raised in angry shouts. A horse attached to some sort of vehicle galloped down the road. The guests started to their feet. A violent struggle was taking place outside the dining-room door. McAllister sprang up just in time to see the Baron break away from Blair's coachman and cover him with his pistol. The jehu threw up his hands. He was a sorry spectacle, collarless, and without his coat. Damp earth clung to his lower limbs and his defiant eyes glowed under tousled hair, while a bloody, swollen nose protruded between them.

"Here! What's all this?" shouted Blair. "Put up that pistol! Who are you, sir?" Then the host rubbed his eyes and looked again.

"By George! It's the Baron!" yelled Wainwright.

"The Baron! The Baron!" exclaimed the others.

33

"Baron—nothin'!" gasped Barney, still covering the coachman, while with the other hand he tried to rearrange his neckwear. "I'm Conville of the Central Office, and this man has aided in an escape. I'm arrestin' him for felony!"

The detective's own features had evidently made a close acquaintance with mother earth, and one sleeve was torn almost to the shoulder. His eye presently fell upon McAllister, and he gave vent to an exclamation of bewilderment.

"You! You! How did you get out of that wagon so quick? I've got you now, anyway!" And he shifted his gun in McAllister's direction. The women shrieked and crowded back into the dining-room.

The coachman, who had not dared to remove his eyes from the detective, now began to jabber hysterically.

"Hi think 'e's mad, I do, Mr. Blair! Hi think we all are! First hout comes Mr. McAllister, whom I brought from the station only an 'our ago an' says as 'ow 'e must go back at once to New York. So I 'arnesses up Lady Bird in the spyder an' sends Jeames to put hon 'is livery. Just as Jeames comes back an' Mr. McAllister jumps in, hout comes this party 'ere an' yells somethin' about Welch an' tries to climb in arter Mr. McAllister. Jeames gives the mare a cut an' haway they go. Then this 'ere party begins to run arter 'em and commences shootin'. Hi tackles 'im! 'E knocks me down! Hi grabs 'im by the leg, an' 'ere we are, sir, axin' yer pardon—Hello, why 'ere's Mr. McAllister now! May I ask as 'ow you got 'ere, sir?"

But Barney had suddenly dropped the pistol.

"Quick!" he shouted wildly. "Harness another horse! We've still got time. I can't lose my man this way!"

"Well, who is he? Who was it you shot at?"

"Welch! Fatty Welch!" shrieked the Baron. "There's two of 'em! But the one I want has started for the station. I must catch him!"

"Excuse me, sir," interrupted the old butler, who alone had preserved his equanimity, addressing Mr. Blair. "My impression is, sir, that it must have been Manice, sir—the new third man, sir. I saw him step out. He must have taken Mr. McAllister's coat and hat!"

There was an immediate chorus of assent. Of course that was it. The man had disguised himself in McAllister's clothes.

"He's got the necklace!" wailed Mildred. "Oh, I know he has!"

"Yes! Yes!"

"Of course he's got it!"

"After him! After him!"

"Necklace! What necklace?" inquired Barney, more bewildered than ever.

"My mother's pearl necklace! She bought it in Rome. And now it's gone. He's got it."

Barney made a move for the door.

"Run and harness up, William!" directed Blair. "Put in the Morgan ponies. Hustle now. The train isn't due for fifteen minutes and you can reach the station in ten. Don't spare the horses!"

William, with a defiant look at the detective, hastened to obey the order.

Barney was running his hands through his hair. He certainly had stumbled on to somethin', by Hookey! If he could only catch that feller it would mean certain promotion! He had to admit that he had been mistaken about McAllister, but this was better.

"You see, I was right!" remarked our hero to the detective in his usual suave tones. "You should have done just what I said. You stayed too long upstairs. However, there's still a running chance of your catching our man at the station. Here, take a drink, and then get along as fast as you can!"

He handed Barney a glass of champagne, and the detective hastily gulped it down. He needed it, for the fifteen-foot jump from the bath-room window had shaken him up badly.

"Trap's ready, sir!" called William, coming into the hall, and Barney turned without a word and dashed for the door. The whip cracked and McAllister was free.

"Well, well, well!" remarked Blair. "Don't let's lose our dinner, anyway! Come, ladies, let's finish our meal. We at least know who the thief is, and there's a fair chance of his being caught. I will notify the White Plains police at once! Don't despair, Miss Benson. We'll have the necklace for you yet!"

But Mildred was not to be comforted and clung to Mrs. Blair, with the tears welling in her eyes, while her hostess patted her cheek and tried to encourage a belief that the necklace in some mysterious way would return.

"No, it's gone! I know it is. They'll never catch him! Oh, it's dreadful! I would give anything in the world to have that necklace back!"

"Anything, Miss Benson?" inquired McAllister gayly, as he rose from his place and held up the softly shining cord of pearls. "But perhaps if I held you to the letter of your contract you might claim duress. Allow me to return the necklace. It's a great pleasure, I assure you!"

"Hooray for Chubby!" shouted Wainwright. The company gasped with astonishment as Miss Benson eagerly seized the jewels.

"By George, McAllister! How did you do it?" inquired his excited host.

"Yes, tell us! How did you get 'em? Where did you get 'em?"

"Who was the Baron?"

"How on earth did you know?"

They all suddenly began to shout, asking questions, arguing, and exclaiming with astonishment.

McAllister saw that some explanation was in order.

"Just a bit of detective work of my own," he announced carelessly. "I don't care to say anything more about it. One can't give away one's trade secrets, don'cher know. Of course that assistant of mine made rather a mess of it, but after all, the necklace was the main thing!" And he bowed to Miss Benson.

Beyond this brilliant elucidation of the mystery no one could extract a syllable from the hero of the occasion. The Baron did not return, and his absence was not observed. But Joe Wainwright voiced the sentiments of the entire company when he announced somewhat huskily that McAllister made Sherlock Holmes look like thirty cents.

"But, say," he muttered thickly an hour later to his host as they sauntered into the billiard-room for one last whiskey and soda, "did you notice how much that butler feller that ran away looked like McAllister? 'S livin' image! 'Pon my 'onor!"

"You've been drinking, Joe!" laughed his companion.

THE ESCAPE OF WILKINS

I

"Party to see you, sir, in the visitors' room. Didn't have a card. Said you would know him, sir."

Although Peter spoke in his customary deferential tones, there was a queer look upon his face that did not escape McAllister as the latter glanced up from the afternoon paper which he had been perusing in the window.

"Hm!" remarked the clubman, gazing out at the rain falling in torrents. Who in thunder could be calling upon him a day like this, when there wasn't even a cab in sight and the policemen had sought sanctuary in convenient vestibules. It was evident that this "party" must want to see him very badly indeed.

"What shall I say, sir?" continued Peter gently.

McAllister glanced sharply at him. Of course it was absurd to suppose that Peter, or anyone else, had heard of the extraordinary events at the Blairs' the night before, yet vaguely McAllister felt that this stranger must in some mysterious way be connected with them. In any case there was no use trying to duck the consequences of the adventure, whatever they might prove to be.

"I'll see him," said the clubman. Maybe it was another detective after additional information, or perhaps a reporter. Without hesitation he crossed the marble hall and parted the portières of the visitors' room. Before him stood the rain-soaked, bedraggled figure of the valet.

"Wilkins!" he gasped.

The burglar raised his head and disclosed a countenance haggard from lack of sleep and the strain of the pursuit. Little rivers of rain streamed from his cuffs, his (McAllister's) coat-tails, and from the brim of his master's hat, which he held deprecatingly before him. There was a look of fear in his eyes, and he trembled like a hare which pauses uncertain in which direction to escape.

"Forgive me, sir! Oh, sir, forgive me! They're right hafter me! Just houtside, sir! It was my honly chance!"

McAllister gazed at him horrified and speechless.

"You see, sir," continued Wilkins in accents of breathless terror, "I caught the train last night and reached the city a'ead of the detective. I knew 'e'd 'ave telegraphed a general halarm, so I 'id in a harea all night. This mornin' I thought I'd given 'im the slip, but I walked square into 'im on Fiftieth Street. I took it on a run hup Sixth Havenue, doubled 'round a truck, an' thought I'd lost 'im, but 'e saw me on Fifty-third Street an' started dead after me. I think 'e saw me stop in 'ere, sir. Wot shall I do, sir? You won't give me hup, will you, sir?"

Before McAllister could reply there was a commotion at the door of the club, and he recognized the clear tones of Barney Conville.

"Who am I? I'm a sergeant of police—Detective Bureau. You've just passed in a burglar. He must be right inside. Let me in, I say!"

Wilkins shrank back toward the curtains.

There was a slight scuffle, but the servant outside placed his foot behind the door in such a position that the detective could not enter. Then Peter came to the rescue.

"What do you mean by trying to force your way into a private club, like this? I'll telephone the Inspector. Get out of here, now! Get away from that door!"

"Inspector nothin'! Let me in!"

"Have you got a warrant?"

The question seemed to stagger the detective for a moment, and his adversary seized the opportunity to close the door. Then Peter knocked politely upon the other side of the curtains.

"I'm afraid, Mr. McAllister, I can't keep the officer out much longer. It's only a question of time. You'll pardon me, sir?"

"Of course, Peter," answered McAllister.

He stepped to the window. Outside he could see Conville stationing two plain-clothes men so as to guard both exits from the club. McAllister's breath came fast. Wilkins crouched in terror by the centre-table. Then a momentary inspiration came to the clubman.

"Er—Peter, this is my friend, Mr. Lloyd-Jones. Take his coat and hat, give me a check for them, and then show him upstairs to a room. He'll be here for an hour or so."

"Very good, sir," replied Peter without emotion, as he removed Wilkins's dripping coat and hat. "This way, sir."

Casting a look of dazed gratitude at his former master, the valet followed Peter toward the elevator.

"Here's a nice mess!" thought McAllister, as he returned to the big room. "How am I ever going to get rid of him? And ain't I liable somehow as an accomplice?"

He wrinkled his brows, lit a Perfecto, and sank again into his accustomed place by the window.

"That policeman wants to see you, sir," said the doorman,

suddenly appearing at his elbow. "Says he knows you, and it's somethin' very important."

The clubman smothered a curse. His first impulse was to tell the impudent fellow to go to the devil, but then he thought better of it. He had beaten Conville once, and he would do so again. When it came to a show-down, he reckoned his brains were about as good as a policeman's.

"All right," he replied. "Tell him to sit down—that I've just come in, and will be with him in a few moments."

"Very good, sir," answered the servant.

McAllister perceived that he must think rapidly. There was no escape from the conclusion that he was certainly assisting in the escape of a felon; that he was an accessory after the fact, as it were. The idea did not increase his happiness at all. His one experience in the Tombs, however adventitious, had been quite sufficient. Nevertheless, he could not go back on Wilkins, particularly now that he had promised to assist him. McAllister rubbed his broad forehead in perplexity.

"The officer says he's in a great hurry, sir, and wants to know can you see him at once, sir," said the doorman, coming back.

"Hang it!" exclaimed our hero. "Yes, I'll see him."

He got up and walked slowly to the visitors' room again, while Peter, with a studiously unconscious expression, held the portières open. He entered, prepared for the worst. As he did so, Conville sprang to his feet, leaving a pool of water in front of the sofa and tossing little drops of rain from the ends of his mustache.

"Look here, Mr. McAllister, there's been enough of this. Where's Welch, the crook, who ran in here a few moments ago? Oh, he's here fast enough! I've got your club covered, front and behind. Don't try to con me!"

McAllister slowly adjusted his monocle, smiled affably, and sank comfortably into an armchair.

"Why, it's you, Baron, isn't it! How are you? Won't you have a little nip of something warm? No? A cigar, then. Here, Peter, bring the gentleman an Obsequio. Well, to what do I owe this honor?"

Conville glared at him enraged. However, he restrained his wrath. A wise detective never puts himself at a disadvantage by giving way to useless emotion. When Peter returned with the cigar, Barney took it mechanically and struck a match, meanwhile keeping one eye upon the door of the club.

"I suppose," he presently remarked, "you think you're smart. Well, you're mistaken. I had you wrong last night, I admit—that is, so far as your identity was concerned. You're a real high-roller, all right, but that ain't the whole thing, by a long shot. How would you like to wander down to Headquarters as an accomplice?"

A few chills played hide-and-seek around the base of the clubman's spine.

"Don't be an ass!" he finally managed to ejaculate.

"Oh, I can't connect you with the necklace! You're safe enough there," Barney continued. "But how about this little game right here in this club? You're aiding in the escape of a felon. That's felony. You know that yourself. Besides, when you locked me in the bathroom last night you assaulted an officer in the performance of his duty. I've got you dead to rights, see?"

McAllister laughed lightly.

"By jiminy!" he exclaimed, "I thought you were crazy all the time, and now I know it. What in thunder are you driving at?"

Conville knocked the ashes off his cigar impatiently.

"Drivin' at? Drivin' at? Where's Welch—Fatty Welch, that ran in here five minutes ago?"

McAllister assumed a puzzled expression.

"Welch? No one ran in here except myself. I came in about that time. Got off the L at Fiftieth Street, footed it pretty fast up Sixth Avenue, and then through Fifty-third Street to the club. I got mighty well wet, too, I tell you!"

"Don't think you can throw that game into me!" shouted Conville. "You can't catch me twice that way. It was Welch I saw, not you."

"You don't believe me?"

McAllister pressed the bell and Peter entered.

"Peter, tell this gentleman how many persons have come into the club within the hour."

"Why, only you, sir," replied Peter, without hesitation. "Your clothes was wringin' wet, sir. No one else has entered the club since twelve o'clock."

"Bah!" exclaimed Conville. "If it was you that came in," he added cunningly, "suppose you show me your check, and let me have a look at your coat!"

"Certainly," responded McAllister, beginning to regain his equanimity, as he drew Wilkins's check from his pocket. "Here it is. You can step over and get the coat for yourself."

Barney seized the small square of brass, crossed to the coat-room, and returned with the dripping garment, which he held up to the light at the window.

"You ought to find Poole's name under the collar, and my own inside the breast-pocket," remarked Chubby encouragingly. "It's there, isn't it?"

Conville threw the soaked object over a chair-back and made a

40

rapid inspection, then turned to McAllister with an expression of bewilderment.

"I—you—how—" he stammered.

"Don't you remember," laughed his tormentor, "that there was a big truck on the corner of Sixth Avenue?"

Barney set his teeth.

"I see you do," continued McAllister. "Well, what more can I do for you? Are you sure you won't have that drink?"

But Conville was in no mood for drinking. Stepping up to the clubman, he looked searchingly down into his face.

"Mr. McAllister," he hissed, "you think you've got me criss-crossed. You think you're a sure winner. But I know you. I know your face. And this time I don't lose you, see? You're in cahoots with Welch. You're his side-partner. You'll see me again. Remember, you're a common felon."

The detective made for the door.

"Don't say 'common,'" murmured McAllister, as Conville disappeared. Then his nonchalant look gave place to one of extreme dejection. "Peter," he gasped, "tell Mr. Lloyd-Jones I must see him at once."

Peter soon returned with the unexpected information that "Mr. Lloyd-Jones" had gone to bed and wouldn't get up.

"Says he's sick, sir," said Peter, trying hard to retain his gravity.

McAllister made one jump for the elevator. Peter followed. Of course, he had known Wilkins when the latter was in McAllister's employ.

"I put him in No. 13, sir," remarked the majordomo.

Sure enough, Wilkins was in bed. His clothes were nowhere visible, and the quilt was pulled well up around his fat neck. He seemed utterly to have lost his nerve.

"Oh, sir!" he cried apologetically, "I was hafraid to come down, sir. Without my clothes they never could hidentify me, sir!"

"What on earth have you done with 'em?" cried his master.

"Oh, Mr. McAllister!" wailed Wilkins, "I couldn't think o' nothin' else, so I just threw 'em hout the window, into the hairshaft."

At this intelligence Peter, who had lingered by the door, choked violently and retired down the hall.

"Wilkins," exclaimed McAllister, "I never took you for a fool before! Pray, what do you propose to do now?"

"I don't know, sir."

"Can't you see what an awkward position you've placed me in?" went on McAllister. "I'm liable to arrest for aidin' in your

41

escape. In fact, that detective has just threatened to take me to Headquarters."

"'Oly Moses!'" moaned Wilkins. "Oh, wot shall I do? If you honly get me haway, sir, I promise you I'll never return."

McAllister closed the door, sat down by the bed, and puffed hard at his cigar.

"I'll try it!" he muttered at length. "Wilkins, you remember you always wore my clothes."

"Yes, sir," sighed Wilkins.

"Well, to-night you shall leave the club in my dress-suit, tall hat, and Inverness—understand? You'll take a cab from here at eleven-forty. Go to the Grand Central and board the twelve o'clock train for Boston. Here's a ticket, and the check for the drawing-room. You'll be Mr. McAllister of the Colophon Club, if anyone speaks to you. You're going on to Mr. Cabot's wedding to-morrow, to act as best man. Turn in as soon as you go on board, and don't let anyone disturb you. I'll be on the train myself, and after it starts I'll knock three times on the door."

"Very good, sir," murmured Wilkins.

"I'll send to my rooms for the clothes at once. Do you think you can do it?"

"Oh, certainly, sir! Thank you, sir! I'll be there, sir, never fail."

"Well, good luck to you."

McAllister returned to the big room downstairs. The longer he thought of his plan the better he liked it. He was going to the Winthrops' Twelfth Night party that evening as Henry VIII. He would dress at the club and leave it in costume about nine o'clock. Conville would never recognize him in doublet and hose, and, when Wilkins departed at eleven-forty, would in all likelihood take the latter for McAllister. If he could thus get rid of his ex-valet for good and all it would be cheap at twice the trouble. So far as spiriting away Wilkins was concerned the whole thing seemed easy enough, and McAllister, once more in his usual state of genial placidity, ordered as good a dinner as the chef could provide.

II

The revelry was at its height when Henry VIII realized with a start that it was already half after eleven. First there had been a professional presentation of the scene between Sir Andrew Aguecheek and Sir Toby Belch that had made McAllister shake with merriment. He thought Sir Andrew the drollest fellow that he had seen for many a day. Maria and the clown were both good, too. McAllister had a fleeting wish that he had essayed Sir Toby. The champagne had been excellent and the characters most amusing, and, altogether, McAllister did not blame himself for having overstayed his time—in fact, he didn't care much whether he had or not. He had intended going back to his rooms for the purpose of changing his costume, but he had plenty of clothes on the train, and there really seemed no need of it at all. He bade his hostess good-night in a most optimistic frame of mind and hailed a cab. The long ulster which he wore entirely concealed his costume save for his shoes, strange creations of undressed leather, red on the uppers and white between the toes. As for his cap and feather, he was quite too happy to mind them for an instant. The assembled crowd of lackeys and footmen cheered him mildly as he drove away, but Henry VIII, smoking a large cigar, noticed them not. Neither did he observe a slim young man who darted out from behind a flight of steps and followed the cab, keeping about half a block in the rear. The rain had stopped. The clouds had drawn aside their curtains, and a big friendly moon beamed down on McAllister from an azure sky, bright almost as day.

The cabman hit up his pace as they reached the slope from the Cathedral down Fifth Avenue, and the runner was distanced by several blocks. McAllister, happy and sleepy, was blissfully unconscious of being an actor in a drama of vast import to the New York police, but as they reached Forty-third Street he saw by the illuminated clock upon the Grand Central Station that it was two minutes to twelve. At the same moment a trace broke. The driver sprang from his seat, but before he could reach the ground McAllister had leaped out. Tossing a bill to the perturbed cabby, our hero threw off his ulster and sped with an agility marvellous to behold down Forty-third Street toward the station. As he dashed across Madison Avenue, directly in front of an electric car, the hand on the clock slipped a minute nearer. At that instant the slim man turned the corner from Fifth Avenue and redoubled his speed. Thirty seconds later, McAllister, in sword, doublet, hose, and feathered cap, burst into the waiting-room, carrying an ulster, clearing half its length in six strides, threw himself through the revolving door to the platform, and sprang past the astonished gate-man just as he was sliding-to the gate.

"Hi, there, give us yer ticket!" yelled the man after the retreating form of Henry VIII, but royalty made no response.

The gate closed, a gong rang twice, somewhere up ahead an engine gave half a dozen spasmodic coughs, and the forward section of the train began to pull out. McAllister, gasping for breath, a terrible pain in his side, his ulster seeming to weigh a thousand pounds, stumbled upon the platform of the car next the last. As he did so, the slim young man rushed to the gate and commenced to beat frantically upon it. The gate-man, indignant, approached to make use of severe language.

"Open this gate!" yelled the man. "There's a burglar in disguise on that train. Didn't you see him run through? Open up!"

"Whata yer givin' us?" answered Gate. "Who are yer, anyhow?"

"I'm a detective sergeant!" shrieked the one outside, excitedly exhibiting a shield. "I order you to open this gate and let me through."

Gate looked with exasperating deliberateness after the receding train; its red lights were just passing out of the station.

"Oh, go to—!" said he through the bars.

"Is this car 2241?" inquired the breathless McAllister at the same moment, as he staggered inside.

"Sho, boss," replied the porter, grinning from ear to ear as he received the ticket and its accompanying half-dollar. "Drawin'-room, sah? Yes-sah. Right here, sah! Yo' frien', he arrived some time ago. May Ah enquire what personage yo represent, sah? A most magnificent sword, sah!"

"Where's the smoking compartment?" asked McAllister.

"Udder end, sah!"

Now McAllister had no inclination to feel his way the length of that swaying car. He perceived that the smoking compartment of the car behind would naturally be much more convenient.

"I'm going into the next car to smoke for a while," he informed the darky.

No one was in the smoking compartment of the Benvolio, which was bright and warm, and McAllister, throwing down his ulster, stretched luxuriously across the cushions, lit a cigar, and watched with interest the myriad lights of the Greater City marching past, those near at hand flashing by with the velocity of meteors, and those beyond swinging slowly forward along the outer rim of the circle. And the idea of this huge circle, its circumference ever changing with the forward movement of its pivot, beside which the train was rushing, never passing that mysterious edge which fled before them into infinity, took hold on McAllister's imagination, and he fancied, as he sped onward, that in some mysterious way, if he could only square that circle or calculate its radius, he could solve the problem of existence. What was it he had learned when a boy at St. Andrew's about the circle? Pi R—one—two—two Pi R! That was it! "$2\pi r$." The smoke from his cigar swirled thickly around the Pintsch light in the ceiling, and Henry VIII, oblivious of the anachronism, with his sword and feathered cap upon the sofa beside him, gazed solemnly into space.

"Br-r-clink!—br-r-clink!" went the track.

"Two Pi R!" murmured McAllister. "Two Pi R!"

III

Under the big moon's yellow disk, beside and past the roaring train, along the silent reaches of the Sound, leaping on its copper thread from pole to pole, jumping from insulator to insulator, from town to town, sped a message concerning Henry VIII. The night operator at New Haven, dozing over a paper in the corner, heard his call four times before he came to his senses. Then he sent the answer rattling back with a simulation of indignation:

"Yes, yes! What's your rush?"

Special—Police—Headquarters—Newn Haven. Escaped ex-convict Welch on No. 13 from New York. Notify McGinnis. In complete disguise. Arrest and notify. Particulars long-distance 'phone in morning.

Ebstein.

The operator crossed the room and unhooked the telephone. "Headquarters, please."

"Yes. Headquarters! Is McGinnis of the New York Detective Bureau there? Tell him he's wanted, to make an important arrest on board No. 13 when she comes through at two-twenty. Sorry. Say, tell him to bring along some cigars. I'll give him the complete message down here."

Then the operator went back to his paper. In a few moments he suddenly sat up.

"By gum!" he ejaculated.

BOLD ATTEMPT AT BURGLARY IN COUNTRY HOUSE

It was learned to-day that a well-known crook had been successful recently in securing a position as a servant at Mr. Gordon Blair's at Scarsdale. Last evening one of the guests missed her valuable pearl necklace. In the excitement which followed the burglar made his escape, leaving the necklace behind him. The perpetrator of this

45

bold attempt is the notorious Fatty Welch, now wanted in several States as a fugitive from justice.

"By gum!" repeated the operator, throwing down the paper. Then he went to the drawer and took out a small bull-dog revolver, which he carefully loaded.

"Br-r-clink!—br-r-clink!" went the track, as the train swung round the curve outside New Haven. The brakes groaned, the porters waked from troubled slumbers in wicker chairs, one or two old women put out their arms and peered through the window-shades, and the train thundered past the depot and slowly came to a full stop. Ahead, the engine panted and steamed. Two gnomes ran, Mimi-like, out of a cavernous darkness behind the station and by the light of flaring torches began to hammer and tap the flanges. The conductor, swinging off the rear car, ran into the embrace of a huge Irishman. At the same moment a squad of policemen separated and scattered to the different platforms.

"Here! Let me go!" gasped the conductor. "What's all this?"

"Say, Cap., I'm McGinnis—Central Office, New York. You've got a burglar on board. They're after wirin' me to make the arrest."

"Burglar be damned!" yelled the conductor. "Do you think you can hold me up and search my train? Why, I'd be two hours late!"

"I won't take more'n fifteen minutes," continued McGinnis, making for the rear car.

"Come back there, you!" shouted the conductor, grasping him firmly by the coat-tails. "You can't wake up all the passengers."

"Look here, Cap.," expostulated the detective, "don't ye see I've got to make this arrest? It won't take a minute. The porters'll know who they've got, and you're runnin' awful light. Have a good cigar?"

The conductor took the weed so designated and swore loudly. It was the biggest piece of gall on record. Well, hang it! he didn't want to take McGinnis all the way to Boston, and even if he did, there would be the same confounded mix-up at the other end. He admitted finally that it was a fine night. Did McGinnis want a nip? He had a bottle in the porter's closet. Yes, call out those niggers and make 'em tell what they knew.

The conductor was now just as insistent that the burglar should be arrested then and there as he had been before that the train should not be held up. He rushed through the cars telling the various porters to go outside. Eight or ten presently assembled upon the platform. They filled McGinnis with unspeakable repulsion.

The conductor began with car No. 2204.

"Now, Deacon, who have you got?"

The Deacon, an enormously fat darky, rolled his eyes and replied that he had "two ole women an' er gen'elman gwine ortermobublin with his cheffonier."

The conductor opined that these would prove unfertile candidates for McGinnis. He therefore turned to Moses, of car No. 2201. Moses, however, had only half a load. There was a fat man, a Mr. Huber, who travelled regularly; two ladies on passes; and a very thin man, with his wife, her sister, a maid, two nurses, and three children.

"Nothin' doin'!" remarked the captain. "Now, Colonel, what have you got?"

But the Colonel, a middle-aged colored man of aristocratic appearance, had an easy answer. His entire car was full, as he expressed it, "er frogs."

"Frenchmen!" grunted McGinnis.

The conductor remembered. Yes, they were Sanko's Orchestra going on to give a matinée concert in Providence.

The next car had only five drummers, every one of whom was known to the conductor, as taking the trip twice a week. They were therefore counted out. That left only one car, No. 2205.

"Well, William, what have you got?"

William grinned. Though sleepy, he realized the importance of the disclosure he was about to make and was correspondingly dignified and ponderous. There was two trabblin' gen'elmen, Mr. Smith and Mr. Higgins. He'd handled dose gen'elmen fo' several years. There was a very old lady, her daughter and maid. Then there was Mr. Uberheimer, who got off at Middletown. And then— William smiled significantly—there was an awful strange pair in the drawin'-room. They could look for themselves. He didn't know nuff'n 'bout burglars in disguise, but dere was "one of 'em in er mighty curious set er fixtures."

"Huh! Two of 'em!" commented McGinnis.

"That's easy!" remarked the mollified conductor.

The telegraph operator, who read Laura Jean Libbey, now approached with his revolver.

McGinnis, another detective, and the conductor moved toward the car. William preferred the safety of the platform and the temporary distinction of being the discoverer of the fugitive. No light was visible in the drawing-room, and the sounds of heavy slumber were plainly audible. The conductor rapped loudly; there was no response. He rattled the door and turned the handle vigorously, but elicited no sign of recognition. Then McGinnis rapped with his knife on the glass of the door. He happened to hit three times. Immediately there were sounds within. Something very

47

much like "All right, sir," and the door was opened. The conductor and McGinnis saw a fat man, in blue silk pajamas, his face flushed and his eyes heavy with sleep, who looked at them in dazed bewilderment.

"Wot do you want?" drawled the fat man, blinking at the lantern.

"Sorry to disturb you," broke in McGinnis briskly, "but is there any wan else, beside ye, to kape ye company?"

Wilkins shook his head with annoyance and made as if to close the door, but the detective thrust his foot across the threshold.

"Aisy there!" he remarked. "Conductor, just turn on that light, will ye?"

Wilkins scrambled heavily into his berth, and the conductor struck a match and turned on the Pintsch light. Only one bed was occupied, and that by the fat man in the pajamas. On the sofa was an elegant alligator-skin bag disclosing a row of massive silver-topped bottles. A tall silk hat and Inverness coat hung from a hook, and a suit of evening clothes, as well as a business suit of fustian, were neatly folded and lying on the upper berth.

At this vision of respectability both McGinnis and the conductor recoiled, glancing doubtfully at one another. Wilkins saw his advantage.

"May I hinquire," remarked he, with dignity, "wot you mean by these hactions? W'y am I thus disturbed in the middle of the night? It is houtrageous!"

"Very sorry, sir," replied the conductor. "The fact is, we thought two people, suspicious characters, had taken this room together, and this officer here"—pointing to McGinnis—"had orders to arrest one of them."

Wilkins swelled with indignation.

"Suspicious characters! Two people! Look 'ere, conductor, I'll 'ave you to hunderstand that I will not tolerate such a performance. I am Mr. McAllister, of the Colophon Club, New York, and I am hon my way to hattend the wedding of Mr. Frederick Cabot in Boston, to-morrow. I am to be 'is best man. Can I give you any further hinformation?"

The conductor, who had noticed the initials "McA" on the silver bottle heads, and the same stamped upon the bag, stammered something in the nature of an apology.

"Say, Cap.," whispered McGinnis, "we've got him wrong, I guess. This feller ain't no burglar. Anywan can see he's a swell, all right. Leave him alone."

"Very sorry to have disturbed you," apologized the conductor humbly, putting out the light and closing the door.

48

"That nigger must be nutty," he added to the detective. "By Joshua! Perhaps he's got away with some of my stuff!"

"Look here, William, what's the matter with you? Have you been swipin' my whisky. There ain't two men in that drawin'-room at all—just one—a swell," hollered the conductor as they reached the platform.

"Fo' de Lawd, Cap'n, I ain't teched yo' whisky," cried William in terror. "I swear dey was two of 'em, 'n' de udder was in disguise. It was de fines' disguise I eber saw!" he added reminiscently.

"Aw, what yer givin' us!" exclaimed McGinnis, entirely out of patience. "What kind av a disguise was he in?"

"Dat's what I axed him," explained William, edging toward the rim of the circle. "I done ax him right away what character he done represent. He had on silk stockin's, an' a colored deglishay shirt, an' a belt an' moccasons, an' a sword an'——"

"A sword!" yelled McGinnis, making a jump in William's direction. "I'll break yer black head for ye!"

"Hold on!" cried the conductor, who had disappeared into the car and had emerged again with a bottle in his hand. "The stuff's here."

"I tell ye the coon is drunk!" shouted the detective in angry tones. "He can't make small av me!"

"I done tole you the trufe," continued William from a safe distance, his teeth and eyeballs shining in the moonlight.

"Well, where did he go?" asked the conductor. "Did you put him in the drawin'-room?"

"I seen his ticket," replied William, "an' he said he wanted to smoke, so he went into the Benvolio, the car behin'."

"Car behind!" cried McGinnis. "There ain't no car behind. This here is the last car."

"Sure," said the conductor, with a laugh; "we dropped the Benvolio at Selma Junction for repairs. Say, McGinnis, you better have that drink!"

IV

McAllister was awakened by a sense of chill. The compartment was dark, save for the pale light of the moon hanging low over what seemed to be water and the masts of ships, which stole in and picked out sharply the silver buckles on his shoes and the buttons of his doublet. There was no motion, no sound. The train was apparently waiting somewhere, but McAllister could not

49

hear the engine. He put on his ulster and stepped to the door of the car. All the lights had been extinguished and he could hear neither the sound of heavy breathing nor the other customary evidences of the innocent rest of the human animal. He looked across the platform for his own car and found that the train had totally disappeared. The Benvolio was stationary—side-tracked, evidently, on the outskirts of a town, not far from some wharves.

"Jiminy!" thought McAllister, looking at his uncheerful surroundings and his picturesque, if somewhat cool, costume.

For a moment his mental processes refused to answer the heavy draught upon them. Then he turned up his coat-collar, stepped out upon the platform, and lit a cigar. By the light of the match he looked at his watch and saw that it was four o'clock. Overhead the sky glowed with thousands of twinkling stars, and the moon, just touching the sea, made a limpid path of light across the water. At the docks silent ships lay fast asleep. A mile away a clock struck four, intensifying the stillness. It was very beautiful, but very cold, and McAllister shivered as he thought of Wilkins, and Freddy Cabot, and the wedding at twelve o'clock. So far as he knew he might be just outside of Boston—Quincy, or somewhere—yet, somehow, the moon didn't look as if it were at Quincy.

He jumped down and started along the track. His feet stung as they struck the cinder. His whole body was asleep. It was easy enough to walk in the direction in which the clock had sounded, and this he did. The rails followed the shore for about a hundred yards and then joined the main line. Presently he came in sight of a depot. Every now and then his sword would get between his legs, and this caused him so much annoyance that he took it off and carried it. It was queer how uncomfortable the old style of shoe was when used for walking on a railroad track. His ruffle, too, proved a confounded nuisance, almost preventing a satisfactory adjustment of coat-collar. Finally he untied it and put it in the pocket of his ulster. The cap was not so bad.

The depot had inspired the clubman with distinct hope, but as he approached, it appeared as dark and tenantless as the car behind him. It was impossible to read the name of the station owing to the fact that the sign was too high up for the light of a match to reach it. It was clear that there was nothing to do but to wait for the dawn, and he settled himself in a corner near the express office and tried to forget his discomfort.

He had less time to wait than he had expected. Soon a great clattering of hoofs caused him to climb stiffly to his feet again. Three farmers' wagons, each drawn by a pair of heavy horses, backed in against the platform, and their drivers, throwing down the reins, leaped to the ground. All were smoking pipes and chaffing one another loudly. Then they began to unload huge cans of milk. This looked encouraging. If they were bringing milk at this hour there must be a train—going somewhere. It didn't matter where to McAllister, if only he could get warm. Presently a faint humming came along the rails, which steadily increased in volume until the approaching train could be distinctly heard.

"Pretty nigh on time," commented the nearest farmer.

McAllister stepped forward, sword in hand. The farmer involuntarily drew back.

"Wall, I swan!" he remarked, removing his pipe.

"Do you mind telling me," inquired our friend, "what place this is and where this train goes to?"

"I reckon not," replied the other. "This is Selma Junction, and this here train is due in New York at five. Who be you?"

"Well," answered McAllister, "I'm just an humble citizen of New York, forced by circumstances to return to the city as soon as possible."

"Reckon you're one o' them play-actors, bean't ye?"

"You've got it," returned McAllister. "Fact is, I've just been playing Henry VIII—on the road."

"I've heard tell on't," commented the rustic. "But I ain't never seen it. Shakespeare, ain't it?"

"Yes, Shakespeare," admitted the clubman.

At this moment the milk-train roared in and the teamsters began passing up their cans. There were no passenger coaches—nothing but freight-cars and a caboose. Toward this our friend made his way. There did not seem to be any conductor, and, without making inquiries, McAllister climbed upon the platform and pushed open the door. If warmth was what he desired he soon found it. The end of the car was roughly fitted with half a dozen bunks, two boxes which served for chairs, and some spittoons. A small cast-iron stove glowed red-hot, but while the place was odoriferous, its temperature was grateful to the shivering McAllister. The car was empty save for a gigantic Irishman sitting fast asleep in the farther corner.

Our hero laid down his sword, threw off his ulster, and hung his cap upon an adjacent hook. In a moment or two the train started again. Still no one came into the caboose. Now daylight began to filter in through the grimy windows. The sun jumped suddenly from behind a ridge and shot a beam into the face of the sleeper at the other end of the car. Slowly he awoke, yawned, rubbed his eyes, and, catching the glint of silver buttons, gazed stupidly in McAllister's direction. The random glance gradually gave place to a stare of intense amazement. He wrinkled his brows, and leaned forward,

51

scrutinizing with care every detail of McAllister's make-up. The train stopped for an instant and a burly brakeman banged open the door and stepped inside. He, too, hung fire, as it were, at the sight of Henry VIII. Then he broke into a loud laugh.

"Who in thunder are you?"

Before McAllister could reply McGinnis, with a comprehensive smile, made answer:

"Shure, 'tis only a prisoner I'm after takin' back to the city!"

"Mr. McAllister," remarked Conville, two hours later, as the three of them sat in the visitors' room at the club, "I hope you won't say anything about this. You see, I had no business to put a kid like Ebstein on the job, but I was clean knocked out and had to snatch some sleep. I suppose he thought he was doin' a big thing when he nailed you for a burglar. But, after all, the only thing that saved Welch was your fallin' asleep in the Benvolio."

"My dear Baron," sympathetically replied McAllister, who had once more resumed his ordinary attire, "why attribute to chance what is in fact due to intellect? No, I won't mention our adventure, and if our friend McGinnis—"

"Oh, McGinnis'll keep his head shut, all right, you bet!" interrupted Barney. "But say, Mr. McAllister, on the level, you're too good for us. Why don't you chuck this game and come in out of the rain? You'll be up against it in the end. Help us to land this feller!"

McAllister took a long pull at his cigar and half-closed his eyes. There was a quizzical look around his mouth that Conville had never seen there before.

"Perhaps I will," said he softly. "Perhaps I will."

"Good!" shouted the Baron; "put it there! Now, if you get anything, tip us off. You can always catch me at 3100 Spring."

"Well," replied the clubman, "don't forget to drop in here, if you happen to be going by. Some time, on a rainy day perhaps, you might want a nip of something warm."

But to this the Baron did not respond.

A plunge in the tank and a comfortable smoke almost restored McAllister's customary equanimity. Weddings were a bore, anyway. Then he called for a telegraph blank and sent the following:

Was unavoidably detained. Terribly disappointed. If necessary, use Wilkins.

McA.

To which, about noon-time, he received the following reply:
Don't understand. Wilkins arrived, left clothes and departed. You must have mixed your dates. Wedding to-morrow.

F. C.

THE GOVERNOR-GENERAL'S TRUNK

I

McAllister was in the tank. His puffing and blowing as he dove and tumbled like a contented, rubicund porpoise, reverberated loudly among the marble pillars of the bath at the club. It was all part of a carefully adjusted and as rigorously followed regimen, for McAllister was a thorough believer in exercise (provided it was moderate), and took it regularly, averring that a fellow couldn't expect to eat and drink as much as he naturally wanted to unless he kept in some sort of condition, and if he didn't he would simply get off his peck, that was all. Hence "Chubby" arose regularly at nine-thirty, and wrapping himself in a padded Japanese silk dressing-gown, descended to the tank, where he dove six times and swam around twice, after which he weighed himself and had Tim rub him down. Tim felt a high degree of solicitude for all this procedure, since he was a personal discovery of McAllister's, and owed his present exalted position entirely to the clubman's interest, for the latter had found him at Coney Island earning his daily bread by diving, in the presence of countless multitudes, into a six-foot glass tank, where he seated himself upon the bottom and nonchalantly consumed a banana. McAllister's delight and enthusiasm at this elevating spectacle had been boundless.

"Wish I could do any one thing as well as that feller dives down and eats that banana!" he had confided to his friend Wainwright. "Sometimes I feel as if my life had been wasted!" The upshot of the whole matter was that Tim had been forthwith engaged as rubber and swimming teacher at the club.

McAllister had just taken his fifth plunge, and was floating lazily toward the steps, when Tim appeared at the door leading into the dressing-rooms and announced that a party wanted to speak to him on the 'phone, the Lady somebody, evidently a very cantankerous old person, who was in the devil of a hurry, and wouldn't stand no waitin'.

The clubman turned over, sputtered, touched bottom, and arose dripping to his feet. The "old person" on the wire was clearly his aunt, Lady Lyndhurst, and he knew very much better than to irritate her when she was in one of her tantrums. Still, he couldn't imagine what she wanted with him at that hour of the morning. She'd been placid enough the evening before when he'd left her after

53

the opera. But ever since she had married Lord Lyndhurst for her second husband ten years before she'd been getting more and more dictatorial.

"Tell her I'm in this beastly tank; awful sorry I can't speak with her myself, don'cher know, and find out what she wants. And Tim—handle her gently—it's my aunt."

Tim grinned and winked a comprehending eye. As McAllister hurried into his bath-robe and slippers he wondered more and more why she had rung him up so early. He had intended calling on her after breakfast, any way, but "after breakfast" to McAllister meant in the neighborhood of twelve o'clock, for the meal was always carefully ordered the evening before for half-past ten the next morning, after which came the paper and a long, light Casadora, crop of '97, which McAllister had bought up entire. Something must be up—that was certain. He could imagine her in her wrapper and curl-papers holding converse with Tim over the wire. The language of his protégé might well assist in the process for which the curl-papers were required. There was nobody in the world, in McAllister's opinion, so queer as his aunt, except his aunt's husband. The latter was a stout, beefy nobleman of sixty-five, with a walrus-like countenance, an implicit faith in the perfection of British institutions, and about enough intelligence to drive a watering-cart. He had been rewarded for his unswerving fidelity to party with the post of Governor-General at a small group of islands somewhere near the equator, and had assumed his duties solemnly and ponderously, establishing the Bertillon system of measurements for the seven criminals which his islands supported, and producing quarterly monographs on the flora, fauna, and conchology of his dominion. Just now they were en route for England (via Quebec, of course), and were stopping at the Waldorf.

Tim presently reappeared.

"She says you've got to hike right down to the hotel as fast as you can. She's terrible upset. My, ain't she a tiger?"

"But what's the bloomin' row?" exclaimed McAllister.

Tim looked round cautiously and lowered his voice.

"The Lyndhurst Jewels has been stole!" said he.

II

The Lyndhurst Jewels stolen! No wonder Aunt Sophia had seemed peevish, for they were the treasured heirlooms of her husband's family, cherished and guarded by her with anxious eye.

54

McAllister had always said the old man was an ass to go lugging 'em off down among the mangoes and land-crabs, but the Governor-General liked to have his lady appear in style at Government House, and took much innocent pleasure in astonishing the natives by the splendor of her adornment. The jewelry, however, was the source of unending annoyance to himself, Sophia, and everybody else, for it was always getting lost, and burglar scares occurred with regularity at the islands. It had been still intact, however, on their arrival in New York.

The clubman found his uncle and aunt sitting dejectedly at the breakfast-table in the Diplomatic Suite.

The atmosphere of gloom struck a cold chill to our friend's centre of vivacity. There were also evidences of a domestic misunderstanding. His aunt fidgeted nervously, and his uncle evaded McAllister's eye as they responded half-heartedly to his cheerful salutation. That the matter was serious was obvious. Clearly this time the jewels must be really gone. In addition, both the Governor-General and his lady kept looking over their shoulders fearfully, as if dreading the momentary assault of some assassin. McAllister inquired what the jolly mess was, incidentally suggesting that their hurry-call had deprived him of any attempt at breakfast. His hint, however, fell on barren ground.

"That fool Morton has packed all the jewelry in the big Vuitton!" exclaimed his uncle, nervously jabbing his spoon into a grape-fruit. "To say the least, it was excessively careless of him, for he knows perfectly well that we always carry it in the morocco hand-bag, and never allow it out of our sight." The Governor-General paused, and took a sip of coffee.

"Well," said McAllister, rather impatiently, "why don't you have him unpack it, then?" He couldn't for the life of him see why they made such a row about a thing of that sort. It was clear enough that they were both more than half mad.

"Ah, that's the point! It was sent to the station with the rest of the luggage last evening. Heaven knows it may all have been stolen by this time! Think of it, McAllister! The Lyndhurst Jewels, secured merely by a miserable brass check with a number on it—and the railroad liable by express contract only to the extent of one hundred dollars!" Before Uncle Basil had attained his present eminence he had been called to the bar, and his book on "Flotsam and Jetsam" is still an authority in those regions to which later works have not penetrated. "You see we're leaving at three this afternoon, but why send it all so early unless for a purpose?" Lord Lyndhurst nodded conclusively. He had the air of one who had divined something.

Still Chubby failed to see the connection. Someone, a valet

55

evidently, had packed the jewelry in the wrong place, and then sent the load off a little ahead of time. What of it? He recalled vividly an occasion when the jewels had been stuffed by mistake into the soiled-clothes basket, but had turned up safe enough at the end of the trip.

"If that is all," replied McAllister, "all you have to do is to send your man over to the station and have the trunk brought back. Send the fellow who packed the trunk—this Morton—whoever he is."

"No," said his uncle, studiously knocking in the end of a boiled egg. "There are reasons. I wish you would go, instead. The fact is I don't wish Morton to leave the rooms this morning; I—I need him." Lord Lyndhurst again evaded the clubman's inquiring glance, and eyed the egg in an embarrassed fashion.

McAllister laughed. "I guess your jewelry's all right," said he cheerfully. "Certainly I'll go. Don't worry. I'll have the trunk and the jewels back here inside of fifty minutes. Who's Morton, anyhow?"

"My valet," replied Lord Lyndhurst, lowering his voice, and looking over his shoulder. "You wouldn't recall him. I engaged the man at Kingston on the way out. As a servant I have had absolutely no fault to find at all. You know it's very hard to get a good man to go to the Tropics, but Morton has seemed perfectly contented. Up to the present time I haven't had the slightest reason to suspect his honesty!"

"Well, I don't see that you have any now," said McAllister. "I guess I'll start along. I haven't had anythin' to eat yet. Have you the check?"

Uncle Basil gingerly handed him the bit of brass.

"I secured it from Morton," he remarked, attacking the egg viciously.

"Secured it?" exclaimed McAllister.

The Governor-General nodded ambiguously.

Aunt Sophia during the course of the recital had become almost hysterical, and now sat wringing her hands in the greatest agitation. Suddenly she broke forth:

"I told Basil he had been too hasty! But he would have it that there was nothing else to do! Oh, dear! Oh, dear! Why don't you tell him what you've done?"

"What in thunder have you done?" asked McAllister, now convinced beyond peradventure that his uncle was a candidate for the nearest insane asylum.

Lord Lyndhurst became very red, stammered, and jerked his thumb over his shoulder.

"Yes, secured it! Morton, if you must know it, is locked in the clothes-closet. I locked him!"

"He's in there!" suddenly wailed Aunt Sophia. "Basil put him in! And now the jewelry's no one knows where, and there's a man in the room, and I'm afraid to stay and Basil's afraid to go for fear he may get out, and——"

She was interrupted by a smothered voice that came from within the closet. McAllister was startled, for there was something faintly, vaguely familiar about it.

"It's a bloomin' houtrage, it is! Look 'ere, sir, I'll 'ave you to hunderstand that I gives notice at once, sir, 'ere and now, sir! It's a great hindignity you are a-puttin' me to, sir! Won't you let me hout, sir?" The voice ceased momentarily.

"Isn't it awful!" exclaimed Aunt Sophia. "He's been like that for over an hour!"

"Yes!" added Uncle Basil. "At times he's been actually abusive." But McAllister was lost in an effort to recall the hazy past. Where had he heard that voice before?

"'Ang it, sir! Won't you let me hout, sir," continued Morton. "I'm stiflin' in 'ere, an' I thinks there's a rat, sir. O Lawd! Let me hout!"

McAllister jumped to his feet. Of course he recognized the voice! Could he ever forget it? Had anyone ever said "O Lawd!" in quite the same way as the majestic Wilkins? It could be no other! By George, the old man wasn't such a fool after all! And the jewels! He smote his fist upon the table, while his uncle and aunt gazed at him apprehensively. There was no use exciting their fears, however. It was all plain to him, now. The clever dog! Well, the first thing was to see what had become of the jewels.

"Damn!" came in vigorous tones from the closet, as Wilkins endeavored to assert himself. "It's a bloomin' houtrage, it is! I'll 'ave you arrested for hassault an' bat'ry, I will, if you are a guv'nor! Let me hout, I say!"

III

McAllister lost no time in getting to the Grand Central Station. He was looking for a big Vuitton trunk, and he wanted to find it quick. For this purpose he enlisted the services of a burly young porter, who, for the consideration of a half-dollar, piloted the clubman through the crowded alleys of the outgoing baggage-room, until they came upon the familiar collection of Lord Lyndhurst's paraphernalia of travel. Eagerly he recognized the luggage of his uncle's official household. There were his boot-boxes, his hat-boxes, his portable desk, his dumb-bells, his bath-tub, his medicine chest, the secretary's trunk, the typewriter in its case; there were his aunt's basket trunks, and—yes—there was the big Vuitton. McAllister heaved a sigh of relief. The next thing was to get it back to the hotel as fast as possible.

"That's it," said he to the porter. "Heave it out!" They were standing in a little open space some distance from the entrance. The big Vuitton lay at one side, and about it a row of other trunks roughly in a semicircle. The porter made but one step in the desired direction, then jumped as if he had seen a ghost, for a big basket trunk, standing alone upon its end apart, suddenly shook violently, its lock clicked, the cover swung open, and out jumped a slender, sharp-featured young man with a black mustache. It was Barney Conville, although at first McAllister failed to recognize him.

"Look here you! Don't touch that trunk!" he exclaimed. Then he perceived McAllister, and a look of intense disgust overspread his face.

"It's the Baron!" ejaculated McAllister. "Now what the devil do you suppose he's been doin' in that trunk? Howd'y', Baron," he added pleasantly, holding out his hand. "Hardly expected to see you here. Do you take your rest that way?" pointing to the trunk from which Conville had emerged.

The detective eyed him with disapproval.

"Say," he remarked, disdainfully, "you give me a pain—always buttin' in an' spoilin' everythin'! This here is a plant. I'm waitin' fer a thief—Jerry, the Oyster. They're goin' to try an' lift that big striped trunk over there. It belongs to an old party up to the Waldorf. He's a diplomatico."

"He's my uncle!" cried McAllister.

"Your aunt!" snorted Barney.

"But I want to take that trunk back with me."

"On the level?"

"Sure!"

"Can't help it! This is an important job. The Oyster's the cleverest thief in the business. Works in with all the butlers and valets. Why he's got away with more'n three thousand pieces of baggage. He's the——"

Barney did not finish the sentence. Suddenly he ducked, and grabbing McAllister by the shoulder, pulled him down with him.

"There he is now! Into the trunk! There's no other way! Plenty of room!" He shoved his fat companion inside and stepped after him. McAllister, utterly bewildered, tried to convince himself that he was not dreaming. He was quite sure he had taken only one

58

Scotch that morning, but he pinched himself, and was relieved to get the proper reaction. When he became used to the dim light he discovered that he was ensconced in a dress-box of immense proportions, made of basket work, and covered with waterproofing. Placed on end, with a seat across the middle, it afforded a very comfortable place of concealment. Conville turned the key and locked the cover. Then he poked McAllister in the ribs.

"Great joint, ain't it? Idee of the cap's. Makes a fine plant," he whispered, affixing his eye to a narrow slit near the top.

"Sh-h!" he added; "he's here. There's another peeper over on your side."

McAllister followed his example, gluing his eye to the improvised window, and discovered that they commanded the approach to the big Vuitton. And inside that innocent piece of luggage reposed the glory of his uncle's family, the heirlooms of four centuries! He made an involuntary movement.

"Keep still!" hissed Conville, and McAllister sank back obediently.

A young Anglican clergyman in shovel-hat and gaiters, carrying a dainty silver-headed umbrella in one hand and a copy of The Churchman in the other, had approached the counter. He seemed somewhat at a loss, gazed vaguely about him for a moment, and then stepping up to the head baggage-man, an oldish man with white whiskers, addressed him anxiously.

"I say, my man, I'm really in an awful mess, don't you know! I don't see my box anywhere. I sent it over from the hotel early this morning, and I'm leavin' for Montreal at three. The luggage-man says it was left here by ten o'clock. Do you keep all the boxes in this room?"

The head baggage-man nodded.

"Sorry you've lost your trunk," said he. "If it ain't here we haven't got it, but like as not it's mixed up in one of them piles. If you'll wait for about ten minutes I'll see if I can find it for your Reverence."

The Anglican looked shocked.

"Thanks, I'm sure," he murmured stiffly. He was a slight young man with a monocle and mutton-chops.

"It's very good of you," he added after a pause, with more condescension. "Awfully awkward to be without one's luggage, for I have a service in Montreal to-morrow, and all my vestments are in my box. I fear I shall miss my train."

"Oh, I guess not!" replied the baggage-man encouragingly. "I'll be with you presently. You come in and look around yourself,

59

and if you don't see it I'll help you. This way, sir," and he lifted a section of the counter and allowed the clergyman to pass in.

"My! Ain't he clever!" whispered Barney delightedly.

The clergyman now began a rather dilatory investigation of the contents of the baggage-room, bending over and examining every trunk in sight, and even tapping the one in which they were ensconced with the silver head of his umbrella, but after a few moments, in apparent despair, he took his stand beside the big trunk marked "B. C. L.," and gazed despondently about him. There was nothing in his appearance to suggest that he was other than he seemed, but Barney directed McAllister's attention to the copy of The Churchman, from the leaves of which protruded two diminutive pieces of string, put there, as it might appear, for a book-mark. And now as the Anglican shifted from one foot to the other, ostensibly waiting for the porter, he placed his hands behind him and took a step or two backward toward the big trunk. Chubby was by this time all agog. What would the fellow do? He certainly couldn't be goin' to shoulder the trunk and try to walk off with it!

Suddenly McAllister saw the daintily gloved hands slip a penknife from among the leaves of the magazine and quickly sever the check from the handle of the trunk. The Anglican altered his position and waited until the baggage-man was once more engaged at the other end of the counter. Again this amiable representative of the cloth shuffled backward until the handle was within easy reach, and with a dexterity which must have been born of long practice deftly tied the two ends of string around it. With a quick motion he stepped away in the direction of the counter, and out from the leaves of The Churchman fell and dangled a new check stamped "Waistcoat's Express, No. 1467."

"My good fellow," impatiently drawled the clergyman, approaching the baggage-man, "I really can't wait, don'cher know. I've looked everywhere, and my box isn't here. I don't know whether to blame that beastly luggage-man, or whether it's the fault of this disgustin' American railroad. It's evident someone's at fault, and as I assume that you are in charge I shall report you immediately."

The elderly baggage-man regarded the robust champion of religion before him with scorn.

"Well, son, you can report all you like. I've worked in this baggage-room eighteen years, and you're not the first English crank who thought he owned the hull Central Railroad," and he turned on his heel, while the clergyman, with an expression of horror, ambled quickly out of the side door.

McAllister had watched this remarkable proceeding with

enthusiastic interest, his round face shining with the excitement of a child.

"Jiminy, but this is great!" he exclaimed, slapping Barney upon the back. "And to think of your doin' it for a livin'! Why I'd sit here all day for nothin'! What happens next? And what becomes of the feller that's just gone out?"

"Oh, you ain't seen half the show yet!" responded Conville, pleased. "It is pretty good fun at times. But, o' course, this is a star performance, and we're sure of our man. Oh, it beats the theayter, all right, all right! Truth's stranger than fiction every time, you bet. Now take this Oyster—why he's a regular cracker-jack! Got sense enough to be an alderman, or president, or anythin', but he keeps right at his own little job of liftin' trunks, an' he ain't never been caught yet. His pal'll be along now any minute."

"How's that?" inquired Chubby with eagerness.

"Why, don'cher see? Jerry's cut off the reg'lar tag, and now the other feller'll present a duplicate of the one Jerry's just hitched on. Great game, 'Foxy Quiller,' eh?"

McAllister admitted delightedly that it was a great game. By George, it beat playin' the horses! At the same time he shivered as he realized how nearly the famous jewels had actually been lost. Wilkins must be an awful bad egg to go and tie up to a gang of that sort!

The baggage-man, serenely unconscious of all that had been taking place behind his back, and apparently not soured by his little set-to with the Englishman, was genially assisting the great American public to find its effects, and beaming on all about him. People streamed in and out, engines coughed and wheezed; from outside came the roar and rattle of the city.

Presently there bounced in a stout person in a yellow and black suit, with white waistcoat and green tie, who mopped his red face with a large silk handkerchief. Rushing up to a porter who seemed to be unoccupied, he threw down a pasteboard check, together with a shining half-dollar, and shouted, "Here, my good feller, that trunk, will you? Quick! The big one with the red letters on it—'B. C. L.' They sent it here from the Astoria instead of to the steamboat dock, and my ship sails at twelve. Now, get a move on!"

The porter grabbed the check and the half-dollar, and falling upon the big Vuitton, rolled it end over end out into the street, followed by its perspiring claimant.

"That's right, that's right," shouted the bounder. "Chuck it on behind. Mus'n't miss the boat!" and throwing the porter another half-dollar, the sportive traveller jumped into the hack, yelling, "Now drive like the devil!" The door closed with a bang, and the vehicle quickly disappeared among the tracks and wagons of Forty-second Street.

McAllister for the first time felt distinctly uneasy.

"Look here," he whispered feverishly, "is it right to let him walk off like that? Hurry! Open the trunk, or he'll get away!"

"Sit still, and don't get excited!" commanded Barney. "It's all right," he added condescendingly, remembering that McAllister was unfamiliar with such mysteries. "We've got him covered. He couldn't get away to save his neck. An' as for follerin' him, why he'll carry that trunk half over New York before he lands it where it's goin'!"

"All right!" sighed the clubman; "you're the doctor. But it seems to me you're takin' a lot of risk. Your brother officer might lose track of him, or he might drop the trunk somehow, and then where would the jewels be?"

"Right exactly where they are now," replied Barney with a grin. "In the office safe at the Waldorf. They ain't never left the hotel. There wasn't any need of it, and if I hadn't taken 'em out I'd 've had to watch 'em here all night. Now everythin's all right.

"And say," he added, chuckling at the joke of it, "I forgot to tell you. Who do you suppose is workin' with Jerry? Fatty Welch! 'Wilkins,' you'd call him. He's turned up again an' hooked on, somehow, to the Gov'nor. Me and my side-partner's been trailin' 'em both ever since your uncle hit New York. I had the room opposite him at the Waldorf. Yesterday mornin' I saw Welch pack the jewelry. I was togged out as a bell-boy, and was cleanin' the winders. The Gov'nor's kind of figgity you know, and I thought we'd better not mention anythin' to him. Of course I didn't have any idea you'd come waltzin' along this way."

McAllister solemnly held out his hand to the detective. He was as demonstrative as his narrow quarters rendered possible.

"Baron," said he, "you're a corker! I've learned a heap this morning."

"There's lots of things you never dream of, Horace," replied Barney politely.

"Do you remember, Baron, the last time we met asking me to help you nab Wilkins?" continued McAllister. "Well, I'm goin' to make good. I've got him safely locked in a closet at the hotel. He promised not to come back, and now I'm done with him. What do you say to that?"

"Good work!" ejaculated Barney. "Keep it up! In time you might make a pretty good detective."

From Barney such a concession was high praise, and showed intense appreciation. On their way back to the Waldorf he explained that the "Oyster" was one of a very few "guns" able effectively to make use of a disguise, this being in part due to the fact that he was the son of a clergyman, and educated for the stage.

They were met at the door of the apartment by Lady Lyndhurst.

"Basil has disappeared!" she gasped. "And that awful man in the closet has become so blasphemous that I can't remain with decency in the room."

McAllister partially pacified her by stating that the jewelry was entirely safe. He wondered what on earth had become of the Governor. Once inside the suite conversation became practically impossible, owing to the sounds of inarticulate rage which proceeded from the closet.

Barney decided to place the valet immediately under arrest and take him to Police Headquarters. The sooner they did so the more likely he would be to "squeal." He requested McAllister to arm himself with a walking-stick, and to stand ready to come to his assistance if, on opening the door, he should find himself unable to cope with the prisoner alone. Aunt Sophia was relegated to her bedroom, the door leading to the corridor was closed and locked, and the two prepared for the conflict. The detective, of course, had his pistol, which he cocked and held ready.

"Don't fire 'till you see the whites of his eyes!" murmured McAllister.

"Fire—nothin'!" muttered Barney, throwing open the closet door.

"Hands up, or I'll shoot!" yelled the detective, as a fat, wild-eyed individual sprung from within and burst upon their astonished gaze. The Governor-General stood before them.

Speechless with rage, he glowered from one to the other—then in response to their surprised inquiries broke into incoherent explanation. He had waited on guard some ten minutes after McAllister's departure, and Sophia had gone to her bedroom to finish dressing, when suddenly the expostulations of Morton had seemed to grow fainter. Finally they had died entirely away, and in their place had come terrible gasps and gurgles. He had remembered that there was no means of renewing the air supply in the closet, and had become alarmed. Presently all sounds had ceased. He was convinced that Morton was being suffocated. Opening the door, he had found the valet apparently lying there unconscious, and had dragged him forth, whereupon Morton had suddenly returned to life, and before he knew it had jammed him into the closet and locked the door.

"He was most impertinent, too, when he got on the outside, I can assure you," concluded Lord Lyndhurst indignantly. "Gave me a lot of gratuitous advice!"

McAllister and the detective endeavored to calm his troubled spirit, and soothe his ruffled dignity, informing him that the jewels had been in the hotel safe all the time. The Governor, however, refused to take any stock whatever in their explanation. Nothing of the sort could possibly have happened in England. It took them an hour to persuade him that they were not lying. The only things that appeared to convince him at all were the disappearance of Morton, a large bump on his own forehead, and the actual presence of the jewelry in the safe downstairs. Even then he sent to Tiffany's for a man to examine it.

Barney he regarded with unconcealed suspicion, subjecting him to an exhaustive cross-examination upon his antecedents and occupation. The Governor declared he was astounded at his impudence. The idea of opening his private luggage! He would address a communication to the authorities! It was little better than grand larceny. It was grand larceny, by Jupiter! Hadn't Conville abstracted the jewels vi et armis? Of course he had! Damme, he would see if the sacred rights of an English official should be trampled on! It was trespass anyway—Trespass ab initio! Did Conville know that? It was grand larceny and trespass. He would lock him up.

Barney grinned, and the Governor again became almost apoplectic.

He snorted scornfully at the detective's explanation about this Jerry "What-do-you-call-him—the Clam." Pooh! Did they expect him to believe that? Conville was a confounded, hair-brained busybody—He dwindled off, exhausted.

At that moment there came a sharp rap upon the door, and an officer in roundsman's uniform entered.

"Gentleman called at the precinct house and reported a jewelry theft in this suite. Said the thief had been caught and locked up in a closet, so I thought I'd drop over and see how things stood."

He looked inquiringly at McAllister, significantly at the Governor-General, and then caught sight of Barney.

"Hello, Conville!" he exclaimed. "You on the case? Well, then I'll drop out. Got your man, I see!" He glanced again at the dishevelled scion of nobility before him.

"Everythin's all right," answered the detective with a chuckle. "I guess they was fakin' you round at the house. By the way, I want you to meet a friend of mine—Roundsman McCarthy, let me present you to his Nibs—the Governor-General."

The Governor glared immobile, his stony eyes shifting from

the now red and stammering roundsman to Conville's beaming countenance, and back again.

"Gentlemen," he remarked sternly, "do you prefer Scotch or rye? You will find cigars on the sideboard. The drinks, as you Yankees say, are upon me!"

"By the way," he added to McCarthy, as McAllister filled the glasses, "would you be so obliging as to describe the individual who so thoughtfully notified you in regard to the loss of the jewelry?"

"Rather stout, well-dressed man, fat face, gray eyes," answered McCarthy, lighting a cigar. "Looked somethin' like this gentleman here," indicating the clubman. "Spoke with a kind of English accent. Nice appearin' feller, all right."

"By George! Wilkins!" ejaculated McAllister.

"Damn!" exploded Uncle Basil.

"The nerve of him!" muttered Barney.

THE GOLDEN TOUCH

I

McAllister, with his friend Wainwright, was lounging before the fire in the big room, having a little private Story Teller's Night of their own. It was in the early autumn, and neither of the clubmen were really settled in town as yet, the former having run down from the Berkshires only for a few days, and the latter having just landed from the Cedric. The sight of Tomlinson, who appeared tentatively in the distance and then, receiving no encouragement, stalked slowly away, reminded Wainwright of something he had heard in Paris.

"I base my claim to your sympathetic credence, McAllister, upon the impregnable rock of universally accepted fact that Tomlinson is a highfalutin ass. I see that you agree. Very good, then; I proceed. In the first place, you must know that our anemic friend decided last spring that the state of his health required a trip to Paris. He therefore went—alone. The reason is obvious. Who should he fall in with at the Hotel Continental but a gentleman named Buncomb—Colonel C. T. P. Buncomb, a person with a bullet-hole in the middle of his forehead, who claimed to belong to a most exclusive Southern family in Savannah. Incidentally he'd been in command of a Georgia regiment in the Civil War and had been knocked in the head at Gettysburg—one of those big, flabby fellows with white hair. If all Tomlinson says about his capacity to chew Black Strap and absorb rum is accurate, I reckon the Colonel was right up to weight and could qualify as an F. F. V. He knew everybody and everything in Paris; passed up our friend right along the Faubourg Saint Germain; and introduced him to a lot of duchesses and countesses—that is, Tomlinson says they were. Can't you see 'em, swaggerin' down the Champs-Élysées arm in arm? In addition, he took our mournful acquaintance to all the cafés chantants and students' balls, and gave him sure things on the races. Oh, that Colonel must have been a regular doodle-bug!

"In due course Tomlinson gathered that his new friend was a mining expert taking a short vacation and just blowing in an extra half million or so. He believed it. You see, he had never met any of them at the Waldorf at home. He was also introduced to a young man in the same line of business, named Larry Summerdale, who seemed to have plenty of money, and was likewise au fait with the aristocracy.

"Well, one night, after they had been to the Bal Boullier and had had a little supper at the Jockey Club, the Colonel became a trifle more confidential than usual, and let drop that their friend Summerdale had a brother employed as private secretary by a copper king who owned a wonderful mine out in Arizona called The Silver Bow. The stock in this concern had originally been sold at five dollars a share, but recently a rich vein had been struck and the stock had quadrupled in value. No one knew of this except the officers of the company, who, of course, were anxious to buy up all they could find. They had located most of it easily enough, but there were two or three lots that had thus far eluded them. Among these was the largest single block of stock in existence, owned by the son of the original discoverer of the prospect. He had two thousand shares, and was blissfully ignorant of the fact that they were worth forty thousand dollars. Just where this chap was no one seemed to know, but his name was Edwin H. Blake, and he was supposed to be in Paris. It appeared that the Colonel and Larry were watching out for Blake with the charitable idea of relieving him of his stock at five, and selling it for twenty in the States.

"Next day, if you'll believe it, the Colonel didn't remember a thing; became quite angry at Tomlinson's supposing he'd take advantage of any person in the way suggested; explained that he must have been drinking, and begged him to forget everything that might have been said. Of course, Tomlinson dropped the subject, but after that the Colonel and he rather drifted apart. Then quite by accident, two or three weeks later, our friend stumbled on Blake himself—met him right on the race-track, through a Frenchman named Depau.

"Now our innocent friend had been sort of lonely ever since he'd lost sight of Buncomb, and this Blake turned out to be an awfully good sort. Tomlinson naturally inquired if he'd ever met the Colonel or Larry Summerdale, but he never had, and finally they took an apartment together."

"He must have been pleased when Tomlinson told him about the value of his stock," remarked McAllister, lighting another cigar.

"I'm comin' to that," replied Wainwright. "It seems that Tomlinson so far forgot his early New England traditions as to covet that stock himself. Shockin', wasn't it?

"One day, when they were lunching at the Trois Freres, our friend hinted that he was interested in mining stock. Blake laughed, and replied that if Tomlinson owned as much as he did of the stuff he wouldn't want to see another share as long as he lived, and added that he was loaded up with a lot of worthless stock—two thousand shares—in an old prospect in Arizona that he had inherited from his father, and wasn't worth the paper the certificate was printed on. The leery Tomlinson admitted having heard of the mine, but gave it as his impression that it had possibilities.

"Then he had a sudden headache, and went out and cabled to The Silver Bow offices at the World building here in New York to find out what the company would pay for the stock. In an hour or two he got an answer stating that they were prepared to give twenty dollars a share for not less than two thousand shares. Good, eh?

"Well, next day he led the conversation round again to mining stocks, and finally offered to buy Blake's holdings for five dollars a share. When the latter hesitated, Tomlinson was so afraid he'd lose the stock that he almost raised his bid to fifteen; but Blake only laughed, and said that he had no intention of robbing one of his friends, and that the old stuff really wasn't worth a cent. Tomlinson became quite indignant, suggested that perhaps he knew more about that particular mine than even Blake did, and finally overcame the latter's scruples and persuaded him to sell. Then Tomlinson disposed of some bonds by cable, and that evening gave Blake a draft for fifty thousand francs in exchange for his two thousand share certificate in The Silver Bow of Arizona. He told me it had a picture of a miner with a pick-ax and a mule standing against the rising sun on it. Sort of allegorical, don't you think?

"Blake continued to protest that our friend was being cheated, and offered to buy it back at any time; but Tomlinson's one idea was to get to New York as fast as possible. He had cabled that the stock was on the way, and that very night he slid out of Paris and caught the Norddeutscher Lloyd at Cherbourg. I inferred that he occupied the bridal chamber on the way back all by himself.

"The instant they landed he jumped in a cab and started for the World building; but when he got there he couldn't find any Silver Bow Mining Company. It had evaporated. It had been there right enough—for ten days—the ten days Tomlinson calculated that it had taken Blake to sell him the stock. But no one knew where it had gone or what had become of it.

"Well, of course," kept on Wainwright, "he nearly went crazy; cabled the police in Paris and had 'em all arrested, including Colonel Buncomb; and took the next steamer back. He says they had the trial in a little police court in the Palais de Justice. Buncomb had hired Maître Labori to defend him. Everybody kept their hats on, and apparently they all shouted at once. The Judge was the only one that kept his mouth shut at all. Tomlinson told his story through an interpreter, and charged Buncomb, Summerdale, and Blake with conspiracy to defraud.

"When the Colonel realized what it was all about he jumped into the middle of the room, pushed his silk hat back of his ears, flapped his coat-tails, and sailed into 'em in good old Southern style. I tell you he must have made the eagle scream. He was a Colonel in the Confederate Army, he was—the Thirtieth Georgia. The whole thing was a miserable French scheme to blackmail him. He'd appeal to the American Ambassador. He'd see if a parcel of French soup-makers and a police judge could interfere with the Constitution of the United States. Every once in a while he'd yell 'Conspuez' or 'À bas' and sort of froth at the mouth. He made a great big impression. Then Maître Labori got in his licks. He said Tomlinson was a wolf in sheep's clothing—a rascal—a 'vilain m'sieur,' whatever that is.

"Finally he inquired, with a very unpleasant smile, if Buncomb had ever asked him to buy any stock?

"Tomlinson had to say 'No.'

"Did Larry Summerdale?

"'No'

"Didn't Blake tell him the stock was worthless?

"'Yes.'

"How did he know the stock wasn't worth what he paid for it?

"'Well, he didn't absolutely.'

"The Labori said something with a long rattling 'r' in it like a snake, and turned with a gesture of extreme contempt to the Judge. He remarked that one glance of comparison between Colonel Buncomb and Tomlinson would show which was the gentleman and which was the rogue. Then the first thing our friend knew the court had adjourned—they had all been turned out—discharged—acquitted. But the thing that most disgusted Tomlinson was that as he was coming away he saw the whole push, the Colonel and Larry and Blake, all piling into a big Panhard autocar. They passed him going about eighty miles an hour. You see, Tomlinson had paid for that car, and he'd always wanted one to run himself. The last he heard of 'em they were tearing up the Riviera."

"And what did Tomlinson do then?" asked McAllister.

"There was nothing he could do in Paris, so he came home on a ten-day boat and went to visit his uncle up at Methuen, Mass. Gay place, Methuen! Saturday night you can ride down to Lawrence on the electric car for a nickel and hear the band play in front of the gas works. But the simple life has done him good."

One evening, several months later, McAllister and a party of friends dropped into Rector's after the theatre for a caviare sandwich before turning in. The hostelry, as usual, was in a blaze of light and crowded, but after waiting for a few moments they were given a table just vacated by a party of four. McAllister, having given their order, noticed a couple seated directly in his line of vision who instantly challenged his attention. The girl was ordinary—slender, dark-haired, sharp-featured, and clad in a scarlet costume trimmed with ermine—obviously an actress or vaudeville "artist." It was her companion, however, that caused McAllister to readjust his monocle. Curious! Where had he seen that face? It was that of a heavy man of approximately sixty, benign, smooth-shaven, full-featured, and with an expanse of broad white forehead, the centre of which was marked in a curious fashion by a deep dent like a hole made by dropping a marble into soft putty. It gave him the appearance of having had a third eye, now extinct. It fascinated McAllister. He was sure he had met the old fellow somewhere—he couldn't just place where. But that hole in the forehead—yes, he was certain! Listening abstractedly to his friends' conversation, the clubman studied his neighbor, becoming each moment more convinced that at some time in the past they had been thrown together. Presently the pair arose, and the man helped the woman into her ermine coat. The hole in his forehead kept falling in and out of shadow, as McAllister, his eyes fastened upon it like some bird charmed by a reptile, watched the head waiter bow them ostentatiously out.

"Fellows!" exclaimed McAllister, "look at those people just going out; do you know who they are?"

"Why, that's Yvette Vibbert, the comedienne," said Rogers. "She's at Hammerstein's. I don't know her escort. By George! that's a queer thing on his forehead."

McAllister beckoned the head waiter to him.

"Alphonse, who's the gentleman with Mademoiselle Vibbert?"

Alphonse smiled.

"Zat is Monsieur Herbert." He pronounced it Erbaire.

"Well, who's Monsieur Erbaire?"

Alphonse elevated his eyebrows, shrugged his shoulders, protruded his lips, and extended the palms of his hands.

"Alphonse says," remarked McAllister, turning to the group around the table, "Alphonse says that you can search him."

70

III

McAllister had speculated for a day or two upon the probable identity of the man with the hole in his forehead, and then had finally given it up as a bad job. One didn't like to dig up the past too carefully, anyhow. You never could tell exactly what you might exhume.

The next Sunday afternoon, while running his eyes carelessly over the "personals," his notice was attracted to the following:

> Business Opportunities.—Advertiser wants party with four thousand dollars ready cash; can make twelve thousand dollars in five weeks; no scheme, strictly legitimate business transaction; will bear thorough investigation; must act immediately; no brokers; principals only.
>
> Herbert, 319 Herald.

The name sounded familiar. But he didn't know any Herbert. Then there hovered in the penumbra of his consciousness for a moment the ghost of a scarlet dress, an ermine hat. Ah, yes! Herbert was the man with the hole in his forehead that night at Rector's, that Alphonse didn't know. But where had he known that man? He raised his eyes and caught a glimpse of Tomlinson, the saturnine Tomlinson, sitting by a window. Of course! Buncomb—Colonel C. T. P. Buncomb—Tomlinson's high-rolling friend of the Champs-Élysées—turned up in New York as Mr. Herbert—a man who'd triple your money in five weeks! The chain was complete. If he kept his wits about him he might increase the reputation achieved at Blair's. It would require finesse, to be sure, but his experience with Conville had given him confidence. Here was a chance to do a little more detective work on his own account. He replied to the advertisement, inviting an interview. The "Colonel" would probably call, try some old swindling game, McAllister would lure him on, and at the proper moment call in the police. It looked easy sailing.

Accordingly the appointed hour next day found the clubman waiting impatiently at his rooms, and at two o'clock promptly Mr. Herbert was announced. But McAllister was doomed to disappointment. The visitor was not the Colonel at all, and didn't even have a bullet-hole in his forehead. A short, thick-set man, arrayed carefully in a dark blue overcoat, bowed himself in. In his hand he carried a glistening silk hat, and his own countenance was no less shining and urbane. Thick bristly black hair parted mathematically in the middle drooped on either side of his forehead above a pair of snappy black eyes and rather bulbous nose.

71

McAllister somewhat uneasily invited his guest to be seated.

Mr. Herbert smilingly took the chair offered him.

"Mr. McAllister?" he inquired affably.

"Ye-es," replied the clubman. "I noticed your advertisement in the Herald, and it occurred to me that I might like to look into it."

Mr. Herbert smiled slightly in a deprecating manner.

"I admit my method savors a trifle of charlatanism," he remarked, "but the situation was unusual and time was of the essence. Are we quite alone?"

"Oh, yes, certainly! Will you smoke?"

Mr. Herbert had no objection to joining McAllister in a cigar.

"The gist of the matter is this," he explained, holding the weed in the corner of his mouth as he spoke—a trick McAllister had never acquired. "I have a brother who is employed in a confidential capacity by the president of a large mining company—The Golden Touch. The stock has always sold at around four or five. Recently they struck a very rich lode. It was kept very quiet, and only the officers of the company actually on the field know of it. Needless to say, they are buying in the stock as fast as they can."

"Of course," answered McAllister sympathetically. He felt as if he had run across an old friend again. Things were looking up a bit.

"Well, I have located a block of which they know absolutely nothing. It was issued to an engineer in lieu of cash for services at the mine. He suddenly developed sciatica, and is obliged to go to Baden-Baden. At present he is laid up at one of the hotels in this city. Of course he is ignorant of the find made since he left Arizona, and of the fact that his stock, once worth only five dollars a share, is now selling at twenty."

"Well, he's a richer man than he supposes," commented McAllister naively.

Mr. Herbert smiled with condescension.

"Exactly. That is the point. If I had five thousand dollars I could buy his thousand shares to-morrow and sell it to the company at fifteen thousand dollars' profit. You furnish the funds, I the opportunity, and we divide even. I've a sure thing! What do you think of it?"

"By George!" exclaimed the clubman, slapping his knee delightedly, "I've a mind to go you! . . . But," he added shrewdly, "I should want to see the prospective buyer of my stock before I purchased it."

"Right you are; right you are, Mr. McAllister," instantly returned Mr. Herbert. "Now, I'm dead on the level, see? To-morrow morning you can go down and see the president of The Golden Touch yourself. The offices are in the New York Life Building."

"All right," answered McAllister. "To-morrow? Wait a minute; I've an engagement. Why can't we go now?"

Mr. Herbert nodded approvingly. Ah, that was business! They would go at once.

McAllister rang for Frazier, who assisted him into his coat and summoned a cab. On their way down-town Herbert waxed even more confidential. He believed, if they could land this block of stock, they might perhaps dig up a few more hundred shares. Conscientious effort counted just as much in an affair of this sort as in any other. McAllister displayed the deepest interest.

Arrived at the New York Life Building, the two took the elevator to the fifth floor, where Herbert led the way to a large suite on the Leonard Street side. McAllister rarely had to go down-town— his lawyer usually called on him at his rooms—and was much impressed by the marble corridors and gilt lettering upon the massive doors. Upon a door at the end of the hall the clubman could see in large capitals the words,

THE GOLDEN TOUCH MINING CO.

Office of the President.

They turned to the left and paused outside another door marked "Entrance." Herbert thought he'd better remain in the corridor—the President might smell a rat; so McAllister decided to enter alone. In an adjoining suite he could see some men testing a fire-escape consisting of a long bulging canvas tube, which reached from the window in the direction of the street below. Someone was preparing to make a descent. McAllister wished he could stop and see the fellow slide through; but business was business, and he opened the door.

Inside he found himself in a large, handsome office. Three gum-chewing boys idled at desks in front of a brass railing, behind which several typewriters rattled continuously. On learning that McAllister desired to see the President, one of the boys penetrated an inner office, and presently beckoned our friend into another room hung with large maps and photographs and furnished with a mahogany table, around which were ranged a dozen vacant but impressive chairs. In the room beyond, evidently the holy of holies, he could see an elderly man at a roll-top desk smoking a large cigar.

McAllister was beginning to lose his nerve; everything seemed so methodical and everybody so busy. Telephones rang incessantly; buzzers whirred; the machines clacked; and the man inside smoked on serenely, unperturbed, a wonderful example of the superiority of

73

mind over matter. Who was he? McAllister began to fear that he was going to make an ass of himself. Then the magnate slowly raised his eyes; retreat became no longer possible. With a start, McAllister found himself face to face with the man with the bullet-hole in his forehead. The latter bowed slightly.

"I am President Van Vorst," he announced in a dignified manner.

McAllister hastily tried to assume the expression and manner of a yokel.

"Er—er—" he stammered; "you see, the fact is, I want to sell some stock."

The Colonel eyed him sternly.

"Stock? What stock?"

"In the Golden Touch."

The President slightly elevated his eyebrows.

"Stock in The Golden Touch? How much have you got?"

"About a thousand shares."

"Nonsense!" remarked the Colonel.

"No, it isn't," replied McAllister. "I have, really. What'll you pay for it?"

"Five dollars a share."

"No, no," said McAllister, edging nervously toward the door. "I think it's worth more than that."

"Come back here," muttered the other, getting up from his chair and scowling. "What do you know about the value of The Golden Touch, I should like to know?"

"Perhaps I know more than you think," answered McAllister, with an inane imitation of airy nonchalance.

"See here," said the Colonel excitedly, "is this on the level? Can you deliver a thousand?"

"Certainly."

The President sank back in his chair.

"Then you have located Murphy's stock!" he exclaimed. "You've beaten us! That cursed certificate was issued just before—" He paused, and looked sharply toward McAllister.

"Just before you made that strike," finished the clubman significantly.

"Hang you!" cried the Colonel angrily. "What do you ask?"

"Eighteen."

"Too much. Give you ten."

McAllister started for the door.

At that instant a telegraph-boy entered and handed the President a flimsy yellow paper.

"Give you twelve," added the Colonel, casting his eye rapidly over the telegram.

"Can't do business on that basis."

"Well, you've got us cornered. I'll break the record. I'll give you fifteen."

McAllister hesitated.

"All right," said he rather reluctantly. "Cash down?"

"Of course," replied the Colonel. "I'll wait here for you. You might as well look at this now." And he showed the clubman the paper.

Stafford, Arizona.

Struck very rich ore on the foot-wall. Recent assays show eight per cent. copper, carrying five dollars in gold to the ton. Try and locate Murphy's stock.

"You see," added the Colonel, "I've got to get it, if it busts me!"

"Well, you shall have it in half an hour," replied McAllister.

Out in the corridor Herbert wanted to know exactly what had happened, and laughed heartily when McAllister described the interview. Oh, that old Van Vorst was a sly dog! He'd steal the gold out of your teeth if you gave him the chance. Carrying five dollars in gold to the ton! That was even better than his brother had advised him. Well, the next thing was to capture Murphy's stock.

On their way to the Astor House to see the sick engineer, McAllister stopped at the Chemical National Bank, on the pretext of procuring the money to pay for the stock, and there called up Police Headquarters. Conville presently came to the wire, and it was arranged between them that the detective should communicate with Tomlinson and bring him at once to the New York Life Building. There they would await the return of McAllister and follow him to the offices of the mining company.

McAllister then rejoined Mr. Herbert in the cab and drove at once to the hotel. The polite clerk informed the strangers that Mr. Murphy was bad, very bad, and that they would have to secure permission from the trained nurse before they could visit him. They might, however, go upstairs and inquire for themselves.

Mr. Murphy's room proved to be at the extreme end of a musty corridor, in which the pungent odor of iodoform and antiseptics, noticeable even at the elevator, gave evidence of his lamentable condition. A soft knock brought an immediate response from a muscular male nurse, who was at last persuaded to allow them to interview his patient on the express condition that their call should be limited to a few moments' duration only. Inside, the smell of medicine became overpowering. McAllister could discern by the dim light a figure lying upon a bed in the far corner shrouded in bandages, and moaning with pain. Near at hand stood a table covered with liniment and bottles.

"Wot is it?" whined the sick engineer. "Carn't yer leave me in peace? Wot is it, I s'y?"

For the third time in his life McAllister's heart nearly stopped beating at the sound of that voice. It was, however, unmistakable. Should it come from the heavens above, or the caverns of the hills, or the waters beneath the earth, it could originate in but one unique, extraordinary individual—Wilkins! It was a startling complication, and for an instant McAllister's brain refused to cope with the situation.

"You really must pardon us!" Herbert began, "but we've come to see if you wouldn't sell some of your Golden Touch mining stock."

"'Oly Moses!" wailed the sick engineer, turning his head to the wall. "Oh, my leg! Wot do you come 'ere for, about stock, when I'm almost dead? Go aw'y, I s'y!"

McAllister pulled himself together. He had intended buying the stock, and on returning to the company's offices to have Conville arrest Herbert and the Colonel, without bothering about the sick engineer. He was pretty sure he had evidence enough. But now, with Wilkins to assist him, he undoubtedly could force a confession from them both.

"Go ahead," he whispered to Herbert; "I'm no good at that sort of thing."

So Mr. Herbert started in to persuade his invalid confederate to part with his valueless stock for McAllister's money. He waxed eloquent over the glories of the Continent and the miraculous cures effected at Baden-Baden, as well as upon the uncertainties of this life, and mining stock in particular.

Meanwhile the sick man tossed in agony upon his pallet and cursed the inconsiderate strangers who forced their selfish interests upon him at such a moment. Outside the door the nurse coughed impatiently. At last, after an unusually persistent harangue on the part of Herbert, the invalid, inveighing against the sciatica that had placed him thus at their mercy, and more to get rid of them than anything else, reluctantly yielded. Fumbling among the bed-clothes, he produced a soiled certificate, which he smoothed out and regarded sadly.

"'Ere, tyke it," he muttered. "Tyke it! Gimme yer money, an' go aw'y!"

As yet he had not recognized McAllister, who had remained partially concealed behind his companion.

"Now's your chance!" whispered the latter. "Take it while you can get it. Where's the money?"

McAllister drew out the bills, which crackled deliciously in his hands, and stepped square in front of the sick engineer, between him and Herbert.

"Mr. Murphy"—he spoke the words slowly and distinctly—"I'm the person who's buying your stock. This gentleman has merely interested me in the proposition." Then, fixing his eyes directly on those of Wilkins, he held out the bills. A look of terror came over the face of the valet, and he half-raised himself from the pillow as he stared horrified at his former master. Then he sank back, and turned away his head.

"Now answer me a few questions," continued McAllister. "Are you the bona fide owner of this stock?"

Wilkins choked.

"S' 'elp me! Got it fer services," he gasped.

"And it's worth what you ask—five thousand dollars?"

Wilkins glanced helplessly at Herbert, who was examining a bottle of iodine on the mantelpiece. Then he rolled convulsively upon his side.

"Oh, my leg!" he groaned, thrashing around until his head came within a few inches of McAllister's face. "It's rotten," he whispered under his breath. "Don't touch it! . . . Oh, my pore leg! . . . Just pretend to pass me the money. . . . 'Ere, tyke yer stock, if yer 'ave to! . . . I wouldn't rob yer, sir, indeed I wouldn't! . . . W'ere's yer money?"

A gentle smile came over McAllister's placid countenance. Who said there was no honor among thieves? Who said there was no such thing as gratitude and self-sacrifice? He did not realize at the moment that it was the only thing Wilkins could possibly have done to save himself. His simple faith accepted it as an act of devotion upon the other's part. With a swift wink at his old servant, McAllister stepped back to where Herbert was standing.

"I don't know," he said doubtfully. "How can I be sure this sick man's name is really Murphy, or that he is the fellow that worked at the mine? I guess I'd better have him identified before I give up my money."

"Don't be foolish!" growled Herbert. "Of course he's the man! My brother gave his description in the letter, and he fits it to a T. And then he has the certificate. What more do you want?"

"I don't know," repeated McAllister hesitatingly. He shook his head and shifted from one foot to the other. "I don't know. I guess I won't do it."

Herbert seemed annoyed.

"Look here," he demanded of the sick engineer, "are you so awful sick you can't come over to the company's offices and be identified?"—adding sotto voce to McAllister, "if he does, old Van Vorst will probably buy the stock himself, and we'll lose our chance."

The sick man moaned and grumbled. By 'ookey! 'Ere was impudence for yer. Come an' rob 'im of 'is stock, an' then demand 'e be identified.

"We'll take you in our cab. It ain't far," urged Herbert, nodding vigorously at Wilkins from behind McAllister.

"Oh, I'll go!" responded the engineer with sudden alacrity. "Anything to hoblige."

He hobbled painfully out of bed. The nurse had by this time returned, and was demanding in forcible language that his patient should instantly get back. Seeing that his expostulations had no effect, he assisted Wilkins very ungraciously to get into his clothes. With the aid of a stout cane the latter tottered to the elevator and was finally ensconced safely in the cab. All this had occupied nearly an hour; twenty minutes more brought them to the New York Life Building.

As McAllister and Herbert assisted their supposed victim into the building, the clubman caught a glimpse of the lean Tomlinson and athletically built Conville standing together behind the pillars of the portico. The elevator whisked them up to the fifth floor so rapidly that the sick man swore loudly that he should never live to come down again. As they turned into the corridor toward the entrance of the office, McAllister saw his confederates emerge from the rear elevator. Things were going well enough, so far. Now for the coup d'état!

The boy admitted them at once into the inner sanctum. As before, President Van Vorst sat there calmly smoking a cigar. At his right, in a corner by the window, stood a heavy iron safe.

"Well," said McAllister briskly, "I've brought the stock, and I've brought its former owner with it. Do you recognize him?"

"Well, well!" returned the President, stepping forward with great cordiality and clasping Wilkins's hand in his. "If it isn't my old engineer, Murphy! How are you, Murphy, old socks? It's nearly a year, isn't it, since you were at Stafford?"

"Yes," replied Wilkins tremulously, "an' I'm a very sick man. I've got the skyathicer somethin' hawful."

McAllister produced the stock from his coat-pocket.

"Do you identify this certificate?" inquired the clubman.

"Of course! Now think of that! I've been lookin' for that thousand shares ever since Murphy left the mine," said the Colonel with a show of irritation.

"Well, are you ready to pay for it?" demanded McAllister sharply.

The Colonel hesitated, looking from one to the other. Clearly he could not determine just how matters stood.

"Well," he remarked finally, "I can't pay for it just this minute, but I'll go right out and get the money. You see, I didn't expect you back quite so soon. Who does the stock belong to, anyhow—you, or Murphy?"

"At present it belongs to me," said the clubman.

As McAllister spoke he stepped in front of the door leading into the directors' room. From below came faintly the rattle of the street and the clang of electric cars, while in the outer office could be heard the merry tattoo of the typewriters. Could it be possible that in this opulently furnished office, with its rosewood desk and chairs, its Persian rugs and paintings, its plate glass and heavy curtains, he was confronting a crew of swindlers of whom his own valet was an accomplice? It was almost past belief. Yet, as he recalled Wainwright's vivid description of the fall of Tomlinson, the scene at Rector's, the advertisement in the Herald, and the strange occurrences of the morning, he perceived that there could be no question in the matter. He was facing three common—or rather most uncommon—thieves, all of whom probably had served more than one term in State prison—desperate characters, who would not hesitate to use force, or worse, should it appear necessary. For a moment the clubman lost heart. He might be murdered, and no one be the wiser. Then a vague shadow flickered against the opaque glass of the main door, and McAllister gained new courage. Conville was just outside, with Tomlinson—although the latter could not be regarded as a valuable auxiliary in the event of a hand-to-hand struggle. Was he safe in counting on Wilkins? What if the ex-convict should go back on him? How did the valet know but that, by assisting his master, he was sending himself to State prison? McAllister had a fleeting desire to turn and dart from the room. What business had a middle-aged clubman turning detective, anyway? Then he braced himself, took a good grip of his stout walking-stick, and turned to the Colonel with an assumption of calmness which he was very far from feeling. The noonday sun streamed into the windows and threw into strong relief the muscular figures of the group about him.

"I'm afraid you've been deceived in Murphy," he remarked coolly. "He isn't an engineer at all; he's just an ex-convict."

The Colonel uttered a swift oath and snatched a Colt from an open drawer of the desk. Herbert turned fiercely upon the clubman. Wilkins dropped his crutch.

"What are you giving us!" cried the Colonel.

"I'll leave it to him," added McAllister. "By the way, his name isn't Murphy at all—it's Wilkins—or Welch, if you prefer."

"What's this—a plant?" yelled Herbert. "By God, if——"

"Don't be upset, Mr. Summerdale," said the clubman. "You might lay down that pistol, Colonel Buncomb. Wilkins is an old friend of mine—in fact he used to work for me."

The two thieves glared at him, speechless. Wilkins picked up his crutch by the small end, remarking:

"Better go easy there, Buncomb."

"I think you gentlemen had the pleasure of meeting another friend of mine last summer, a Mr. Tomlinson," continued McAllister. "He's told me a good deal about you. I am under the impression that he paid for an automobile and a little trip you took on the Riviera. How would you like to turn back the money?"

Buncomb stood in the middle of the room pale and motionless, while the clubman opened the door into the hall and called Tomlinson's name.

"Yaas, I'm here, McAllister. What do you want?" replied the club bore as his lank figure entered the room. At the sight of Buncomb, Summerdale, and Wilkins he stopped short.

"By Jove!" he drawled, "I'm dashed if it ain't the Colonel—and Larry!"

"Look here, you—you—chappie!" snarled Buncomb, "clear out of here! And you, too, Tomlinson. Understand?" He waved the revolver threateningly.

"Colonel," remarked McAllister, "I'm here for just one purpose, and that's to collect the debt you gentlemen owe my friend Mr. Tomlinson. Wilkins, or Welch, or Murphy, or whatever you call him, is ready to turn state's evidence against you. I promise him immunity. There's an officer just outside. Shall I call him?"

"Is that straight, Fatty?" cried Summerdale, his face livid with fright and anger. "Are you going to squeal on us?"

"Sure!" replied Wilkins. "I'm through with you, you miserable shell-gamers! The best thing for you is to hopen the old coal-box hover there and count hout what's left of that ten thousand."

"Curse you!" hissed Summerdale. "How do we know you won't have us pinched whether we pay up or not?"

"I reckon we'd better take a chance," muttered the Colonel,

laying down his revolver and dropping on his knees before the safe. The little knob spun around, the lock clicked, and the heavy door swung open, but at the same moment there was a terrific crash of glass behind them.

"Excuse noise," exclaimed Conville, thrusting his face through the broken pane and covering Buncomb with a long black weapon. "Kindly keep your arms up, Colonel—and you too, Larry. How stout you've grown! Thank you! I was peekin' through the keyhole, and kinder thought this would be a good time to freeze on to what was in the safe without callin' in an expert."

The next instant he had unlocked the door with his other hand and snapped the handcuffs on Summerdale's uplifted wrist. While the detective was doing the same to the Colonel, McAllister caught sight of Wilkins's frightened glance, and gave a slight nod toward the door leading into the next room. Like a flash the valet had jumped through and closed and locked the door behind him. Another door banged. Conville sprang into the hall across the fragments of the shattered glass, with McAllister at his heels. They were just in time to see Wilkins leap into the room where the men were testing the fire-escape.

"Let me try it," said he, and swung himself calmly into the tube. For an instant he delayed his flight, with only his head remaining visible.

"Good-by, Mr. McAllister," he called over his shoulder, "and thank you kindly. I won't forget, sir."

At the same instant Conville bounded through the door and rushed to the window. As he reached the sash Wilkins let go, and plunged downwards. His descent was rapid, his position being discernible from the sagging of the canvas.

Barney started for the elevator in the hope of cutting off the valet's escape below, but he had miscalculated the force of gravitation. As McAllister reached the window he saw the little bulge that represented Wilkins slide gently to the bottom. There was a cheer from the bystanders as the convict stepped lightly to his feet. Then he turned for an instant, and, looking up at McAllister, waved his hand and disappeared among the crowd.

I

"Certainly, sir. Your clothes shall be delivered at the Metropole at nine-forty-five to morrow evenin', sir."

Pondel's dapper little clerk tossed a half-dozen bolts of "trouserings" upon the polished table, and smiled graciously at the firm's best paying customer.

"Here, Bulstead! take Mr. McAllister's waist measure—just a matter of precaution," he added deferentially. "These are somethin' fine, sir—very fine! When they came in, I says to Mr. Pondel: 'If only Mr. McAllister could see that woollen! It's a shame,' I says, 'not to save it for 'im!' An' Mr. Pondel agreed with me at once. 'Very good, Wessons,' says he. 'Lay aside enough of that Lancaster to make Mr. McAllister a single-breasted sack suit, and if he don't fancy it I'll have it made up into somethin' for myself,' he says. Ain't that so, Mr. Pondel?"

The gentleman addressed had graciously sauntered over to congratulate Mr. McAllister upon his selections.

"Ah, very good! Very good indeed! How's that, Wessons? Yes, I told him to keep that piece for you, sir. Lord Bentwood begged for it almost with the tears in his eyes, as I may say, but I assured him that it was already spoken for." He patted the cloth with a fat, ring-covered hand. An atmosphere of exclusive opulence emanated from every inch of his sleek, pudgy person—from the broad white forehead over the glinting steel-gray eyes, from the pointed Van Dyke trimmed to resemble that of a certain exalted personage, from his drab waistcoated abdomen begirdled with its heavy chain and dangling seals, down to the gray-gaitered patent leathers. McAllister distrusted, feared, relied upon him.

The clubman wiped his monocle and glanced out through the plate-glass window. Marlborough Square was flooded with the soft sunshine of the autumn afternoon. Hardly a pedestrian violated the eminently aristocratic silence of St. Timothy's.

"Very thoughtful of you, I'm sure," he replied, not grudging Pondel the extra two guineas which he very well knew the other invariably charged for these little favors. It were cheap at twice the money to feel so much a gentleman.

"But this is Saturday, and it's five o'clock now. I don't see how you can possibly finish all those suits by to-morrow evening. You know I really didn't intend to order anything but the frock-coat. Perhaps you'd just better let the rest go. I can get them some other time."

"Not at all, Mr. McAllister; not at all. We are always delighted to serve you by any means in our power. Did Wessons say they would be finished to-morrow? Then to-morrow they shall be, sir. I'll set my men at work immediately. Pedler! Where's Pedler? Send him here at once!"

A hollow-eyed, lank, round-shouldered journeyman parted the curtains that concealed the rear of the room, and nervously approached his employer. He blinked at the unaccustomed sunlight, suppressing a cough.

"Did you call me, sir?"

"Yes," replied Pondel with the severity of one granting an undeserved favor. "This is Mr. McAllister, of whom you have heard us speak so often. I believe you have cut several of the gentleman's suits. He is to take the Majestic, which sails early Monday morning, and I have promised that his clothes shall be ready to-morrow evening. Can you arrange to stay here to-night and whatever portion of to-morrow is necessary to finish them?"

A worried look passed over the man's face, and his hand flew to his mouth to strangle another cough.

"Certainly, sir; that is—of course— Yes, sir. May I ask how many, sir?"

"Only three, I believe. I was sure it could be arranged. Please ask Aggam to assist you. That is all."

"Yes, sir. Very good, sir." Pedler hesitated a moment as if about to speak, then turned listlessly and plodded back behind the curtains.

"Very obliging man—Pedler. You see, there will be no difficulty, Mr. McAllister."

"Well, I don't see how on earth you're going to do it!" protested McAllister feebly. He wanted the clothes badly, now that he had seen the material. "It's mighty good of you to take all this trouble."

Mr. Pondel made a deprecating gesture.

"We are always glad to serve you, sir!" he repeated, as Wessons escorted the distinguished customer to the door.

"It's a great privilege to be employed by such a man as Mr. Pondel," whispered the salesman. "He thinks an enormous lot of you, sir. Very fine man—Mr. Pondel."

As the hansom jogged rapidly toward the hotel, McAllister reflected painfully upon the enormous sums of money that he annually transferred from his own pockets to those of the lordly

83

tailor. Not that the money made any particular difference. The clubman was well enough fixed, only sometimes the bills were unexpectedly large. The three suits just ordered would average fourteen guineas each. Roughly they would come to two hundred and twenty-five dollars, plus the duty, which he always paid conscientiously. And he was getting off easy at that. He remembered heaps of bills for over two hundred pounds, and that was only the beginning, for he bought most of his clothes right in New York.

Climbing the steps of his hotel, he wondered vaguely how long Pedler and the other fellow would have to work to finish the suits. Of course, they would be paid extra—were probably glad to do it. The chap had a nasty cough, though. Oh, well, that was their business—not his! So long as he put up the money, Pondel could look out for the rest.

However, he felt a distinct sense of relief that his own obligations consisted merely in dressing, dining at the Savoy with Aversly, and then leisurely taking in the Alhambra afterward. Once in his room, he found that the once criminally inclined, but now reformed Wilkins, who had returned to his master's service under a solemn promise of good behavior, had already laid out his clothes. McAllister rather dreaded dressing, for the place was one of those heavily oppressive apartments characteristic of English hotels. Green marble, yellow plush, and black walnut filled the foreground, background, and middle distance, while a marble-topped table, placed squarely in the centre of the room, offered the only oasis in the desert of upholstery, in the form of a single massive book, bound in brown morocco, and bearing the inscription stamped upon its cover in heavy gilt:

HOTEL METROPOLE
HOLY BIBLE
NOT TO BE REMOVED

It fascinated him, recalling the chained hairbrush and comb of the Pacific Coast. There you were offered cleanliness, here godliness, by the proprietors; only the means thereto were not to be taken away. The next comer must have his chance.

As the clubman idly lifted the volume, he suddenly realized that this was the first Bible he had actually touched in over thirty years. The last time he had owned one himself had been at school when he was fifteen years old. Something moved him to carry it to the window. The sun was just dropping over the scarlet chimney-pots of London. Its burnished glare played upon the red gilt edges of the leaves, as McAllister mechanically allowed the book to fall open in his hands. He read these words:

So I returned, and considered all the oppressions that are done under the sun: and behold the tears of such as were oppressed, and they had no comforter; and on the side of their oppressors there was power; but they had no comforter.

The sun sank; the chimneys deadened against the sky-line. When Wilkins, ten minutes later, stole in to see if his master needed his assistance, he found McAllister staring into the darkening west.

II

The bell on St. Timothy's tolled twelve o'clock as McAllister's hansom, straight from the Alhambra, clacked into the moonlit silence of Marlborough Square. A soft breath of distant gardens hung on the cool air. The chimneys rose from the house-tops sharp against a pale blue sky glittering with stars. Here and there a yellow window gleamed for a moment under the eaves, then vanished mysteriously. It was a night for lovers,—calm, still, ecstatic,—for hayfields under the harvest moon,—for white, ghostly reaches of the Thames,—for poetry,—for the exquisite enjoyment of earth's nearest approach to heaven.

The trap above McAllister's head opened.

"Beg pardon, sir. W'ere did you s'y, sir?"

"I said Pondel's," replied McAllister, rather sharply. He knew the cabby must think him a lunatic, but he didn't care. He intended to do the decent thing. Hang it! The fellow could mind his own business.

The hansom crossed the street and reined up in the shadow. All was dark, silent, deserted. Only the brass plate beside the door reflected strangely the moonlight across the way.

"'Ere's Pondel's, sir." The cabby got down and crossed the sidewalk to the door.

"All shut hup!" he commented. "Close at six."

A dark figure emerged quickly from, a neighboring shadow.

"'Ere! Wot is it you want?" demanded the bobby, accosting the cabman with tentative and potential roughness.

"Gent wants Pondel's. I dunno w'y. Ax 'im yerself!" responded cabby in an injured tone.

The bobby turned to the hansom.

"This shop's closed at six o'clock," he announced. "Wot do you want?"

McAllister felt ten thousand times a fool. The beauty of the night, the odoriferous quiet, the peace of the deserted square, all made his errand seem monstrously idiotic. The universe was wheeling silently across the housetops; respectable men and women were in their beds; only night-hawks, lovers, policemen were abroad. It was as if a worm were raising objection to some cardinal law. Why should he try to upset the order and regularity of the London night, clattering into this slumbering section, startling a respectable somnolent policeman, making an ass of himself before his cabby—because somewhere a fellow was working overtime on his trousers. He imagined that as soon as he had made his explanation the bobby and the driver would collapse with merriment, and hale him to a mad-house. But McAllister set his teeth. He was fighting for a principle. He wouldn't "welch" now. He clambered out of the hansom.

"I want to find Pondel, because he's got some fellows working on my clothes, and I don't propose to have anybody working for me on Sunday. Understand? It's Sunday. I don't intend to have folks working on my clothes when they ought to be in bed."

He spoke brokenly, defiantly, catching his breath between words, almost ready to cry; then waited for his auditors to fall upon each other's necks in derisive mirth. He forgot, however, that he was in London. The situation was one apposite to American humor, but evoked no sense of amusement in the policeman. He treated McAllister's explanation with vast respect. Our hero gained confidence. The bobby regretted that the place seemed closed; ventured to express his approval of the clubman's altruistic effort; dilated upon it to the cabby, who was correspondingly impressed. McAllister, immensely cheered, held forth on the wrongs of labor at some length, and, finding a sympathetic audience, produced cigars. The three proved, as it were, a little group of humanitarians united in a common purpose. Then, suddenly, inconsequently, inexcusably, a man coughed. The sound was muffled, but unmistakable. It came from a point directly beneath their feet. The bobby rapped sharply on the pavement several times.

"Hi there, you!" he called. "Hi there, you in Pondel's. Come an' open hup!"

They could hear a dull murmur of conversation, the cough was repeated, a bench dragged across a floor, some fastening was slowly loosed, and a yellow gleam of light shot up through the shadow as a scuttle opened in the sidewalk. A lean, scrawny figure thrust itself upward, sleepily rubbing its eyes, collarless, its shirt open at the breast, its hair tousled, coughing. McAllister, now confident that he had the support of his companions, addressed the ghost, in whom he recognized Pedler, the journeyman from behind the curtains. The clubman's face, however, was concealed in shadow from the other.

"You're working for Pondel, aren't you?"

The ghost coughed again, and shivered, although the air was warm.

"Yes," it answered huskily.

"Are you working on some clothes for a gentleman who's sailing on Monday?"

"Yes," it repeated.

"Then don't, any more," chirped McAllister encouragingly. "Those clothes are for me, and I don't want you to work any longer. You ought to be in bed."

"Wotcher givin' us?" grumbled Pedler. "G'wan! Leave us alone!" He started to descend. But the bobby stepped forward.

"Look 'ere," he said roughly. "Don't you understand? It's just as the gentleman s'ys. You don't 'ave to work any more to-night. You can go 'ome."

"I s'y, wotcher givin' us?" repeated the other. "I cawn't go 'ome. Mr. Pondel's horders is to st'y 'ere until the clothes is finished. M'ybe it's as you s'y, but I cawn't go 'ome."

At this juncture a child began to cry drowsily below, and a woman's voice could be heard striving to comfort it.

"You don't mean you've got a baby down there!" exclaimed McAllister.

"Only little Annie," replied Pedler. "An' the old woman."

"Anyone else?"

"Aggam."

"Let's go down," suggested the bobby. "I can make 'em understand." The ghost descended, dazed, and McAllister, the bobby, and last of all, the cabman, followed down a creaking ladder into a sort of vault under the cellar. A small oil wick gave out a feeble fluctuating light. On one side, cross-legged, sat a shrivelled-up, little old man, his brown beard streaked with gray, stitching. He did not look up, but only worked the faster. A thin woman crouched on a broken chair, holding a little girl in her lap.

"There, there, Annie, don't cry. The bobby's not arter you. It's all right, darlin'!"

Strewn about the cement floor lay the bolts of Lancaster which McAllister had selected, together with patterns, scissors, and unfinished garments.

"Excuse the child, sir," apologized the woman. "She's just a bit sleepy."

"Well," said McAllister, his indignation rising at the scene, and shame burning in his cheeks, "go right home. I won't have you working on these clothes any more." How he wished Pondel was there to get a piece of his mind!

Jim looked wearily at Aggam.

"Wot d'ye s'y, Aggam?"

The other kept on stitching.

"I gets my horders from Pondel," he replied, shortly, "an' I don't tyke no horders from no one helse!"

"But look here," cried McAllister, "the clothes are mine, ain't they? Pondel hasn't anything to do with it! And I tell you to go home."

"Yes," grunted Aggam. "An' then you loses your job, does yer? I don't want no toff mixin' into my affairs. I minds my business, they can mind theirs!"

"I s'y, that's no w'y to speak to the gentleman!" exclaimed the bobby in disgust. "'E's only tryin' to do yer a fyvor! 'Aven't yer got no manners?"

"I minds my business, let 'im mind 'is'n!" repeated Aggam stolidly.

"Well, I must s'y," ejaculated the cabby, "they're a bloomin' grateful lot!"

The tall man seemed to resent this last from one of his own station.

"I appreciates wot the gent wants," he said weakly, "but it's just like Aggam s'ys. Wot can we do? The gent cawn't tell us to go 'ome!"

The child began to cry again. McAllister was exasperated almost to the point of profanity.

"Don't you want to go home?" he exclaimed.

The woman laughed a hollow, mirthless laugh.

"Annie an' me 'ave st'y'd 'ere all the evenin' just to be with Jim. 'E's awful sick. An' 'e'll 'ave to st'y 'ere all d'y to-morrer. Do we want to go 'ome!"

Her husband dashed his shirt-sleeve across his eyes.

"Don't Nell," he muttered. "I ain't sick. I can work. You go 'ome with the kid."

McAllister thrust a handful of bank-notes toward her.

"Where does old Pondel live?" he inquired of the bobby.

"Out in Kew somewheres," replied the officer.

The woman was staring blankly at the money. Suddenly she dropped the little girl and began to sob. Jim broke into a fit of harsh

88

coughing. The cabman climbed up the ladder. The temperature of the vault seemed insufferable to McAllister.

"I suppose you'll go home if Pondel says so?" he suggested.

"Just watch us!" growled Aggam.

"Take that child home, anyhow, and put it to bed," ordered the clubman. "I'll be back in an hour or so."

As he climbed up through the scuttle into the sweet, soft moonlight, and started to enter the hansom, the bobby held out his hand.

"Excuse me, sir. I 'ope you'll pardon the liberty, but, would you mind, I've got a brother in America—Smith's the naime—'e lives in a plaice called Manitoba. Do you 'appen to know 'im?"

"I'm sorry," replied our friend, grasping the other's hand. "I never ran across him."

"Where to now?" asked the cabby.

"To Kew," replied McAllister.

They swung out of the square, leaving the bobby standing in the shadow of Pondel's.

"I'll look out for 'em while you're gone," called the latter encouragingly.

They crossed Bond Street, followed Grosvenor Street into Park Lane, and plunging round Hyde Park corner, past the statue to England's greatest soldier, they entered Kingsbridge. McAllister, all awake from his recent experience, saw things that he had never observed before—bedraggled flower-girls in gaudy hats, with heart-rending faces; drunken laborers staggering along upon the arms of sad-featured women; young girls, slender, painted, strolling with an affectation of light-heartedness along the glittering sidewalks. On they jogged, past narrow streets where, amid the flare of torches, the entire population of the neighborhood swarmed, bargained, swore, and quarrelled; where little children rolled under the costers' carts, fighting for scraps and decaying vegetables; and where their passage was obstructed by the throngs of miserable humanity for whom this was their only park, their only club. It being Saturday night, the butchers were selling off their remnants of meat, and their shrill cries could be heard for blocks. Several times the horse shied to avoid trampling upon some old hag who, clutching her wretched purchase to her breast, hurried homeward before a drunken lout should snatch it from her. McAllister had never imagined the like. It was with a sigh of relief that they left the Hammersmith Road behind and at last reached the residential districts. In about an hour they found themselves in Kew. A cool breeze from the country fanned his cheek. On either hand trim little villas, with smooth lawns, lined the road, and the moonlit air was fragrant with the smell of damp grass, violets, and heliotrope. Here and there could be heard the tinkle of a cottage piano, and the laughter of belated merry-makers on the verandas.

They located Mr. Pondel's villa without difficulty. Standing back some thirty yards from the street, its well-kept garden full of flowering shrubs and carefully tended beds of geraniums, it was a residence typical of the London suburb, with fretwork along the piazza roof, a stone dog guarding each side of the steps, and salmon-pink curtains at the parlor windows. The door stood open, a Japanese lamp burned in the hallway, and the murmur of voices floated out from the door leading into the parlor. McAllister once again felt the overwhelming absurdity of his position. Over his shoulder, as he stood by the hyacinths at the door, floated the same big moon in the same soft heaven. Damp and fragrant, the wind blew in from the lawn and swayed the portières in the narrow hall, behind which, doubtless, sat the lordly Pondel, friend of noblemen, adviser of royalty, entrenched in his castle, a unit in an impregnable system. The whinny of the cab-horse beyond the hedge recalled to McAllister the necessity for action. He realized that he was losing moral ground every instant.

The bell jangled harshly somewhere in the back of the house. A man's voice—Pondel's—muttered indistinctly; there was a feminine whisper in response; someone placed a glass on a table and pushed back a chair. A clock in the neighborhood struck two, and Pondel emerged through the portières—Pondel in a wadded claret-colored dressing-gown embroidered with birds of Paradise, in carpet slippers, with a meerschaum pipe, watery eyes, and slightly disarranged hair. It was rather dim in the hallway, and he did not recognize his visitor.

"What is it? What do you want?" The inquiry was abrupt and a little thick.

"Good evening, Mr. Pondel," stammered McAllister. "I hope you'll excuse me for disturbing you at this hour. It's about the clothes."

"W'o is it?" Pondel peered into his guest's flushed face. "W'y Mr. McAllister, what are you doin' way out 'ere? Excuse my appearance—a little pardonable neglishay of a Saturday evenin'. Come right in, won't you? Great honor, I'm sure. Though, if you'll believe it, I once 'ad the honor of a call from his Grace the Duke of Bashton right in this very 'all. Excuse me w'ile I announce your presence to Mrs. Pondel."

McAllister said something about having to go at once, but Pondel shuffled through the curtains, almost immediately sweeping them back with a lordly gesture of welcome.

"This way, Mr. McAllister." Our miserable friend entered the parlor. "Elizabeth, hallow me to present Mr. McAllister—one of my oldest customers."

Elizabeth—a fat vision of fifty-five, with peroxide hair, and a soft pink of unchanging hue mantling her elsewhere mottled cheeks—arose graciously from the table where she and her husband had been playing double-dummy bridge, and courtesied.

"Chawmed, I'm sure. What a beautiful evenin'! Won't you si' down?" murmured the enchantress.

McAllister took a chair, and Pondel pressed whiskey and water upon him. Oh, Mr. McAllister, needn't be afraid of it; it was the real old thing; Lord Langollen had sent him a dozen. Lizzie would take a nip with 'em—eh, Lizzie? A gen'elman didn't take that long trip every evenin', and a little refreshment would not only do him good, but, as the Yankees said, would show there was no 'ard feelin', eh? He must really take just a drop. Say when!

Lizzie poured out a glass for the much-embarrassed guest. She was in a flowered kimona, even more "neglishay" than her husband, but the bower in which the goddess reclined was a perfect pearl of the decorator's art. Cupids, also "neglishay," toyed with one another around a cluster of electric burners in the ceiling, gay streamers of painted blossoms dangling from their hands and floating down the walls. Gilt chairs, a white and gilt sofa, and a brown etching in a Florentine frame on each wall, were the most conspicuous articles of furniture. At the windows the brilliant salmon-pink curtains bellied softly in the breeze that stole into the chamber and diluted the gentle odor of Parma violets which exuded from the dame in the kimona. To Pondel, McAllister's presence was an evidence of his power; and his pride, tickled mightily, put him in an exquisite good humor. Certainly the occasion required from him, the host, a proper felicitation.

"'Ere's to our better acquaintance," said the tailor, raising his glass sententiously. "Lizzie, drink to Mr. McAllister!"

The three drank solemnly. Then the voluble tailor addressed himself to the task of entertaining his distinguished guest. McAllister could catch at no opening to explain his visit. Pondel chatted gayly of Paris, the Continent, and familiarly of the races and the beau monde. Apparently he knew (by their first names) half the nobility of England, and he endeavored to place his customer equally at his ease with them. He ventured that he knew how most young Americans spent their time in London and Paris; dropped with a wink, that in spite of his present uxoriousness he had been a bit of a dog himself, and ended by suggesting another toast to "A short life and a merry one." The lady of the kimona, grammatically not so strong as her husband, contented herself with expansive smiles and frequent recurrence to the tumbler.

"I must explain my visit," finally broke in McAllister. "It's about the clothes."

Pondel smiled condescendingly.

"My dear Mr. McAllister, you don't need to worry in the slightest. They'll be done promptly to-morrow evenin', take my word for it."

McAllister flushed. How in Heaven's name could he ever make the tailor understand?

"I've decided I don't want 'em!" he stammered.

Pondel's glass went to the table with a bang, and he gazed blankly at his customer. The clubman, not realizing the implication, did not proceed.

"That's all right," finally responded Pondel a trifle coldly. "There's no hurry about settlement. You can take a year, if necessary."

Mrs. Pondel slipped unobtrusively out of the room, leaving a trail of perfume behind her.

"Oh!" exclaimed our friend, catching his breath: "It isn't that. But you see I can't have those men working over night and to-morrow on my account. It's—it's against my principles."

Pondel brightened. A load had been taken from his heart. So long as McAllister's bank account was good, any idiosyncrasy the American might exhibit did not matter. He had always regarded McAllister, however, as a man of the world, and had esteemed him accordingly. He perceived that he had been mistaken. His customer was merely a religious crank. He had had experience with them before.

"Pooh! That's all right," said he resuming his former cordiality. "Why, they like to earn the extra money. They're all devoted to my interests, you know."

"Well, I don't want them to work any longer on my clothes," repeated McAllister helplessly.

"I understand," replied Mr. Pondel, rather loftily. "I'm afraid, however, it's too late to stop them now. The cloth 'as been cut, and they would not stop contrary to my direction."

"That's the point," returned McAllister, "I want you to change your orders."

"But, my dear sir," expostulated the tailor, "you can't expect me to go to London this time of night! Besides, they're nearly done by this time. It's impossible!"

"I'll manage that," exclaimed McAllister. "I've been down to

92

the shop already, and they're waiting for me now to come back with your permission to go home; they wouldn't go without it."

"Dear, dear!" replied the tailor, changing his tactics. "How much interest you have taken in their welfare! How kind and thoughtful of you! No, they're faithful men; they wouldn't think of disobeying orders. But what a shame I didn't know of it before! Why, they might 'ave been at 'ome and in their beds. However, I sha'n't forget 'em at the end of the month. Mr. McAllister, I respect you. I have never known of a more unselfish act. Permit me to say it, sir, you are a Christian—a true Christian. I wish there were more like you, sir!"

McAllister arose to his feet. His one thought now was to escape as quickly as possible. The sight of Pondel's smiling countenance filled him with unutterable disgust. Suppose the fellows at the club could see him sitting in this pursy tailor's parlor, with his scented wife, and gilded chairs—

The tailor, however, was anxious to restore the cordiality of their relations, and slopped over in his eagerness to show how kind he was to his men, and how considerate of their well-being. He took McAllister's arm familiarly as he showed him to the door.

"Yes," he added confidentially, "this is a very good locality. Only the best people live in this neighborhood. Rather a neat little property." He proffered McAllister a cigar. The clubman wanted to kick him for a miserable, dirty cad.

"Right back!" he said to the cabby, hardly replying to the tailor's good-night.

London was asleep. Even the streets through which he had driven to Kew were hushed in preparation for the sodden Sunday to come. The moon had lowered over the housetops, and St. Timothy's was in the shadow as once again he drew up in front of Pondel's.

"Back already, sir?" The bobby stepped out to meet him.

"Yes," replied McAllister wearily. "And those fellows down there are going home."

The bobby rapped on the scuttle. Once more Pedler's head protruded above the sidewalk.

"Mr. Pondel says you're to go home," said McAllister.

"The gent's been all the way to Kew for you," interjected the bobby.

"Hi, Aggam!" exclaimed Jim, huskily. "Th' gentleman says we are to go 'ome, Mr. Pondel says." He disappeared. Aggam could be heard muttering below. Presently the light was extinguished, and both emerged from the scuttle and put on their coats. McAllister felt sleepily exultant. Pedler pushed the scuttle into place.

"Well," said McAllister after an awkward pause, "can I give

93

you a lift? Which way do you go? I tell you what: you come back with me to the hotel, and then the hansom can take you both home."

Pedler and Aggam looked doubtfully at one another.

"Oh, come on, you fellows!" exclaimed McAllister, all his natural good spirits returning with a rush. "Get in there, now!"

Pedler and Aggam climbed in, and McAllister directed the driver to go to the Metropole, after stuffing a sovereign into the hand of his friend, the policeman. The stars were still marching across the sky, and the breeze had freshened. Every window was dark; no one was astir. They heard only the echoes of their horse's hoof-beats. Yet the restless silence that precedes the dawn was in the air.

"I lives miles aw'y from 'ere," said Pedler after a meditated period.

"So do I," supplemented Aggam.

"I don't care," replied McAllister. "I've had this cab all night, anyhow, and I want to celebrate. You see, this is the first time I ever got ahead of my tailor."

Another long pause ensued. They were not a talkative lot, surely. McAllister's flow of language absolutely deserted him. He could think of no subject of conversation whatever. Pedler finally came to his assistance.

"I'm thirty-seven year old, an' this is the fust time I've ever ridden in a 'ansom."

"Jiminy!" exclaimed McAllister. "You don't say so! What luck!"

"Fust time for me, too," added Aggam.

After this burst of confidence the three rode in utter silence. At the Metropole the clubman jumped out and bade his companions good-night.

As the cabby gathered up the reins preparatory to a fresh start, Aggam leaned forward rather apologetically.

"You must hexcuse me," he remarked, "but I don't want to sail hunder false colors, and I feel as if I hort to s'y that while I'm a Socialist, I 'ave no particular sympathy with Sabbatarianism."

"Well, neither have I," replied McAllister encouragingly, an answer which probably puzzled Mr. Aggam for a fortnight.

MCALLISTER'S MARRIAGE

I

The Bar Harbor train slowly came to a stop beside a little wooden station. From over the marshes crept a breath of salty freshness that tried vainly to steal in through the open windows of the Pullman, only intensifying the stifling heat inside.

McAllister arose and made his way to the platform in search of air. A spare, wrinkled octogenarian was in the difficult act of lifting a small girl in a calico dress to the platform of the day coach, the child clinging obstinately to the old gentleman's neck and refusing to disentangle herself.

"Mercy, Abby! Do leggo!" he remonstrated. "Thar, ef ye don't, I'll ask that man thar to hoist ye!"

The little girl reluctantly let go her hold and allowed herself to be placed on the lowest step.

"That's a good girl," continued her guardian; then addressing McAllister, he inquired conversationally:

"Be ye goin' to Bangor?"

"How's that? Ye-es, I believe I am. At least the train passes through," responded McAllister doubtfully, apprehensive of undesirable complications.

The old fellow produced from his waistcoat-pocket a ticket which he placed in the child's hand. Then he turned her around and gave her a little push up the steps.

"Wall, jest keep an eye on Abby, will ye?"

"Good-by, Uncle!" cried the little girl, climbing laboriously up to where the clubman stood and making a little bow, which he gravely returned.

"I don't know . . ." he began.

"That's all right," explained the farmer. "Her aunt'll meet her. Jest see she don't bother no one. Lemme pass ye her duds."

The octogenarian forthwith handed up to McAllister a cloth valise, a pasteboard box, and a large paper bag.

"Her lunch is in the bag," said he. "Don't let her drink none o' that ice-water. My wife says it hez germs into it."

"But I don't . . ." gasped our friend.

"Be keerful o' that box," interrupted her uncle. "There's two dozen hen's eggs in it. If she's good, you might buy her a cent's worth o' peppermints to Portland." He fumbled uncertainly in his breeches' pocket.

"Do you expect me . . ." ejaculated McAllister.

"Give my love to yer aunt," added the other as the train started. "Good-by!" And pulling a large red pocket-handkerchief from his coat-tails he fanned the air vaguely as they moved slowly away from him.

"Oh, isn't it nice!" cried the little girl, who appeared quite at ease with her new acquaintance.

"Ye-es—certainly—of course," he replied, wondering what he should do with his charge. "I suppose we had better go in and sit down, don't you think?"

He stood aside waiting for her to precede him into the parlor car.

"What a lovely place!" she exclaimed as her eyes rested upon the rosewood and the velvet chairs. "Am I really to ride in this?"

"Why, where should you ride, to be sure?" he inquired, beginning to regain his self-possession.

"The car had iron seats before," she informed him.

"How extraordinary!"

"This is an ever so much prettier train," she added. "I'm afraid I'll hurt the plush." She took out a diminutive handkerchief and spread it out to sit upon. The clubman with an amused expression swung round another chair and sat down opposite.

"My name's Abigail Martha Higgins," she said, taking off her little straw hat. "I live in Bangor with my aunt. That old man was Uncle Moses Higgins. Aunt doesn't love his wife."

"Dear me!" sympathized McAllister.

"My father and mother are in heaven," she continued in matter-of-fact tones. "Up there. Wouldn't you hate to live up in the sky and do nothin'?"

"I certainly should," he answered with gravity.

"We all came down from there, you know. Do you think we were born all in one piece, or put together afterward?"

McAllister pondered.

"What's your name?"

"McAllister," he replied.

"That's a funny name!" she commented. "It sounds like McCafferty—that's Deacon Brewer's hired man's name."

"Do you think so?" asked the clubman apologetically, feeling that his parents had done him an irreparable injury.

"I'll call you Mister Mac," added the child, "and you may call me Abby, 'cause I'm only eight. Do you live to Boston?"

"No; New York. An awful way off."

96

"Have they got a Free-Will Meetin'-house there?" she inquired knowingly.

"I'm sure I don't know," he answered, feeling wofully ignorant of all matters of real importance.

"Then it must be a very small place," she decided. "All big places have a Free-Will Meetin'-house, Uncle Moses says."

At this moment Wilkins approached to inquire if his master wanted anything.

"Is there a Free-Will Meetin'-house in New York?" inquired the clubman.

"Yes, sir; I believe so, sir. That is to say, a Baptist place of worship, sir," he answered solemnly.

"Is that your brother?" inquired Abby.

"No—" hesitated McAllister, doubtful as to what the valet's equivalent would be in his little friend's world.

"What's your name?" inquired Abby.

"Wilkins, miss," answered the valet.

"What a lovely name!" cried Abby. "It's much nicer than his'n."

Wilkins stepped back a few paces aghast.

"That box is chuck full of eggs," announced Abby. "I wonder where the hens get them."

"I give it up," said the clubman.

"We have a black horse on our farm," she continued. "It used to be a girl, but now it's a boy."

"Indeed!" exclaimed McAllister.

"Yes, aunt had her tail cut off. Boys have short hair, you know—that's how you tell."

At this Wilkins disappeared rapidly into the background.

"Uncle Moses' wife don't love children," the child continued. "She has the rheumatiz in her thigh."

"But she must like you, Abby," urged her new friend.

"No, she don't. She don't love me 'cause I love Aunt Abby, an' Aunt Abby don't love her."

"I see," said McAllister.

The clubman soon became acquainted with Abby's entire family history, and rapidly realized that the mind of a child was a thing undreamed of in his philosophy. As she pattered on he conversed gravely with her, trying to answer her multitudinous questions. All her world was good save Uncle Moses' wife, and her confidence in the clubman was entire. She admired his clothes, his watch-chain, and his scarf-pin, and ended by directing him to read to her, which McAllister obediently did. None of the magazines seemed to contain suitable articles, so with some misgivings he

97

purchased various colored weeklies, remembering vaguely his own delight in the misadventures of certain chubby ladies and stout gentlemen upon rear pages, perused furtively when waiting at the barber's to get his hair cut as a child. For half an hour her interest remained tense, but then she wearied of using her eyes, and, patting McAllister's fat chin, ordered him to tell her a story. Here was a new difficulty. He had never told a story in his life, but there was no help for it, no escape, as she climbed into his lap.

"Begin with once onup-a-time," she ordered.

"Well," he obeyed "Once 'onup' a time there was a man who lived in a club——"

"A what?" sharply interrupted Abby.

"A big white house with heaps of rooms," he corrected. "And as he had nobody dependent on him, all he had to do was to eat and sleep and look at the sky."

"Didn't he have any children?"

"Nobody in the world," answered McAllister.

"Poor man!" sighed Abby. "Didn't he keep any hens?"

"Not even a hen!"

"I know a big house just like that," said Abby. "Old Captain Barnard used to live in it. Wasn't he lonely?"

"Sometimes."

"Did anyone live with him?"

"His hired man," answered the clubman with a smile, looking down the car to where Wilkins sat in solitary grandeur. "And by and by he got so old and so fat that nobody would marry him, while the wives of other men he knew forgot to ask him to dinner."

"Poor dear man!" murmured Abby, "I should think he'd have wished he hadn't been born."

"Sometimes he did," answered the story-teller. "And he longed for some people to really care for him, and for some little children to keep him company."

"Did he have a cow?"

"No, not even a cow."

Abby laughed sleepily.

"But didn't he ever have any fun?"

"He thought he did, but he didn't, really."

"I'm awful sorry for him!" said Abby. "If I met him I would give him my white hen."

"He used to pay for dinners for people, and send them flowers and candy and go to see them——"

"Sunday afternoons?"

"Yes; Sunday afternoons."

"He was really very nice," said Abby.

98

"Do you think so?" asked McAllister eagerly.

"Why, of course. Don't you think so?"

"So-so," said the clubman.

"But he never hurt anyone?"

"No, never."

"And gave the hired man plenty of victuals?"

"Much more than was good for him," said McAllister with conviction.

"I like that man," said Abby. "He was a good man."

"But some people said he was an idle fellow," insisted McAllister.

"But that didn't do anybody any harm," said Abby.

"No, certainly not."

"And he wasn't cross?"

"No, almost never."

"Then," said Abby, "he was a good man, and I will marry him if he asks me."

And with that she dropped her head on his arm and fell fast asleep.

"Can't I hold the young—person, for you, sir?" inquired the valet in a whisper.

"Certainly not," responded McAllister.

Over the flitting pines circled the crows, black dots against the deep blue; lazy cows stood knee-deep in fields frosted with daisies and watched seemingly without interest the passing train; little puffs of white in serried ranks moved slowly out of the north, never approaching nearer, dissolving at the meridian; on the near horizon a line of indigo mountains tumbled southward; white farm-houses swept slowly by; at dusty crossings gray-whiskered farmers sat loosely holding the reins in amiable conformity with the injunction painted upon weather-worn signs to "Look out for the engine"; at times the train passed over rocky bedded streams dammed for milling, and once or twice across rivers half choked with logs upon which men ran like water-bugs; then through red brick towns, and towns with square granite stores and offices, and towns of white and green, marking the three disconnected periods of the architectural development of Maine; and everywhere the pines.

In the midst of a stretch of thick woods the engine began to whistle frantically. A brakeman, followed closely by a conductor, hurried through the car. The wheels ground harshly and the train gradually ceased to move. Ahead could be heard the loud pounding of the engine and the roar of escaping steam. Volumes of smoke, white and black, rolled over the pines and cast rapidly changing

99

shadows upon the ground. Wilkins, who had gone forth to seek information, now returned.

"There's a freight wreck just a'ead, sir. The conductor says as how we shall be delayed 'ere at least nine hours."

McAllister glanced down at the little form in his arms. It had not moved. Gently he carried her along the aisle, out upon the platform, and down the steps to the ground. Still she did not awake. Up the track he could see groups of excited passengers gesticulating around grotesque piles of wreckage upon which a locomotive lay with its wheels in the air. Beside the track stretched a pine grove, its soft carpet of needles flecked with sunlight. At the foot of one giant tree, on a bed of gray moss, the clubman laid his little charge and threw himself at her feet. An irritable family of nervous crows flapped noisily away to the other side of the track, assembled in angry consultation in a hemlock, deputed a spy, who cautiously reconnoitred, and, on the latter's report, returned. At a safe distance Wilkins sat upon a windfall, and with one eye upon his sleeping master smoked rapidly one of McAllister's cigars.

II

"Yes, Miss Higgins got yer telegram," answered Deacon Brewer, as they drove slowly along the river in the dusty heat of the early July morning. "Ef she hadn't I reckon she'd 'a' gone nigh crazy."

They were in an open two-seated buck-board. McAllister, holding Abby in his lap, occupied the front seat with the Deacon, while Wilkins sat behind with the valise and the pasteboard box.

"It was a tiresome delay and really a very fortunate escape," responded McAllister. "Abby behaved beautifully."

"She's a good child," said the Deacon. "Her mother was a fine woman, and she's goin' to be just like her."

"Are we nearly home?" asked the little girl, rubbing her eyes.

"'Most," answered the Deacon. "Are ye hungry?"

"I got her some bread and milk at a farm-house," explained McAllister, "but none of us have had any breakfast yet."

"Wall, I reckon Miss Higgins'll be prepared for ye," said the Deacon. "She's a liberal woman an' a smart woman, but all the same, the farm's going to be sold for taxes next week."

Abby had fallen asleep, but the clubman started and looked anxiously at her at this piece of intelligence.

"She don't know nuthin' about it," said the farmer. "Miss Higgins can't run a hard-scrabble farm, nor no one can and make a livin' out'n it. It ain't worth five dollars an acre."

"What will she do?" asked the clubman.

"Darn ef I know," responded the other. "She kin help around some, I guess. Deacon Giddings has a powerful lot of company. 'N any woman kin sew. She kin make out, I reckon."

"But the child?" whispered McAllister.

"Her Uncle Moses'll hev to take her," answered the Deacon.

"Jiminy!" ejaculated the clubman, recalling the little girl's description of her uncle's wife. "She won't like that."

"Beggars can't be choosers," said the Deacon dryly.

A turn in the road brought them within view of a small, low farm-house, with good-sized barn, lying in a field between the woods and the river, here about a quarter of a mile in width. The pines grew close to the road upon the left, but upon the other side the land had been well cleared to the Penobscot's bank. Huge piles of stones, ten or twelve feet long, five or so broad, and four or five feet high, were monuments to the energy and industry of some former owner.

"Gosh, how Henery worked to clear this farm!" remarked the Deacon. "He hove stone for twenty years, an' then died. Look at them trees!"

He pointed dramatically to a large orchard containing row upon row of young apple-trees.

At the sound of the wheels a woman came slowly out of the side door and watched their approach. She had the pale, sickly countenance of the wife of the inland Maine farmer, and her limp dress ill concealed the angularity of her form. Her eyes showed that she had passed a sleepless night. McAllister leaped out and lifted Abby down. The woman neither spoke to nor kissed the child, but clutched her tightly in her arms. Then she nodded to the newcomers.

"I'm obliged to ye, Deacon Brewer," she said. "Is this the man who sent the telegram? Won't ye come in and set down?"

"Oh, yes," cried Abby ecstatically. "Get out, Mr. Wilkins! I want to show you the black horse, and all the hens."

"I must be gettin' back," muttered the Deacon.

"Could you let us have a bite of breakfast?" inquired McAllister. "My train doesn't go until twelve o'clock." To return to Bangor at this particular time did not suit him.

"Such as it is," replied Miss Higgins.

"Could you arrange to call out for me in an hour or so?" asked McAllister.

"I reckon I kin," said the Deacon with some reluctance. "I'll hev ter charge ye fifty cents."

"Of course," said McAllister.

Wilkins took down the parcels, and the Deacon drove slowly away.

"I'll scrape somethin' together in a few minutes," said Miss Higgins. "How much was that telegram?"

"Oh, that's all right!" said the abashed clubman.

"No, it ain't. Money's money. Was it ez much ez a quarter?"

McAllister acknowledged the amount.

"I thought so," commented Miss Higgins. "It was wuth it." She had the money all ready and handed it to McAllister.

Etiquette seemed to demand its acceptance.

"Did you say your name was McAllister? Who's this man?"

"His name is Wilkins."

"Well," said Aunt Abby, "one of ye might split up that log, if ye don't mind, while I get the breakfast."

She turned into the house.

McAllister looked doubtfully at the wood-pile.

"Let Mr. Wilkins chop the wood!" shouted Abby; "I want to show you the ba-an."

"Wilkins," said McAllister, "wood-chopping is an art sanctified in this country by tradition."

"Very good, sir," answered Wilkins.

Abby grasped McAllister's hand and tugged him joyfully over the poverty-stricken farm. They visited the orchard, the pig-sty, the hen-house, admired the horse that had been a girl, and ended at the water's edge.

"We ketch salmon here in the spring," explained Abby; "and smelts."

Across the eddying river quiet farms slept in the hot sunshine. Two men in a dory swung slowly up-stream. At their feet the clear water rippled against the stones. In his mind the clubman pictured the stifling city and the squalor of relative existence there.

"It's beautiful, Abby," he said.

"It's the loveliest place in the whole world," she answered, holding his hand tightly. "And I shall never, never go away."

Behind them came the shrill tones of Aunt Abby's voice bidding them to breakfast. Wilkins, coatless, was bearing some mangled fragments of log toward the kitchen. His beaded face spoke unutterable dejection.

"Well, set daown; it's all there is," said Miss Higgins.

McAllister sat, and Abby climbed into a high chair. Wilkins remained standing.

102

"Ain't ye goin' to set?" inquired Miss Higgins.

Wilkins reddened.

"Well, ye be the most bashful man I ever met," remarked the lady. "Set daown and eat yer victuals."

"Sit down," said McAllister, and for the second time master and man shared a meal.

The little room was bare of decoration except for some colored lithographs and wood-cuts, which for the most part represented the funeral corteges of distinguished Americans, with a few hospital scenes and the sinking of a steamship. A rug soiled to a dull drab made a sort of mud spot before the fireplace; a knitted tidy, suggestive of the antimacassar, ornamented the only rocker; at one end stood the stove, and hard by two fixed tubs. Everything except the carpet was scrupulously clean.

Miss Higgins brought to the table a dish of steaming boiled eggs, half a loaf of white bread, and a vegetable dish with a large piece of butter.

"I'll have some coffee for ye in a minute," she remarked as she placed the dishes before them.

McAllister broke some of the eggs into a tumbler and cut the bread.

"What might be your business?" inquired Miss Higgins.

"Er—well—" hesitated McAllister. "I've travelled quite a bit."

"I had a cousin in the hardware line," remarked the hostess reminiscently. "He travelled everywheres. Has it ever taken you ez fur as St. Louis?"

"No," said McAllister. "My line never took me so far."

"Andrew died there—of the water. What's your business?" continued Miss Higgins to Wilkins.

"I'm with Mr. McAllister, ma'am."

"Oh! same firm?"

Wilkins coughed violently and evaded the interrogation.

"Mr. Wilkins handles gents' clothing, underwear, haberdashery, and notions," interposed McAllister gravely.

Wilkins swayed in his seat and grew purple around the gills.

"Oh, Mr. Wilkins!" cried Abby, "what's the matter? You will burst! Take a drink of water."

The valet obediently tried to do as she bade him.

"How much is land worth around here?" asked the clubman. "And what do you raise?"

Miss Higgins looked at him suspiciously.

"We raise pertaters, some corn and oats, and get a purty fair apple crop in the autumn."

103

"Must have been hard work clearing the farm," added McAllister, "if one can judge by the piles of stones."

"Work? I guess 'twas work!" sniffed Miss Higgins. "You travellin' men hain't got no idee of what real work is. There ain't a stone in the nineteen acres of farm land. Henery picked 'em all up by hand."

"Are you Abby's guardian?" asked McAllister.

"Yes," said Miss Higgins. "I'm all the folks she's got, except Moses, down to Portsmouth, and a lot of good he is with that wife he's got!"

Wilkins now asked awkwardly to be excused.

"That friend of yourn seems to be a dummy!" remarked Miss Higgins after the valet had disappeared.

"He isn't much in the social line," admitted his master. "But he knows his business."

"I'm goin' out to show Mr. Wilkins the beehive," cried Abby, slipping down from her chair. "Come right along, won't you?"

"I'll be there in just a minute," said McAllister.

Abby grabbed up her sunbonnet and ran skipping out of the kitchen.

"She's a dear little girl," said McAllister. "I hope she'll have a chance to get a good education."

"Education behind a counter in Bangor is all she'll get," answered her aunt.

They sat in silence for a moment, and then McAllister, feeling the craving induced by habit, drew an Obsequio from his pocket, and asked:

"Do you object to smoking?"

Miss Abby bristled.

"I don't want none o' them se-gars in this house, so long's I'm in it!" she exclaimed. "Ain't out-doors good enough for you, without stinkin' up the kitchen?"

"I didn't mean any offence," apologized McAllister. "I'll wait till I go out, of course."

"One of the devil's tricks!" sniffed Miss Abby.

McAllister, terribly embarrassed, got up and stepped to the window. The coffee had been execrable, but a benign influence animated him. Down the slope toward the gently flowing Penobscot little Abby was leading Wilkins by the hand. The boy-horse kicked his heels in a daisy-flecked pasture beyond the barn.

"What did you say the farm was worth?" asked the clubman.

"There's a hundred and eighty-one acres o' woodland, and the cleared land just makes two hundred. It ought to be worth eighteen hundred dollars."

"I know a man who wants a farm. He says some day all this river front will be valuable for a summer resort. I'm authorized to buy for him. I'll give you sixteen hundred and fifty. Is it a bargain?"

Miss Abby turned pale.

"Oh, I don't know! It seems dreadful to sell it, after all the years Henery put into cleanin' of it up. I was hopin' somehow that maybe I could get work on the farm from them as bought it and keep Abby here for a while longer."

"That's all right," said McAllister. "My principal is buying it on a speculation. You can stay indefinitely."

"How about rent?" asked Miss Abby.

"You can take care of the farm, and he won't charge you any rent."

The terms having been finally arranged to Miss Abby's satisfaction, McAllister drew a small check-book from his pocket and filled out a voucher for the amount.

"We can sign the papers later," said he with a smile.

Miss Abby took the slip of paper doubtfully.

"How do I know I ain't gettin' cheated?" she asked. "Suppose this should turn out to be no good?"

"Then you'd have the farm," said McAllister.

He fumbled in his pocket until he found a clean letter-back and with his stylographic pen rapidly wrote the following:

"I hereby give and convey the Henry Higgins farm, heretofore purchased by me, to my friend Abigail Martha Higgins, in consideration for much of value of which no one knows but myself. In witness whereof I sign my name and affix a seal."

He found a used postage-stamp that still had a trifle of gum on its back and made use of it as a fragmentary seal.

While in some doubt as to the legal sufficiency of this instrument, McAllister felt that its intendment was unmistakable. Having replaced his pen, he carefully folded the document and thrust it into his pocket. Just at this moment Miss Higgins announced the return of Deacon Brewer, who was wheeling slowly into the gate. Toward the orchard McAllister could see, as he stepped to the door, little Abby still tugging along Wilkins, whose massive and emotionless face was glistening with the heat.

"Hit's very 'ot, sir!" he remarked tentatively to his master. "I've been to see the 'ives."

"How funny Mr. Wilkins talks!" said Abby. "He told me he knew a boy once who got stung, and said the bee bit 'im in 'is 'ead! Do all drummers talk like that?"

"Drummers!" exclaimed Wilkins.

"Aunt said you were both drummers; I s'pose you left your

105

drums somewhere. I don't like 'em; they make too much music. They have them in the circus parade in Bangor every year."

"Be you folks ready to start?" inquired Deacon Brewer. "Purty nice view of the water from here, ain't they? There's a good well on the place, too, and a few boat-loads of manure would give you crops to beat—all. Don't know enybody thet wants to speckalate a little in farmin' land, do ye? This here is a good, likely place. Reckon you kin buy it cheap."

"Sh-h!" said McAllister, laying his finger on his lips.

"No one sha'n't ever buy this farm," said Abby; "I'm goin' to live here always."

"Wall," said the Deacon, "better be movin'. I don't like to keep the mare standin' in the sun."

"Are you goin' away?" cried Abby in agonized tones. "You'll come back soon, won't you?"

"I hope so, very soon," said McAllister. "Don't you want to show me the boy-horse before I start?"

"Oh, yes, yes!" she cried, seizing his hand.

The stout clubman and the little girl walked slowly across the grass-grown drive to the daisy field beside the barn, talking busily.

"Your friend's bought this farm," announced Miss Abby to Wilkins.

"'Oly Moses!" ejaculated the valet.

"By gum!" exclaimed the Deacon. "What did he give?"

"Sixteen hundred and fifty dollars."

"Gee!" said the Deacon.

"An' we're to stay on rent-free 's long 's we want!"

"I swan!" commented the pillar of the local Baptist Church. "Some folks doos hev luck!"

He went over to adjust a bit of harness.

"It'll keep 'em out o' the poor farm," he muttered. "But, by gosh, thet feller must be a fool!"

Over in the daisy field, McAllister, to the wonder of the boy-horse, pulled the despised cigar from his pocket, cut off the end, and began to smoke with infinite satisfaction.

"What a beautiful, beautiful, lovely ring!" exclaimed Abby joyfully, examining with delight the embossed paper of red and gold.

"Do you remember about the lonely man who lived in the big white house I told you of?" asked McAllister.

"Of course I do," sighed Abby. "Poor man! he was so good, and nobody loved him."

"Do you love him?" asked McAllister.

"Dear man! I love him, all my heart!" cried the child.

"Then the man is very, very happy," said McAllister softly.

Overhead a single black crow, wheeling out of a stumpy pine, circled to investigate this strange love-scene. Satisfied of its propriety, he cawed loudly and resettled himself upon the shaking topmost bough.

McAllister drew the golden band from his cigar and took the folded paper from his pocket.

"Here's a love-letter," said he. "Your aunt will read it for you when I've gone."

Abby took it sadly.

"Now hold up your left hand," said McAllister, smiling. As he slipped the paper circle over her fourth finger he said gravely:

"'With this ring I thee wed, and with all my worldly goods I thee endow.' Give me a kiss."

She did so, in wonder.

"Now we are married," said he.

THE JAILBIRD

I

Now it had come, he was not quite sure that he wanted it. For a moment he longed to go back and join the men marching away to the shoe-shop. Inside those walls he had never had to think of what he should eat or drink, or wherewithal he should be clothed.

Over against the gray parapet echoed the buzzing of the electric cars, a strange sound to ears accustomed only to the tramp of marching feet, the harsh voices of wardens, and the clang of iron doors. Below him the harbor waves danced and sparkled, ferry-boats rushed from shore to shore, big ships moved slowly toward the distant islands and the still more distant sea, while near at hand the busy street flowed like a river, which he was compelled to swim but in which he already felt the millstone of his past dragging him down.

His heart sank as he asked himself what life could hold for him. How often, sitting on his prison bed with his head in his hands, he had pictured joyously the present moment! Now he felt like a child who has lost its parent's hand in the passing throng.

There had been a day, the year before, when his old mother's letter had not come, and, instead, only a line of stereotyped consolation from the country pastor to the village ne'er-do-well. No one had seen him choke over his bowl of soup and bread, or noticed the tears that trickled down upon the shoe-leather in his hand. She had been the only one who had ever written to him. There was nothing now to take him back to the little cluster of white cottages among the hills where he was born.

As he stood there alone facing the world, he yearned to throw himself once more upon his cot and weep against its iron bars—for three years the only arms outstretched to comfort him.

II

The Judge concluded his charge with the usual, "I leave the case with you, gentlemen," and the jury, collecting their miscellaneous garments, slowly retired. Leary, the County Detective assigned to "Part One," pushed an indictment across the desk, whispering:

"Try him; he's a short one," for it was getting late, and the afternoon sun was already gilding the dingy cornices of the big court-room, now almost deserted save by a lounger or two half asleep on the benches.

"People against Graham," called Dockbridge, the youthful deputy assistant district attorney.

"Fill the box!" shouted the clerk. "James Graham to the bar!" and another dozen "good men and true" answered to their names and settled themselves comfortably in their places.

At the rear the door from the pen opened and the prisoner entered, escorted by an officer. He walked stolidly around the room, passed through the gate held open for him, and took his seat at the table reserved for the defendant and his attorney. There appeared, however, to be no lawyer to represent him.

"Have you counsel?" casually inquired the clerk.

"No," answered the prisoner.

"Mr. Crookshanks, please look after the rights of this defendant," directed the Judge.

The prisoner, a thick-set man of medium height, half rose from his seat, and, turning toward the weazened little lawyer, shook his head rather impatiently. It was obvious that they were not strangers. After a whispered conversation Crookshanks stepped forward and addressed the Court.

"The defendant declines counsel, and stands upon his constitutional right to defend himself," he said apologetically.

There was a slight lifting of heads among the jury, and a few sharp glances in the direction of the prisoner, which seemed in no wise to disconcert him.

"Very well, then; proceed," ordered the Court.

The prosecutor rapidly outlined his case—one of simple "larceny from the person." The People would show that the defendant had taken a wallet from the pocket of the complaining witness. He had been caught in flagrante delicto. There were several eye-witnesses. The case would occupy but a few moments, unless, to be sure, the prisoner had some witnesses. The young assistant, who seemed slightly nervous at the unusual prospect of conducting a trial against a lawyerless defendant (savoring as it did of a hand-to-hand combat in the days of trial by battle), started to comment upon the novelty of the situation, gave it up, and to cover his retreat called his first witness.

Dockbridge was very young indeed. He was undergoing the process of being "whipped into shape" by the Judge, a kind but unrelenting observer of all the technicalities of the criminal branch, and this was one of his first cases. He could work up a pretty fair argument in his office, but he now felt his inexperience and began to wish it was time to adjourn, or that his senior, "Colonel Bob," the stout Nestor of Part One, whose long practice made him ready for any emergency, would return. But "Colonel Bob" could have proved an excellent alibi at that moment, and the battle had to be fought out alone.

The prisoner, meanwhile, was sitting calm but vigilant, pen in hand. His face, square and strong, with firmly marked mouth and chin, showed no sign of emotion, but under their heavy brows his black eyes played uneasily between the Court and jury. Evidently not more than thirty years of age, his attitude and expression showed intelligence and alert capacity.

"Go on, Mr. District Attorney," again admonished the Judge; and Dockbridge, pulling himself together, commenced to examine the complainant.

The prisoner was now straining eye and ear to catch every look and word from the witness-stand. Hardly had the complainant opened his mouth before the defendant had objected to the answer, the objection had been sustained, and the reply stricken out. He continued to object from time to time, and his points were so well taken that he dominated not only the examination but the witness as well, and the jury presently found themselves listening to a cross-examination as skilfully conducted as if by a trained practitioner.

But, although the defendant showed himself a better lawyer than his adversary, it was apparent that his battle was a losing one. Point after point he contested stubbornly, yet the case loomed clear against him.

The People having "rested," the defendant announced that he had no witnesses, and would go to the jury on the evidence, or, rather "failure of evidence," as he put it, of the prosecution. It was done with great adroitness, and none of the jury perceived that, by refusing to accept counsel, he had made it impossible to take the stand in his own behalf, and had thus escaped the necessity of subjecting himself to cross-examination as to his past career.

If the spectators had expected a piteous appeal for mercy or a burst of prison rhetoric, they were disappointed. The prisoner summed his case up carefully, arguing that there was a reasonable doubt upon the evidence to which he was entitled; begged the jury not to condemn him merely because he appeared before them as one charged with a crime; appealed to them for justice; and at the close, for the first time forgetting the proprieties of the situation, exclaimed, "I did not do it, gentlemen! I did not do it! There is an absolute failure of proof! You cannot find that I took the purse from the old gentleman on such evidence! It is all a lie!"

It was his one false touch. To raise the issue of veracity is usually a mistake on the part of a defendant, and the defiant look in Graham's eyes might well have suggested conscious guilt.

As he paused for a moment after this concluding sentence, an Italian band came marching down Centre Street playing the dead march. Some patriot was being borne to his last sleep in an alien land. Outside the court-house it paused for a moment with one melancholy crash of funeral chords. It seemed a vibrant echo of the discord of his own fruitless life. At the same moment a ray from the red sun setting over the Tombs fell upon the prisoner's face.

Dockbridge summed the case up in the stock fashion, and then for half an hour the Judge addressed the jury in a calm and dispassionate analysis of the evidence, not hesitating to compare the abilities of the prosecutor and prisoner to the disadvantage of the former, saying in this respect: "Neither must you be influenced by any feeling of admiration at the capacity shown by this defendant to conduct his own case. If he has appeared more than a match for the prosecution, it must not affect the weight which you give to the evidence against him."

"More than a match for the prosecution!" That had been rather rough, to be sure, and the fifth juror had looked at Dockbridge and grinned.

The jury filed out, the prisoner was led back to the pen, the Judge vanished into his chambers, and the prosecutor, his feet on the counsel table, lit a cigar and indulged in retrospection. The benches were deserted. There was no one but himself left in the court-room. Usually, when a jury retired, there was some mother or wife or daughter, with her handkerchief to her eyes, waiting for them to come back, but this fellow had none such. He had fought alone. Well, damn him, he deserved to! But who the deuce was he? It had been clever on his part not to take the stand. Strange to be trying a man you had never seen before—of whom you knew nothing, who had merely side-stepped into your life and would soon back out of it. "Poor devil!" thought the deputy as he lit another Perfecto.

Now the jury, as juries sometimes do, wanted to talk and had a consuming desire to smoke, so they both smoked and talked; and when O'Reilly came to turn on the lights in the court-room, they were still out, and Dockbridge had fallen fast asleep.

III

At half past ten o'clock the big court-room still remained almost empty. Inside the rail the clerk and the stenographer, having returned from a short visit to Tom Foley's saloon across the way, were languidly discussing the condition of the stock-market. A nebulous illumination in the vastness above only served to increase the shadowy dimness of the room. The talk of the pair made a scarcely audible whisper in the great silence. Outside, an electric car could be heard at intervals; within, only the slam of iron doors, subdued by distance, echoed through the corridors.

Dockbridge had awakened, and, lounging before his table, was trying to get up a case for the morrow. The Judge had gone home for dinner. One by one the court attendants had strayed away, coming back to push open the heavy door, and, after a furtive glance at the empty bench, as silently to depart.

Below in the stifling pen, alone behind the bars, James Graham sat staring vacantly at the stained cement floor. A savage rage surged through him. Curse them! That infernal Judge had not given him half a chance. Once more he recalled that day when he had stepped out into the sunlight a free man. Again he saw his iron bed, his cobbling bench, his coarse food, his hated stripes. He choked at the thought of them. Only two months before he had been at liberty. Think of it! Good clothes, good food, pleasure! God, what a fool! A dull pain worked through his body; he remembered that he had not eaten since seven that morning.

Outside in the corridor the keeper was smoking a cigar. The fumes of it drifted in and mingled with the stench of the pen. It almost nauseated him. He leaned his head against the wall and closed his eyes. The act brought rushing back the memories of his childhood, and of how, every night, he would lay his head upon his mother's knee and say, "Have I been a good boy to-day?" A sob shook him, and he pressed closer against the wall.

A sound of moving feet roused him suddenly. A door swung open, shut again, and voices came with a draught of air from the corridor.

The keeper waiting outside stirred and stood up, looking regretfully at his cigar.

"Get up there, you!"

The prisoner obeyed perfunctorily, and followed the officer heavily up the stairs and down the dirty passage to the court-room. Outside, he shrank from entering. Those eyes—those eyes! That hard, pitiless Judge! But he was pushed roughly forward. Then his old pugnacity returned; he set his teeth, and entered.

He trudged around the room and stopped at the bar before the clerk. On his right sat the twelve silent men. On the bench the white-haired Judge was gazing at him with sad but penetrating eyes.

It was different from the mellow glow of the afternoon. They were all so still—like ghosts—and all around, all about him! He wanted to shout out at them, "Speak! for God's sake, speak!" But something stifled him. The overwhelming power of the law held him speechless.

The clerk rose without looking at the prisoner.

"Gentlemen of the jury, have you agreed upon a verdict?"

"We have," answered the foreman, rising and standing with his eyes upon the floor.

"How say you, do you find the defendant guilty, or not guilty?"

"Guilty of grand larceny in the first degree."

The prisoner involuntarily pressed his hand to his heart. He had weathered that blast before and could do so again. Dockbridge gave him a look full of pity. Graham hated him for it. That child! That snivelling little fool! He wanted none of his sympathy! His breath came faster. Must they all look at him? Was that a part of his trial—to be stared down? He glared back at them. The room swam, and he saw only the stern face on the bench above.

"Name?" broke in the harsh voice of the clerk.

"James Graham."

"Age?"

"Twenty-eight."

"Married, or unmarried?" "Temperate?" came the pitiless questions, all answered in a monotone.

"Ever convicted before?"

"No," said the prisoner in a low voice, but the word sounded to him like a roaring torrent. Then came once more that awful silence. The dread eye of the Judge seared his soul.

"Graham, is that the truth?"

"Yes, sir."

"Are you quite sure?"

That merciless question! What had that to do with it? Why should he have to tell them? That was not his crime. He was ready to suffer for what he had done, but not for the past; that was not fair—he had paid for that. He must defend himself.

"Yes, sir."

"Swear him," said the Judge.

The officer took up the soiled Bible and started to place it in Graham's hand. But the hand dropped from it.

113

"No, no, I can't!" he faltered; "I can't—I—I—it is no use," he added huskily.

"When were you convicted?"

"I served six months for petty larceny in the penitentiary six years ago."

"Is that all?"

"Yes, sir."

"Are you sure?"

"Yes, sir."

"Quite sure? Think again!"

"Yes, sir," almost inaudibly.

"Swear him."

Again the book was forced toward the unwilling hand, and again it was refused.

"Have you no pity—no mercy?" his dark eyes seemed to say. Then they gave way to a look of utter hopelessness.

"I served three years in Charlestown for larceny, and was discharged two months ago."

"Is that all?"

"O, God! Isn't that enough?" suddenly groaned the prisoner. "No, no; it isn't all! It's always been the same old story! Concord, Joliet, Elmira, Springfield, Sing Sing, Charlestown—yes, six times. Twelve years. . . . I'm a jailbird." He laughed harshly and rested wearily against the wooden bar.

"Have you anything to say why judgment should not be pronounced against you?"

"Your Honor, will you hear me?" Graham choked back a dry sob.

The Judge slightly inclined his head.

"Yes. I'm a jailbird," uttered the prisoner rapidly. "I'm only out two months." There was no defiance in his voice now, and his eyes searched the face of the Judge, seeking for mercy. "I had a good home—no matter where—and a good father and mother. My father died and didn't leave anything, and I had to work while my mother kept house. I worked on the farm, winter and summer, summer and winter, early and late. I got sick of it. I quit the farm and went to the city. I worked hard and did well. I learned shorthand, and finally got a job as a court stenographer. That's how I know about the rules of evidence. Then I got started wrong, and by and by I took a fifty-dollar note and another fellow was sent up for it. After that I didn't care. I had a good time—of its kind. It was better than a dog's life on the farm, anyway. By and by I got caught, and then it was no use. Each time I got out I swore I'd lead an honest life. But I couldn't. A convict might as well try to eat stones as to find a job. But when I

114

got free this time I made up my mind to starve rather than get back again. I meant it, too. I tried hard. It was no use in Boston—they're too respectable. All a convict can do there is to get a two weeks' job sawing wood. At the end of that time he's supposed to be able to take care of himself. I had to give it up and come to New York.

"It was August, and I went the rounds of the offices for three weeks, looking for work. No one wanted a stenographer, and there was nothing else to do that I could find. Once I thought I had something on the water-front, but the man changed his mind. A woman told me to go to Dr. Westminster, so I went. He was kind enough, said he was very busy, but would do all he could for me; that there was a special society for just such cases, and he would give me a card. I thanked him, and took the card and went to the society. The young woman there gave me two soup tickets, and said she would do all she could for me. Next day she reported that there was nothing doing just then, but if I could come back in about a month they could probably do better. Then she gave me another soup ticket. I drank the soup and then I went back to Dr. Westminster. He was rather annoyed at seeing me again, and said that he had done all that he could, but would bear me in mind; meantime, unless I heard from him, it would be no use to call again. I'd lived on soup for two days.

"I got a meal by begging on the avenue. Then another woman told me to go to Dr. Emberdays, and I went to him. By this time I must have been looking pretty tough. He said that he would do what he could, and that there was a society to which he would give me a line. They asked me a devil of a lot of questions, and gave me a flannel undershirt. It made me sick! An undershirt in August, when I wanted bread and human sympathy!

"It was no use. I gave up parsons and tried the river-front again. I didn't get over one meal a day, and my head ached all the time. I heard of a job at One Hundred and Sixty-ninth Street, carrying lumber. I got a nickel for holding a horse, and went up. It was a gang of niggers. They got a dollar a day. The boss was a nigger, too, and didn't want cheap white trash. I almost went down on my knees to him, and finally he said I might come the next day. I slept in a field under a tree without anything to eat that night, and started in at seven the next morning. The thermometer went up to ninety-six, and we worked without stopping. I had to lug one end of a big stick, with a nigger under the other end, one hundred yards, then go back and get another. I got so I didn't know what I was doing. At eleven o'clock I fainted, and then I was sick, dreadfully sick. At three the boss nigger kicked me and said I had to stop faking or I wouldn't get paid, and so I got up and lugged until six. But I was so ill I knew it was no use. I couldn't do that kind of work.

"It was an awfully hot night. I got off the 'L' at Thirty-fourth Street and walked through to the avenue. When I got to the Waldorf I stopped and looked in the windows. There were men and women in there, and flowers and everything to eat—just what I could eat if I chose. And I had been working with niggers, Judge, all day long until I fainted, heaving timber. I just stood and waited, and when a chance came to snatch a roll of bills I took it. They couldn't catch me. I was good for ten of 'em, Judge.

"After that it was easy. I met some of the fellows that had served time with me and got back into the old life. Judge, it's no use. I don't blame you for what you are going to do, nor I don't blame the jury. Anyone could see through the bluff I put up. I'm guilty. I'm a jailbird, I say. I'm done. Only I've had no chance, Judge. Give me another; let me go back to the farm. I'll go, I swear I will! It'll kill me to go to prison. I'm a human being. God meant me to live out of doors, and I've spent half of my life inside stone walls. Let me go back to the country. I'll go, Judge. I'm a human being. Give me one more chance."

There was no sound when the prisoner stopped speaking. The judge did not reply for a full minute. His face wore its habitual look of sadness. Then he spoke in a very low tone, but one which was distinctly audible in the silence of the court-room.

"Graham, you have read your own sentence. You have confessed that you cannot lead an honest life. Your fault is that you will not work. There are a thousand farms within a hundred miles, where you could earn a livelihood for the asking. Your intelligence is of a high order. By ordinary application you could have risen far above your fellows. You are a dangerous criminal—all the more dangerous for your ability. You almost outwitted the jury, and conducted your own case more ably than nine out of ten lawyers would have done. You have ruined your own life, and cast away a pearl of price. You have my pity, but I cannot allow it to affect my duty. Graham, I sentence you to State Prison for ten years."

The prisoner shivered, and covered his face with his hands. Then the officer clapped him on the shoulder and pushed him toward the door.

"Gentlemen, you are excused." The Judge bowed to the jury.

"Hear ye! Hear ye!" bawled the attendant: "all persons having business with Part One of the General Sessions of the Peace, held in and for the County of New York, may now depart. This Court stands adjourned until to-morrow morning at half past ten o'clock."

IN THE COURSE OF JUSTICE

"The Law is a sort of hocuspocus science that smiles in yer face while it picks yer pocket; and the glorious uncertainty of it is of mair use to the professors than the justice of it."

I

A trim, neatly dressed young man, holding in one of his carefully gloved hands a bamboo cane, sat upon a bench in Union Square one brilliant October morning some ten years ago. All about him swarms of excited sparrows chattered and fought among the yellow leaves. A last night's carnation languished in his button-hole, and his smoothly shaven lantern-jaw and high cheekbones suggested the type of upper Broadway and the Tenderloin. In spite of this, the general effect was not unpleasing, especially as his sparse curly hair, just turning gray at the temples, disclosed a forehead suggestive of more than usual intelligence in a face otherwise ordinary. A shadowy, inscrutable smile from time to time played upon his features, at one moment making them seem good-naturedly sympathetic, at another, sinister. The casual observer would have classed him as a student or actor. He was both, and more.

From a large jewelry store across the way presently emerged a diminutive messenger-boy carrying a small, square bundle, and turned into Broadway. The man on the bench, known to his friends as "Supple Jim," rose unobtrusively to his feet. The apostle of Hermes stopped to buy a cent's worth of mucilaginous candy from the Italian on the corner, and then, whistling loudly, dawdled upon his way. The man followed, manœuvring for position, while the boy, now in the chewing stage and struggling violently, lingered to inspect a mechanical toy. The supple one accomplished a flank movement, approached, touched him on the shoulder, and displayed a silver badge beneath his coat.

"Young man, I'm from the Central Office, and need your help. About a block from here a feller will come runnin' after you and say they've given you the wrong bundle—see? He'll hand you another, and tell you to give him the one you've got. He's a crook—'Paddy the Sneak'—old game! see?"

117

The boy was all attention, his jaws motionless.

"Yep!" he replied, his eyes glistening delightedly.

"Well, I'll be right behind you; and when he throws the game into you, just pretend you fall to it an' hand him your box. Then I'll make the collar. Are you on?"

"Say, that's easy!" grinned the boy.

"Show us what you're good for, then, and I'll have the Inspector send you some passes for the theayter."

The boy started on in business-like fashion. As his interlocutor had predicted, a hatless "feller" overtook him, breathless, and entered into voluble explanation. The messenger exchanged bundles, and then, eyes front, continued up the street until the detective should pounce upon his victim. For some strange reason no such event took place. At the end of the block he cast a furtive glance behind him. Both Paddy and the Central Office man had vanished, to dispose in a Bowery pawnshop of the fruits of their short hour of toil, dividing between them one hundred and sixty dollars as the equivalent of the diamond stud which the box had contained.

Half an hour later, drawn by a fascination which he found irresistible, the hero of this legal memoir took a car to the Criminal Courts Building, and made his way to the General Sessions.

"Forgot my subpœna, Cap'n. I'm a witness. Just let me in, please!" he said, with a smile of easy good-nature.

Old Flaherty, the superannuated door-keeper, known as The Eagle, eyed the young man suspiciously for a moment, and then, grumbling, allowed him to enter the court-room. The thief who had so easily secured admittance, fought his way persistently through the throng, elbowed by the gruff officer at the inner gate, and selecting the best seat on the front bench, compelled its earlier occupants to make room for him with a calm assurance and matter-of-course superiority which they had not the courage to oppose.

Supple Jim listened with interest to the call of the calendar. A few lawyers, with their witnesses, whose cases had gone over until the morrow, struggled out through the crush at the door, with no perceptible diminution in the throng within. The clerk prepared to call the roll of the jury.

"Trial jurors in the case of 'The People against Richard Monohan,' please answer to your names."

The twelve, in varying keys, had all replied; the trial was "on" again, having been interrupted, evidently, by the adjournment of the afternoon before. A venerable complainant now resumed the story of how two young men, whose acquaintance he had made in a saloon the previous Sunday evening, had followed him into the street, assaulted him on his way home and robbed him of his ring. He positively identified the prisoner as the one who had wrenched it from his finger.

Next, an officer testified to having arrested the defendant upon the old gentleman's description, and to having found in his pocket a pawn-ticket calling for the ring in question.

The case, in the vernacular of the courts, was "dead open and shut."

The People "rested," and the defendant, a miserable specimen of those wretched beings that constitute the penumbra of crime, took the stand. His defence was absurd. He denied ever before having seen his accuser, had not been in the saloon, had not taken the ring, had not pawned it, had bought the ticket from a man on the corner who, he remembered, had told him he was getting a bargain at three dollars. He could not describe this "man," or account for his own whereabouts on the evening in question. He had been drunk at the time. It was a story as old as theft itself.

The prosecutor winked at the jury, and the Judge once more summoned the apostolic-looking complainant to the chair.

"You realize, sir, the terrible consequences to this young man should you be mistaken? Are you quite sure that he is one of the persons who robbed you?" he inquired with becoming gravity.

The witness raised himself by his cane, and stepping down to where the prisoner sat, gazed searchingly into his stolid face.

"God knows," said he, "I wouldn't harm a hair of his head. But by all that's holy, I swear he's the man who took my ring."

A wave of interest passed over the assembled attorneys. That was business for you! No use to cross-examine an old fellow like him. There was a great nodding of heads and shuffling of feet.

"Do you think you could identify your other assailant if you should see him?" continued the judge.

"I'm sure of it," calmly replied the witness.

"Very well, sir," continued his Honor; "see if you can do so."

Half of the audience moved uneasily, and glanced longingly toward the closed means of exit. A woman tittered hysterically. The witness slowly descended, and, escorted by a policeman, began his inspection, scrutinizing each face with care. Quietly he moved along the first bench, and then, gently shaking his head, along the second. The interest became breathless. A sigh of relief rippled along the settees after him. The only spectator unmoved by what was taking place was Supple Jim, who smiled genially at the old gentleman as the latter glanced at him and passed on. Four rows—five rows—six rows—seven rows. At last there was but one bench left, and the excitement reached the point of ebullition. Would he find him?

Were they going to be disappointed after all? Only half a bench left! Only two men left! Ah! what was that? People shoved one another in the back, craning their heads to see what was doing in the distant corner where the complainant stood. Suddenly the searcher faced the Judge, and, pointing to the last occupant of the rear settee, announced with conviction:

"Your Honor, this is the other man!"

A murmur travelled rapidly around the court-room. Honors were even between a Judge who could thus unerringly divine the presence of a malefactor and a patriarch who, out of so great a multitude, was able unhesitatingly to pick out a midnight assailant.

The "criminal" attorneys whispered among themselves: "Well, say! what do you think of that! All right, eh? Well, I guess! Well, say!"

This picturesque digression concluded, interest again centred in the defendant, of whose ultimate conviction there could no longer be any doubt.

Not that the identification of the accomplice had any real significance, since the man so ostentatiously picked out by the patriarch in court had been caught red-handed at the time of the robbery within a block of the saloon, was already under indictment as a co-defendant, and being out on bail had merely been brought in under a bench warrant and placed among the spectators. But the performance had a distinct dramatic value, and the jury could not be blamed for making the natural deduction that if the complainant was right as regards the one, ipso facto he must be as to the other. That the complainant had already identified him at the police-station and at the Tombs seemed a matter of small importance. The point was, apparently, that the old fellow had a good memory, and one upon which the jury could safely rely.

The Judge charged the law, and the jury retired, returning almost immediately with a verdict of "Guilty of robbery in the first degree."

The prisoner at the bar swayed for an instant, steadied himself, and stood clinging to the rail, while his counsel made the usual motions for a new trial and in arrest of judgment.

"Clear the box! Clear the box!" shouted the clerk, and the jury, their duty comfortably discharged, filed slowly out.

The court-room rapidly emptied itself into the corridors. Supple Jim waited on the steps of the building until a young woman, carrying a baby, came wearily out, and, as she passed, thrust a roll of bills into her hand.

"Your feller's been done dirt!" he growled. "Take that, and put it out of sight. Don't give it to any lawyer, now! You'll need it yourself." Then he sprang lightly upon the rear platform of a surface car as it whizzed by, and vanished from her astonished gaze.

Thus was an innocent man convicted, while crime triumphant played the part of benefactor.

II

The next morning Supple Jim, sitting in the warm sunshine in the bay-window of his favorite restaurant, lazily finished a hearty breakfast of ham and eggs, glancing casually, meanwhile, at the morning paper which lay open before him. At a respectful distance his attendant awaited the moment when this important guest should snap his fingers, demand his damage, and call for a Carolina Perfecto. These would be forthcoming with alacrity, for Mr. James Hawkins was more of an autocrat on Fourteenth Street than a Pittsburg oil magnate at the Waldorf. Just now the Supple James was reading with keen enjoyment how, the day before, a quick-witted old gentleman had brought a malefactor to justice. At one of the paragraphs he broke into a gentle laugh, perusing it again and again, apparently with intense enjoyment.

Had ever such a farce been enacted in the course of justice! He tossed away the paper and swore softly. Of course, the only thing that had rendered such a situation possible at all was the fact that the aged Farlan was a superlative old ass. To hear him tell his yarn on the stand, you would have thought that it gave him positive pain to testify against a fellow being. Did you ever see such white hair and such a big white beard? Why, he looked like Dowie or Moses, or some of those fellows. When Jim had tripped him up and slipped off the ring, the old chap had already swallowed half a dozen "County Antrims," and wasn't in a condition to remember anything or anybody. The idea of his going so piously into court and swearing the thing on to Monohan; it gave you the creeps! A fellow might go to "the chair" as easy as not, in just the same way. Of course, Jim had not intended to get the young greenhorn into any trouble when he had sold him the pawn-ticket. He had been just an easy mark. And when the police had arrested him and found the ticket in his pocket, there was not any call for Jim to set them straight. That was just Monohan's luck, curse him! Let him look out for himself.

But to see the patriarch carefully forging the shackles upon the wrong man, had filled Jim with a wondering and ecstatic bewilderment. The stars in their courses had seemed warring in his behalf.

Think of it! That fellow Monohan could get twenty years! It made him mad, this infernal conspiracy, as it seemed to him, between judges and prosecutors. It mattered little, apparently, whether they got the right man or not, so long as they got someone! What business had they to go and convict a fellow who was innocent, and put him, "Jim," the cleverest "gun" in the profession, in such a position? He wondered if folks in other lines of business had so many problems to face. The stupidity of witnesses and the trickery of lawyers was almost beyond belief. It was a perennial contest, not only of wit against wit, strategy against strategy, but, worst of all, of wit against impenetrable dulness. Why, if people were going to be so careless about swearing a man's liberty away, it was time to "get on the level." You might be nailed any time by mistake, and then your record would make any defence impossible. You had the right to demand common honesty, or, at least, intelligence, on the part of the prosecution.

But the main question was, What was going to become of Monohan? Well, the boy was convicted, and that was the end of it. It was quite clear to Jim that, had he been victimized in the same way, no one would have bothered about it at all. It was simply the fortune of war.

But twenty years! His own pitiful aggregate of six, with vacations in between, as it were, looked infinitesimal beside that awful burial alive. He'd be fifty when he came out—if he ever came out! Sometimes they died like flies in a hot summer. And then there was always Dannemora—worst of all, Dannemora! It would kill him to go back. He couldn't live away from the main stem now. Why, he hadn't been in stir for five years. All his prison traits, the gait, the hunch, were effaced—gone completely. His brows contracted in a sharp frown.

"What's the use?" he muttered as he rose to go. "He ain't worth it! I can stake his wife and kids till his time's up! But, God! I could never go back!"

Yet the same irresistible force which had directed him to the court-room the day before, now led him to the Grand Central Station. Like one walking in a dream, he bought a ticket and took the noon train alone to Ossining.

Following a path that led him quickly to a hill above the town not far from the prison walls, he threw himself at full length beside a bowlder, and gazed upon the familiar outlook. Across the broad, shining river lay the dreamy blue hills he had so often watched while working at his brushes. Here and there a small boat skimmed down the stream before the same fresh breeze that sent the red and brown leaves fluttering along the grass. The sunlight touched everything with enchantment, the cool autumn air was an intoxicant—it was the Golden Age again. No, not the Golden Age! Just below, two hundred yards away, he noticed for the first time a group of men in stripes breaking stones. Some were kneeling, some crouching upon their haunches. They worked in silence, cracking one stone after another and making little piles of the fragments. At the distance of only a few feet two guards leaned upon their loaded rifles. Jim shut his eyes.

III

The day of sentence came. Once more Jim found himself in the stifling court. He saw Monohan brought to the bar, and watched as he waited listlessly for those few terrible words. The Court listened with grim patience to the lawyer's perfunctory appeal for mercy, and then, as the latter concluded, addressed the prisoner with asperity.

"Richard Monohan, you have been justly convicted by a jury of your peers of robbery in the first degree. The circumstances are such as to entitle you to no sympathy from the Court. The evidence is so clear and positive, and the complainant's identification of you so perfect, that it would have been impossible for a jury to reach any other verdict. Under the law you might be punished by a term of twenty years, but I shall be merciful to you. The sentence of the Court is—" here the Judge adjusted his spectacles, and scribbled something in a book—"that you be confined in State Prison for a period of not less than ten nor more than fifteen years."

Monohan staggered and turned white.

The whole crowded court-room gasped aloud.

"Come on there!" growled the attendant to his prisoner. But suddenly there was a quick movement in the centre of the room, and a man sprang to his feet.

"Stop!" he shouted. "Stop! There's been a mistake! You've convicted the wrong man! I stole that ring!"

"Keep your seats! Keep your seats!" bellowed the court officers as the spectators rose impulsively to their feet.

Those who had been present at the trial two days before were all positive now that they had never taken any stock in the old gentleman's identification.

"Silence! Silence in the court!" shouted the Captain pounding vigorously with a paper-weight.

"What's all this?" sternly demanded the Judge. "Do you claim that you robbed the complainant in this case? Impossible!"

"Not a bit, yer 'Onor!" replied Jim in clarion tones. "You've nailed the wrong man, that's all. I took the ring, pawned it for five dollars, and sold the ticket to Monohan on the corner. I can't stand for his gettin' any fifteen years," he concluded, glancing expectantly at the spectators.

A ripple of applause followed this declaration.

"Hm!" commented his Honor. "How about the co-defendant in the case, identified here in the court-room? Do you exonerate him as well?"

"I've nothin' to do with him," answered Jim calmly. "I've got enough troubles of my own without shouldering any more. Only Monohan didn't have any hand in the job. You've got the boot on the wrong foot!"

Young Mr. Dockbridge, the Deputy Assistant District Attorney, now asserted himself.

"This is all very well," said he with interest, "but we must have it in the proper form. If your Honor will warn this person of his rights, and administer the oath, the stenographer may take his confession and make it a part of the record."

Jim was accordingly sworn, and informed that whatever he was about to say must be "without fear or hope of reward," and might be used as evidence against him thereafter.

In the ingenious and exhaustive interrogation which followed, the Judge, a noted cross-examiner, only succeeded in establishing beyond peradventure that Jim was telling nothing but the truth, and that Monohan was, in fact, entirely innocent. He therefore consented, somewhat ungraciously, to having the latter's conviction set aside and to his immediate discharge.

"As for this man," said he, "commit him to the Tombs pending his indictment by the Grand Jury, and see to it, Mr. District Attorney," he added with significance, "that he be brought before me for sentence."

Out into the balconies of the court-house swarmed the mob. Monohan had disappeared with his wife and child, not even pausing to thank his benefactor. It was enough for him that he had escaped from the meshes of the terrible net in which he had been entangled.

From mouth to mouth sprang the wonderful story. It was shouted from one corridor to another, and from elevator to elevator. Like a wireless it flew to the District Attorney's office, the reporters' room, the Coroner's Court, over the bridge to the Tombs, across Centre Street into Tom Foley's, to Pontin's, to the Elm Castle, up Broadway, across to the Bowery, over to the Rialto, along the

124

Tenderloin; it flashed to thieves in the act of picking pockets, and they paused; to "second-story men" plotting in saloons, and held them speechless; the "moll-buzzers" heard it; the "con" men caught it; the "britch men" passed it on. In an hour the whole under-world knew that Supple Jim had squealed on himself, had taken his dose to save a pal, had anteed his last chip, had "chucked the game."

IV

Three long months had passed, during which Jim had lain in the Tombs. For a day or two the newspapers had given him considerable notoriety. A few sentimental women had sent him flowers of greater or less fragrance, with more or less grammatical expressions of admiration; then the dull drag of prison-time had begun, broken only by the daily visit of Paddy, and the more infrequent consultations with old Crookshanks.

The Grand Jury had promptly found an indictment, but when the District Attorney placed the case upon the calendar in order to allow our hero to plead guilty, Mr. Crookshanks, Jim's counsel, announced that his client had no intention of so doing, and demanded an immediate trial.

Dockbridge, however, now found himself in a situation of singular embarrassment, which made action upon his part for the present impossible. He was at his wits' end, for the law expressly required that no prisoner should be confined longer than two months without trial. And each week he was obliged to face the redoubtable Mr. Crookshanks, who with much bluster demanded that the case should be disposed of.

Thirteen weeks went by and still Jim lived on prison fare. Soon a reporter—an acquaintance of Paddy's—commented upon the fact to his city editor. The policy of the paper happening to be against the administration, an item appeared among the "Criminal Notes" calling attention to the period of time during which Jim had been incarcerated. Other papers copied, and scathing editorials followed. In twenty-four hours Jim's detention beyond the time regulated by statute for the trial of a prisoner without bail had become an issue. The great American public, through its representative, the press, clamored to know why the wheels of justice had clogged, and the campaign committee of the reform party called in a body upon the District Attorney, warning him that an election was approaching and inquiring the cause of the "illegal proceeding which had been brought to their attention." The editor of the Midnight American, with his usual impetuosity, threatened a habeas corpus.

Then the District Attorney sent for the Assistant, and the two had a hurried consultation. Finally the chief shook his head, saying: "There's no way out of it. You'll have to go to trial at once. Perhaps you can secure a plea. We can't afford any more delay. Put it on for to-morrow."

The next day "Part One of the Court of General Sessions of the Peace, in and for the County of New York," was crowded to suffocation, for the dramatic nature of Jim's act of self-sacrifice had not been forgotten, and a keen interest remained in its denouement. It was a brilliant January noon, and the sun poured through the great windows, casting irregular patches of light upon the throng within. High above the crowd of lawyers, witnesses, and policemen sat the Judge; below him, the clerk and Assistant District Attorney conferred together as to the order in which the cases should be tried; to the left reclined a row of non-combatants, "district leaders," ex-police magistrates, and a few privileged spectators; outside the rail crowded the members of the "criminal bar"; while in the main body of the room the benches were tightly packed with loafers, "runners" for the attorneys, curious women, indignant complainants, and sympathizing friends of the various defendants. Here no one was allowed to stand, but nearer the door the pressure became too great, and once more an overplus, new-comers, lawyers who could not force their way to the front, tardy policemen, persons who could not make up their minds to come in and sit down, and stragglers generally, formed a solid mass, absolutely blocking the entrance, and preventing those outside from getting in or anyone inside from getting out.

Around the room the huge pipes of the radiators clicked diligently; full steam was on, not a window open.

Jim was called to the bar, the jury sworn, and Dockbridge, with several innuendoes reflecting upon the moral character of any man who would confess himself a criminal and yet put the county to the expense and trouble of a trial, briefly opened the case.

The stenographer who had taken Jim's confession was the first witness. He read his notes in full, while Dockbridge nodded with an air of finality in the direction of the jury.

"Do you care to cross-examine, Mr. Crookshanks?" he inquired.

The lawyer shook his head.

Jim sat smiling, self-possessed, and silent.

126

The youthful Assistant, still hoping to wring a plea from the defendant, paused and leaned toward the prisoner's counsel.

"Come, come, what's the use?" he suggested benignantly. "Why go through all this farce? Let him plead guilty to 'robbery in the second degree.' He'll be lucky to get that! It's his only chance."

But upon the lean and withered visage of the veteran Crookshanks flickered an inscrutable smile, like that which played upon the features of his client.

"Not on your tin-type!" he ejaculated.

Dockbridge shrugged his shoulders, hesitated a moment, then glanced a trifle uneasily toward the crowd of spectators. Once more he turned in the direction of the prisoner.

"Well, I'll let him plead to grand larceny instead of robbery," he said, with an air of acting against his better judgment.

Crookshanks grinned sardonically and again shook his head.

"Very well, then," said the prosecutor sternly, "your client will have to take the consequences. Call the complainant."

"Daniel Farlan, take the witness' chair."

The crowd in the court-room waited expectantly. The complainant, however, did not respond.

"Daniel Farlan! Daniel Farlan!" bawled the officer.

But the venerable Farlan came not. Perchance he was a-sleeping or a-hunting.

"If your Honor pleases," announced Dockbridge, "the complainant does not answer. I must ask for an adjournment."

But in an instant the old war-horse, Crookshanks, was upon his feet snorting for the battle.

"I protest against any such proceeding!" he shouted, his voice trembling with well-simulated indignation. "My client is in jeopardy. I insist that this trial go on here and now!"

Dockbridge smiled deprecatingly, but the jury and spectators showed plainly that they were of Mr. Crookshanks's opinion. The Judge hesitated for a moment, but his duty was clear. There was no question but that Jim had been put in jeopardy.

"You must go on with the trial, Mr. Dockbridge," he announced reluctantly. "The jury has been sworn, and a witness has testified. It is too late to stop now."

The Assistant was forced to admit that he had no further evidence at hand.

"What!" cried the Judge. "No further evidence! Well, proceed with the defence!"

Dockbridge dropped into a chair and mopped his forehead, while the jury glanced inquiringly in the direction of the defendant. But now Crookshanks, the hero of a hundred legal conflicts, the hope and trust of all defenceless criminals, slowly arose and buttoned his threadbare frock-coat. He looked the Court full in the eye. The prosecutor he ignored.

"If your Honor please," began the old lawyer gently, "I move that the Court direct the jury to acquit, on the ground that the People have failed to make out a case."

The Assistant jumped to his feet. The spectators stared in amazement at the audacity of the request. The Judge's face became a study.

"What do you mean, Mr. Crookshanks?" he exclaimed. "This man is a self-confessed criminal. Do you hear, sir, a self-confessed criminal."

But the anger of the Court had no terrors for little Crookshanks. He waited calmly until the Judge had concluded, smiled deferentially, and resumed his remarks, as if the bench were in its usual state of placidity.

"I must beg most respectfully to point out to your Honor that the Criminal Code provides that the confession of a defendant is not of itself enough to warrant his conviction without additional proof that the crime charged has been committed. May I be pardoned for indicating to your Honor that the only evidence in this proceeding against my client is his own confession, made, I believe, some time ago, under circumstances which were, to say the least, unusual. While I do not pretend to doubt the sincerity of his motives on that occasion, or to contest at this juncture the question of his moral guilt, the fact remains that there has been no additional proof adduced upon any of the material points in the case, to wit, that the complainant ever existed, ever possessed a ring, or that it was ever taken from him."

He paused, coughed slightly, and, removing from his green bag a folded paper, continued: "In addition, it is my duty to inform the Court that a person named Farlan left the jurisdiction of this tribunal upon the day after Monohan's conviction of the offence for which my client is now on trial.

"After such an unfortunate mistake," said Crookshanks with an almost imperceptible twinkle in his "jury eye," "he can hardly be expected to assist voluntarily in a second prosecution. I hold in my hand his affidavit that he has left the State never to return."

The Judge had left his chair and was striding up and down the dais. He now turned wrathfully upon poor Dockbridge.

"What do you mean by trying a case before me prepared in such a fashion? This is a disgraceful miscarriage of justice! I shall lay the matter before the District Attorney in person! Mr. Crookshanks has correctly stated the law. I am absolutely compelled

128

to discharge this defendant, who, by his own statement, ought to be incarcerated in State Prison! I—I—the Court has been hoodwinked! The District Attorney made ridiculous! As for you," casting a withering glance upon the prisoner, "if I ever have the opportunity, I shall punish you as you deserve!"

Dead silence fell upon the court-room. The clerk arose and cleared his throat.

"Mr. Foreman, have you agreed upon a verdict? What say you? Do you find the defendant guilty, or not guilty?"

"Not guilty," replied the foreman, somewhat doubtfully.

There was a smothered demonstration in the rear of the court-room. A few spectators had the temerity to clap their hands.

"Silence! Silence in the court!" shouted the Captain.

The clerk faced the prisoner.

"James Hawkins, alias James Hawkinson, alias Supple Jim, you are discharged."

As our hero stepped from behind the bar, Paddy was the first to grasp his hand.

"You're the cleverest boy in New York!" he muttered enthusiastically; "and say, Jim," he lowered his voice—could it be with a shade of embarrassment?—"you're a hero all right, into the bargain."

"Oh, cut that out!" answered Jim. "Wasn't I playing a sure thing? And wasn't it worth three months,—and ten dollars per to the old guy for staying over in Jersey,—to put 'em in a hole like that?"

And the two of them, relieved by this evasion of an impending and depressing cloud of moral superiority, went out, with others, to get a drink.

THE MAXIMILIAN DIAMOND

Dockbridge yawned, threw down his fountain-pen, whirled his chair away from the window, through which the afternoon sun was pouring a dazzling flood of light, crossed his feet upon the rickety old table whose faded green baize was littered with newspapers, law books, copies of indictments, and empty cigarette boxes, and idly contemplated the graphophone, his latest acquisition. To a stranger, this little office, tucked away behind an elevator shaft under the eaves of the Criminal Courts Building, might have proved of some interest, filled as it was on every side with mementoes of hard-fought cases in the courts below, framed copies of forged checks and notes, photographs of streets and houses known to fame only by virtue of the tragedies they had witnessed, and an uncouth collection of weapons of all varieties from a stiletto and long tapering bread knife to the most modern Colt automatic. On the bookcase stood an innocent-looking bottle which had once contained poison, while above it hung a faded indictment accusing someone long since departed of administering its contents to another who did "for a long time languish, and languishing did die." An enormous black leather lounge, a safe, several chairs, and some pictures of English and American jurists completed the contents of the room. Here Dockbridge had for five years interviewed his witnesses, prepared his cases, and dreamed of establishing a forensic reputation which should later by a shower of gold repay him in part for the many tedious hours passed within its walls. From the grimy windows he could look down upon the court-yard of the Tombs and see the prisoners taking their daily exercise, while from the distance came faintly the din and rattle of Broadway. An air-shaft which passed through the room communicated in some devious manner with the prison pens on the mezzanine floor far beneath, and at times strange odors would come floating up bringing suggestions of prison fare. On such occasions Dockbridge would throw wide both windows, open the transom, and seek refuge in the library.

Taken as a whole, his five years there had been invaluable both from a personal and professional point of view. He had found himself from the very first day in a sort of huge legal clinic, where hourly he could run through the whole gamut of human emotions. It was to him, the embryonic advocate, what hospital service is to the surgeon. He was, as it were, an intern practising the surgery of the law. And what a multitude of cases came there for treatment—every disease of the mind and heart and soul! For a year or two he had been racked nervously and emotionally, forced from laughter in one moment, to tears the next. Then the mere fascination of his trade as prosecutor, the marshalling of evidence, the tactics of trials, the thwarting of conspiracies, the analysis of motives, the exposure of cunning tricks to liberate the guilty, had so possessed his mind that the suffering and sin about him, though keenly realized, no longer cost him sleep and peace of mind. And the stories that he heard! The mysteries which were unravelled before his very eyes, and those deeper mysteries the secrets of which were never revealed, but remained sealed in the hearts of those who, rather than disclose them, sought sanctuary within prison walls!

How he wished sometimes that he could write—if only a little! Through what strange labyrinths of human passion and ingenuity could he conduct his readers! Sometimes he tried to scribble the stories down, but the words would not come. How could you describe your feelings while trying a man for his life, when he sat there at the bar pallid and tense, his hands clutching each other until the nails quivered in the flesh; the groan of the convicted felon; the wail of the heart-broken mother as her son was led away by the officer? He had seen one poor fellow faint dead away on hearing his sentence to the living tomb; and had heard a murderer laugh when convicted and the day set for his execution. Sometimes, in sheer desperation at the thought of losing what he had seen and experienced, he would turn on the graphophone and talk into it, disconnectedly, by the hour. It usually came out in better shape than what he turned off with his pen. If he could only write!

"Dockbridge! Hi, there, Dockbridge!"

The door was kicked open, and the lank figure of one of his associates stood before him. His visitor grinned, and removed his pipe.

"Bob'll be up in a minute. Come along to 'Coney.'"

"Don't feel kittenish enough," answered Dockbridge.

"Oh, come on! It'll do you good."

The sound of rapid steps flew up the stairs, and Bob burst into the room, almost upsetting the first arrival.

"What are you doing up here in this smelly place?" he inquired. "Got a cigarette?"

Dockbridge threw him a package without altering his position.

At this moment the heavily built figure of the chief of staff entered.

"Holding a reception?" he asked good-naturedly.

Bob had slipped behind the owner of the graphophone and

was rapidly surveying his desk. Suddenly he pounced on a pile of yellow paper, and, snatching it up, ran across the room.

"I thought so! He's been writing."

"Here you, Bob, give that back!" cried Dockbridge, springing up. He was blocked by the chief of staff.

"Fair play, now. It may be libellous. The censor demands the right of inspection."

"Oh, I don't mind if you see it!" said Dockbridge, "only I don't intend that cub to snicker over it. It's nothing, anyway."

"'The Maximilian Diamond!'" shouted the thief. "By George, what a rippin' title! Full of gore, I bet!"

"You give that back!" growled its owner.

"Gentlemen, allow me to present the well-known author and brilliant young literary man, Mr. John Dockbridge, whose picture in four colors is soon to appear on the cover of the 'Maiden's Gaslog Companion,'" continued Bob. "I read, 'The villain stood with his dagger elevated for an instant above the bare breast of his palpitating victim.' My, but it's great!"

"You see you'd better read it to us in self-defence," remarked the chief of staff. "Go ahead!"

"Promise, and I'll give it back," said Bob, from the door. "Refuse, and I send it to the 'American.'"

"It wasn't for publication, anyway," explained Dockbridge.

"Of course not," answered Bob. "We'll pass on it. Perhaps we'll send it in for that Five-Thousand-Dollar competition."

"Well, shut up, and I will. Give it here!" Dockbridge recovered the manuscript and returned to his armchair. The others disposed themselves upon the lounge.

"Oyez! Oyez!" cried Bob. "All persons desiring to hear the great American novel, draw near, give your attention and ye shall be heard."

"Keep still!" ordered the chief of staff. "Go ahead, Jack. I'll make him shut up."

"Mind you do," said Dockbridge. "It's about that big diamond, you know. The story begins in this room."

"Well, begin it," laughed Bob.

His companions pulled his head down on the chief's lap and smothered him with a handkerchief.

"Well," said Dockbridge rather sheepishly, "here goes."

THE MAXIMILIAN DIAMOND

A stout, jovial-looking person, with reddish hair, sandy complexion, and watery blue eyes, stood waiting in my office, his wrist attached by means of a nickel-plated handcuff to that of a keeper. My two visitors conducted themselves with remarkable unanimity, and with but a single motion sank into the chairs I offered.

"Well, what's the trouble?" I inquired genially.

The keeper jerked his thumb in the direction of the other, who grinned apologetically and hitched in my direction. Bending toward me, he whispered: "I am the victim of one of the most remarkable conspiracies in history. My story involves personages of the highest rank, and is stranger than one of Dumas' romances. I am a bill-poster."

Not knowing whether he intended to include himself among the illustrious persons alluded to, I nodded encouragingly and produced some cigars.

"My name is Riggs," continued the prisoner, as he bit off the end of his cigar and expelled it through the window. "Got a match?"

The keeper drew a handful from his pocket. I lit a cigar for myself and assumed an attitude of attention.

"My wife is little Flossie Riggs. Don't know her? Why, she dances at Proctor's, and all over. I was doing well at my trade, and would have been doing better, if it hadn't been for that confounded diamond. It was this way. There was a fellow named Tenney, who posted bills with me about five years back, and he finally got a job down in the City of Mexico with a railroad, and I used to correspond with him.

"Among other things, he told me about a great big diamond that the Emperor Maximilian used to wear in the middle of his crown. According to Tenney, it was one of the biggest on record. He said that Maximilian was so stuck on it that he had it taken out and made into a pendant for the Empress Carlotta, and that she used to wear it around at all the court functions, and so on. About the same time he took two other diamonds out of the crown and made them into finger-rings for himself.

"After a while the Mexicans got tired of having an empire and put Maximilian out of business. They stood him and two of his generals up in the parade ground at Queretaro and shot 'em. Now when he was stood up to get shot he had those two rings on his fingers, and the funny part of it was that when the people rushed up to see whether he was dead or not, both the rings were gone. Just about that time, while Carlotta was in prison, the diamond with the big pendant disappeared too. It weighed thirty-three carats. I got all this from Tenney. I don't know where he found out about it. But it all happened way back in '67.

"Somehow or other I used to think quite a lot about that

diamond—partly because I was sorry for Max, who looked to have come out at the small end; and there didn't seem to be any occasion for shooting him anyhow, that I could see.

"Well, I went on bill-posting, and got a good job with the Hair Restorer folks and was doing well, as I said, until one day I happened to take up a paper and read that there were two Mexicans out in St. Louis trying to sell an enormous diamond, but that the dealers there were all afraid to buy it. Finally the police got suspicious, and the Mexicans disappeared. Then all of a sudden it came over me that this must be the diamond that Tenney had wrote about, for all that it had been lost for nearly forty years, and I made up my mind that the Mexicans, having failed in St. Louis, would probably come to New York. I knew they had no right to the diamond anyway, first because it belonged to Maximilian's heirs, and second because it hadn't paid no duty; and I said to myself, 'Next time I write to Tenney he will hear something that will make him sit up.' So every morning, when I started out with my paste-pot and roll of posters, I would keep my eye peeled for the two Mexicans.

"But I didn't hear any more about the diamond for a long time, and I had 'most forgot all about it, until one day I was plastering up one of those yellow-headed Hair Restorer girls in Madison Square, when I saw two chaps cross over Twenty-third Street toward the Park. They were the very gazeebos I'd been looking for. Both were dark and thin and short, and, queerer still, one of them carried a big red case in his hand.

"With my heart rattling against my teeth, I jumped down from the ladder and started after them. They hurried along the street until they came to a jeweller's on Broadway, about a block from the Square. They went in, and I peeked through the window. Presently out they came in a great hurry. They still had the red case, and I made a dash for the door and rushed in. There was the store-keeper with eyes bulgin' half-way out of his head.

"'Say,' says I, 'did those dagoes try to sell you a diamond?'

"'Yes,' says he, 'the biggest I ever saw. They wanted forty thousand dollars for it, and I offered them fifteen thousand, but they wouldn't take it.'

"I didn't give him time for another word, but turned around and made another jump for the door. The Mexicans were almost out of sight, but I could still see them walking toward the Fifth Avenue Hotel, and I hustled after them tight as I could, picked up two cops on the way down, and, just as they were turning in at the entrance, we pounced on 'em.

"'You're under arrest!' I yelled, so excited I didn't really know

134

what I was doing. The fellow with the red case dodged back and handed it over to a big chap who had joined them. This one didn't appear to want to take it, and seemed quite peevish at what was happening. He turned out afterward to have been a General Dosbosco of the Haytien Junta. Well, the cops grabbed all three of them and collared the leather case. Sure enough, so help me—! There inside was the big diamond, and not only that, but a necklace with eighteen stones, and two enormous solitaire rings. The big stone was yellowish, but the others were pure white, sparklin' like one of those electric Pickle signs with fifty-seven varieties. By that time the hurry-up wagon had come, and pretty soon the whole crew of us, diamonds, Mexicans, cops, paste-pot, and me, were clattering to the police-station for fair. There I told 'em all about the diamond, and they telephoned over to Colonel Dudley, at the Custom-house, and the upshot of the whole matter was that the two Mexicans were held on a charge of smuggling diamonds into the United States.

"If you don't believe what I tell you," said Riggs, noticing, perhaps, a suggestion of incredulity in my face, "just look at these"; and fumbling in his pocket, he produced some very soiled and crumpled clippings, containing pictures of Maximilian, the Empress Carlotta, and of a very large diamond which appeared to be about the size of the "Regent." It was then that I dimly remembered reading something of a diamond seizure a short time before, and it was with a renewed interest that I listened to the continuation of my client's story.

"Well," said Riggs, "that was strange, now, wasn't it?

"You can imagine how I felt when I went home and told little Flossie about the diamond; that I was entitled to a fifty per cent. informer's reward; how I was going to give up bill-posting and just be her manager, and how we could take a bigger flat, and all that; and I thought so much about it, and talked so much about it, that I began to feel like I was Rockefeller already, which may account in part for what happened afterward."

At this point the keeper moved uneasily, and I pushed him another cigar.

"Well," continued Riggs, "I just walked on air that afternoon after leaving the Custom-house, and went around blabbing like a poor fool about my good luck. On the way home I stopped in to take a drink. There were a lot of my acquaintances there, and I had something with most of them, and then the first thing I knew everything swam before my eyes. I groped my way into the street and started toward home, but I had only taken a few steps when a gang of strong-arm men attacked me, knocked me down, and robbed me. I struggled to my feet and followed them. They turned

135

and attacked me again. I drew my knife, and then everything got dark, and the next thing I knew I was in the police-station.

"I'll admit that this part of it does seem a little queer." Riggs dropped his voice mysteriously and leaned toward me. "But I have no doubt that I was drugged and beaten for the purpose of getting me locked up in the Tombs as part of a well-planned scheme. You will see for yourself later on.

"Next morning, while I was waiting examination in the prison pen, a man came along who said he was a lawyer and would take my case. I said, All right, but that he would have to wait for his pay. He laughed, and said he guessed there would be no trouble about that; and the next thing I knew I was up before the Judge. My lawyer went up and whispered something to him, and the magistrate said:

"'Five hundred dollars bail for trial.'

"'Look here,' I spoke up, 'ain't I going to have a chance to tell my story?'

"'Keep quiet,' said the lawyer from behind his hand; 'this is just a form. You won't never have to be tried. It's just to get you out.'

"So I said nothing, and went back to the pen and waited; and the next thing I knew the hurry-up wagon had taken me to the Tombs. I tell you it was pretty tough bein' chucked in with a lot of thieves and burglars. The bill of fare ain't above par, you know, and the company's worse. I sat in my cell and waited and waited for my lawyer to show up, for he had said he'd be right over. But he didn't come, and I had to spend the night there. Next morning the keeper told me that my lawyer was in the counsel-room. So down I went with two niggers, who also had an appointment with their lawyers. It's a nasty, unventilated hole, and they lock you and the attorneys all in together. Ever been there?"

I shook my head.

"'Well,' says he, 'now have you got a bondsman?'

"'A what?' says I.

"'A bondsman—someone to go bail for you.'

"'No,' I answered, for I knew nothing about such things.

"'What! I thought you told me you had a lot of friends who had money! You haven't been trifling with me, have you?'

"I knew I hadn't told him anything of the sort, but I thought that maybe he had forgotten; so I said I hadn't any friends who had any money, and knew no one to go bail for me.

"'Bad! very bad!' said he. 'You've got to have money to get out. Isn't there anyone who owes you money, or haven't you got some claim or something?'

"Then all of a sudden it flashed over me about the diamond and my fifty per cent. of the reward, and then something in his eye made me think again. It seemed to me that I had seen him before somewhere. I couldn't remember just where, but the more I hesitated the surer I was. Then it came over me that a few days in jail, more or less, made mighty little difference when I was going to be a rich man so soon, and I decided I had better hang on to what I'd got.

"'No,' said I, 'I ain't got nothin'.'

"'You lie!' says he, growing very red. 'You lie! You've got a claim against the United States Government.'

"Then he saw he'd made a break.

"'Why, they all told me you caught a smuggler, or something, and had a claim against the Government for a hundred dollars.'

"'A hundred!' I yelled. 'Twenty thousand!'

"'Oh!' said he, 'as much as that? Why, I'll get you out this afternoon.'

"'How?' said I.

"'Well, you will have to assign your claim so I can raise the money on it. It's a mere form.'

"But the thought came into my mind, Better stay there ten years than let him have the claim; so I said that I didn't understand such things, and I'd just wait until I could be tried.

"'Tried?' said he. 'Why, you won't be tried for months.'

"My heart sank right down into my boots.

"'Don't be a fool!' he went on. 'Here you are, sick and in prison, and if you don't raise money to get a bondsman you'll stay here a long time. You might die. And if you assign that claim to me, I have a pull with the Judge and I'll have you out by supper-time.'

"'I guess I'll wait awhile,' said I.

"'Think it over, anyway. Now I tell you what I'll do. To-morrow you go up for pleading. You have to say whether you are guilty or not guilty. I'll act as your lawyer and see you through that part of it for nothing, and then if you still don't want to assign the claim, why, you can do as you choose.'

"That seemed fair enough, so I agreed. I spent another night in the cells, and next day about thirty of us were taken across the bridge into the court-room. One by one we were led up to the bar, and the clerk asked us were we guilty or not guilty. The ones that said they were guilty went off to Sing Sing or Blackwell's Island. It scared the life out of me. I was afraid that I might not be able to say 'not,' and so get sent off too, but pretty soon I saw my lawyer.

"'P. Llewellyn Riggs!'

"Up jumped Mr. Lawyer and says, 'Not guilty.'

"'What day?' asked the clerk.

"'The 21st,' says Mr. Lawyer.

"I was dumb for a minute.

"'Look here,' I whispered. 'To-day's only the first—that's three weeks.'

"'Keep quiet,' shouted an officer, and gave me a punch in the back.

"'It's all right,' whispered Mr. Lawyer. 'It's only a form.' And they hustled me out back to the Tombs.

"I didn't hear anything all that day or the next. It seemed as if I should go mad. But at last I was notified that my lawyer was there again, and down I went glad enough for the change. By that time I was feeling pretty seedy.

"'Well, young man,' said he, 'can we do business?'

"'That depends,' I answered.

"'Come, no fooling, now; if you want to get out, give me an assignment of your claim.'

"'Never,' I replied.

"'Then to h—— with you!' he shouted; 'you can rot here alone and try your case by yourself, and I hope you'll get twenty years.'

"I almost sank through the floor. Twenty years!"

Riggs had become quite dramatic, and was again leaning forward looking me straight in the eyes.

"Well, I stood fast, and he cursed me out and left me, and I began to feel that after all maybe I was a fool. I hadn't let my wife know where I was, but now I wrote to her, and she came right down and comforted me. A brave little woman she is, too. And what was more, she said that a nice young lawyer had just moved into our house and had the flat below, and she would go and get him.

"So next morning—I had been in there a week—the young lawyer came. I liked him from the start. When I told him my first lawyer's name he just leaned back and laughed.

"'Old Todd?' he says; 'why, he's the worst robber in the outfit. If he had gotten that assignment he'd have let you lie here forever and been in Paris by this time. You're a lucky man,' says he.

"Well, I thought so too, and laughed with him.

"'But,' he continued, 'you're in an embarrassing position. You can't get out without money, and you can't collect your claim. You'll have to assign it to someone. You can't assign it to your wife. That wouldn't be valid. Haven't you got some friend?'

"'I'm afraid not,' said I.

"'That's unfortunate,' he remarked, looking out where the window ought to be. 'Very unfortunate. I might lend you a couple of hundred myself,' he added. 'I will, too!'

"The blood jumped right up in my throat.'

"'God bless you!' said I, 'you're a true friend!'

"He laid his hand on my shoulder.

"'You're in hard luck, old man, but you're going to win out. I'll stand by you. Here's a five. I'll go out and get the rest right off.'

"Then all of a sudden I began to feel like a king. I could see myself in a new suit, having a bottle up at the Haymarket. I realized that I was a twenty-thousand-dollar millionaire. And just to show my chest, I said:

"'Why, you're an honest man and a true friend. You take my claim and go and collect it this afternoon,' says I.

"'No,' he hesitated, 'it's too much responsibility. I'll trust you for the money and you can pay me afterward.'

"But with that, ass that I was, I fell to begging him to take the claim, and saying he must take it, just to show he believed I trusted him; and so after a while he reluctantly yielded and filled out a paper, and I signed it and got in the warden as a witness, and he rose to go.

"'Well, till this afternoon,' says he.

"'Au revoir,' I laughed, 'get yourself a bottle of wine for me,' says I. And off he goes.

"As I passed back to the cells, who should I see beside the door but my old lawyer.

"I shook my fist in his face.

"'You old robber,' I says, 'we'll see if I can't get along without you!'

"He sneered in my face.

"'Oh, you —— fool!' says he, 'you poor, poor, ——, —— fool!'

"Then he was gone. So I went back to the cell, and sang and whistled and figured on where I should take my little Flossie for dinner. I waited and waited. Six o'clock, and no word. Then I began to get nervous.

"'You poor, poor, ——, —— fool!'

"The words rang around in my cell. Then something sort of gave inside. I knew I'd been robbed, and I yelled and shook the bars of the door and tried to get out. I cried for Flossie. The keepers came and told me to keep still; but I was plump crazy, and kept on yelling until everything got black and I fainted."

"And your lawyer never came back?"

"He never came back!" Riggs exclaimed. "He never came back! I've been robbed! I'm a poor —— fool, just as Todd said I was." Riggs burst into maudlin tears.

I gave him what consolation I could, and promised thoroughly to investigate his story.

The keeper and Riggs arose in unison, the same urbane smile

that had previously illuminated the countenance of the latter restored.

"You couldn't manage to let me have a handful of cigars, could you?" he whispered. I gave him all I had. His cheek was irresistible. I would have given him my watch had he intimated a desire for it.

Then I called up the Custom-house.

"Paid?" came back the voice of the United States District Attorney. "Of course not. The claim is worthless until the diamond is sold; and, anyway, such an assignment as you describe is invalid under our statutes. You had better execute a revocation, however, and place it on file here. Yes, I'll look out for the matter."

One day, about a week later, I was informed that Riggs had been convicted of assault, and sentenced to a year's imprisonment on Blackwell's Island. A jury of his peers had apparently proved less credulous than myself.

Many strange epistles from his place of confinement now reached me, hinting of terrible abuses, starvation, oppression, extortion. He was still the victim of a conspiracy—this time of prison guards and fellow convicts. He prayed for an opportunity to lay the facts before the authorities. I threw the letters aside. It was clear he possessed a powerful imagination, and yet his tale of the discovery of the diamond had been absolutely true. Well, let the law take its course.

A year later a jovial-looking person called at my office, and I recognized my old friend Riggs in a new brown derby hat and checked suit.

After shaking hands warmly, he presented me with a card reading:

P. Llewellyn Riggs,
Private Detective,
— Broadway.

"Yes," he explained in answer to my surprised expression, "I've gone into the detective business. My unfortunate conviction is only a sort of advertisement, you know, and then I was the victim of an outrageous conspiracy!"

"But," said I, "I thought you were going to retire on the proceeds of the diamond."

"Why, haven't you heard?" he replied. "I gave my wife an assignment of the claim with a power of attorney, and when the diamond was sold she ran away."

"Ran away?"

"Yes; she took a friend of mine with her. But I shall find her—just as I did the diamond!" He struck a Sherlock Holmes attitude.

"By the way, if you should ever want any detective work done you'll remember——"

"I am not likely to forget," I answered, "the victim of one of the most remarkable conspiracies in history."

Meantime the Mexicans were tried, convicted, and sent to prison. The jewels themselves were duly made the subject of condemnation proceedings, and whoso peruseth The Federal Reporter for the year 1901 may read thereof under the title "The United States vs. One Diamond Pendant and Two Ear-rings." They were, so to speak, tried, properly convicted, and sold to the highest bidder. The Mexicans are still serving out their time. One turned state's evidence, stating that he was a musician and had won the love of a beautiful señorita in the city of Mexico who had given him the gems to sell in order that they might have money upon which to marry. He also protested that his sweetheart had inherited them from her mother.

Inside the cover of the old red case is printed in gold letters:

LA ESMERALDA.
F. CAUSER ZIHY & CO., MEXICO AND PARIS.

And a faintly scented piece of violet note-paper lies beneath the double lining, containing, in a woman's hand, this:

The diamond necklace is from Maximilian's crown, the Emperor of Mexico. The centre stone has thirty-three and seven-tenths carats, and the eighteen surrounding it no less than one each. The diamond ring, the stone thereof, was in Maximilian's ring at the time he was shot.

But that is all; there is nothing to tell what hand snatched the jewels from the lifeless fingers of the dead Emperor, or who purloined the necklace from the royal household.

In a dusty compartment on my desk there lies a brown manila envelope, and sometimes, when the day's work is over and I have glanced for the last time across the court-yard of the Tombs at the clock tower on the New York Life Building, I take it out and idly read the press story of the famous diamond. And there rises dimly before me the pathetic scene at Queretaro where a brave and good man met his death, and I wonder if perchance there is any truth in the superstition that some stones carry ill-luck with them. But it is a far cry from the Emperor of Mexico to a New York bill-poster.

Dockbridge threw the manuscript on his desk and lit a cigarette.

"Is that all?" asked the lank deputy, stretching himself. "I thought it was going to have some sort of a plot."

"It's a pretty good story," said the chief of staff. "Have you really got any clippings?"

"I think it's rotten!" remarked Bob.

"Well, it's every word of it true, anyway," muttered Dockbridge.

EXTRADITION

I

"Dockbridge," said the District Attorney, coming hurriedly out of his office, "I've got to send you to Seattle. We've just located Andrews there—Sam Andrews of the Boodle Bank. One of Barney Conville's cases, you remember. Here's the Governor's requisition. Barney's down in Ecuador, so McGinnis of the Central Office will go out to make the arrest; but I must have someone to look after the legal end of it—to fight any writ of habeas corpus—and handle the extradition proceedings. They might get around a mere policeman, so I'm going to ask you to attend to it. The trip won't be unpleasant, and the auditor will give you a check for your expenses. Remember, now—your job is to bring Andrews back!"

He handed his assistant a bulky document bedecked with seals and ribbons, and closed the door. Dockbridge gazed blankly after his energetic chief.

"Oh, certainly, certainly! Don't mention it! Delighted, I'm sure! Thank you so much!" he exclaimed with polite sarcasm. Then he turned ferociously to a silent figure sitting behind the railing. "Sudden, eh? Don't even ask me if it's convenient! Exiles me for two months! Just drop over to Bombay and buy him a package of cigarettes! Or run across to Morocco and pick up Perdicaris, like a good fellow! Don't you regard him as a trifle inconsequent?"

Conville's side partner McGinnis, a gigantic Irishman with extraordinarily long arms and huge hands, climbed disjointedly to his feet.

"In-consequence, is it, Mister Dockbridge?" The words came in a gentle roar from the altitudes of his towering form. "Sure, the in-consequence of it is that we're to have the pleasure of travellin' togither." He looked big enough to swing the little Assistant lightly upon one shoulder and stride nimbly across the continent with him.

"An iligant thrip it will be! I'm only regretful I can't take me wife along wid me."

Pat's matrimonial troubles were the common property of the entire force. The only person totally unconscious of their existence was McGinnis himself. His lady, the daughter of fat ex-Detective-Sergeant O'Halloran, made one think inevitably of the small bird that travels through life roosting on the shoulder of the African

143

buffalo. His domestic life would have been one of wild excitement for the average citizen, but McGinnis had a blind and unwavering faith in the perfection of his spouse. Conceive, however, his surprise when the Assistant District Attorney suddenly smote him sharply in the abdomen, and shouted:

"I'll do it!"

"Phwat?" ejaculated Pat.

"Take my wife!"

"Yez have none, ye spalpeen!"

"I'll have one by to-morrow!"

"An' is it Miss Peggy ye mane?"

"No other. The county pays part of the bills. I'll make this my wedding trip!"

"God save us, Mr. Dockbridge!" gasped McGinnis. "Ain't he the little divel!" he added to himself delightedly.

Peggy had at first opposed strenuously Jack's proposition. The idea of going on one's honeymoon with a policeman! Yes, it was all right to combine business and pleasure on occasion, but one did not usually associate business with marriage—at least she hoped she did not—for Jack Dockbridge knew he hadn't a cent, and neither had she. He explained guardedly that that was the principal reason in favor of the plan. They would have part of their expenses paid.

Peggy, being a New Englander, acknowledged the force of the argument but pointed out that there was still the policeman.

Then Dockbridge pictured the West in glowing colors. Why, there were so many bad men out there, one actually needed a body-guard. Had she never heard of the Nagle case? What, not heard of the Nagle case, and she going to marry a lawyer! A newly married pair could not travel alone, unprotected.

Peggy said he was a fraud, an unadulterated fraud—an unabashed liar! Still, she had those furs that had belonged to her mother. She admitted, also, wondering what the Rockies were like. If she did not marry him now, how long would he be gone? Six months?

Jack explained that he might be killed by Indians or desperadoes. In that case the wisdom of her course would undoubtedly be apparent. She could then marry someone else. But that was the reason a policeman would be desirable. And then he was only a sort of policeman himself, anyway. One more would make little difference. In the end they were married.

II

It was a gay little party of three that left Montreal for Vancouver the following Saturday. The red-headed Patrick pruned his speech and proved himself a most entertaining comrade, as he recounted his adventures in securing the return of divers famous criminals under the difficult process of extradition. He had brought safely back "Red" McIntosh from New Orleans, and Trelawney, the English forger, from Quebec; had captured "Strong Arm" Moore in St. Louis, and been an important figure in the old Manhattan Bank cases. He insisted on addressing Dockbridge as "Judge," and introducing him to all strangers as "me distinguished frind, the Disthrick Attorney av Noo York."

There were few passengers for the West, and the triumvirate easily became friendly with the conductors, brakemen, and engine hands upon the various divisions. The trip itself proved one unalloyed delight. Peggy sat for hours spellbound at the windows as the train sang along the frozen rails around the ice-bound shores of Superior and through the snow-mantled forests of Ontario. Sometimes the three in furs and mufflers clung to the reverberating platform of the end car watching the diminishing track, or held their breath in the swaying cab as the engine thundered through the drifts of Manitoba and Assiniboia toward Moose Jaw, Calgary, and the Rockies.

In the monotonous hours across the frozen prairie Peggy learned all the mysteries of the throttle, the magic of the reversing gear, the pressure-valve and the brakes, and once, when there was a clear track for a hundred miles, the driver, with his perspiring brow and frosty back, allowed her slender fingers to guide the dangerous steed. For an hour he stood behind her as she opened and closed the valve, pulled the whistle at his direction, and slackened on the curves. She was undeniably pretty. The driver had been stuck on a girl that looked a bit like her out on the Edmonton run. He opined loudly that by the time they reached Vancouver Peggy could send her along about as well as he could himself. He repeated this emphatically, with much blasphemy, to the fireman.

Peggy lived in an ecstasy of happiness. At odd moments she perused diligently her husband's copy of "Moore on Extradition." She didn't intend to be the man of the family—she was too sensible for that—but she saw no reason why a woman should not know something about her husband's profession, particularly when it was as exciting a one as Jack's.

145

Four days brought them within sight of the mountains, and the next morning, when they stopped for water, the whole range of the Canadian Rockies lay around and above them, their virgin summits sparkling in the winter sun.

"Glad you came, Peg?" shouted Dockbridge, hurling a featherweight snowball in her direction as she stood on the platform in silent wonder at the scene.

She answered only with a deep inspiration of the dry, cold air.

"Shure, ain't we all av us?" inquired McGinnis lighting his pipe. "Say, this beats th' Bowery. Th' Tenderloin ain't in it wid this. I'd loike to camp right here for the rest of me days!"

There was something so unlikely in this, since, apart from the mountains, the only visible object in the landscape was a watering-tank, that they all laughed.

Up they climbed into the glistening teeth of the divide, clearing at last the first Titanic bulwark, now in the darkness of Stygian tunnels, now bathed in glittering ether, until, sweeping down past the whole magnificent range of the Selkirks, they dropped into the boisterous cañon of the Fraser, and knew that their journey was drawing to a close.

The blue shadows of morning melted into the breathless splendor of high noon upon the summit of the world, then, reappearing, faded to purple, azure, gray, until the blazing sun sank in an iridescent line of burning crests. Night fell again, and the stars crowded down upon them like myriads of flickering lamps, while the moon swung in and out behind the giant peaks.

"Shure, 'tis a sad thing we can't ride in a train, drawin' th' county's money foriver!" sighed McGinnis as the sunset died over the foaming rapids.

"Ah, but we've work to do, Pat!" answered Peggy. "You mustn't forget Sam Andrews and the Boodle Bank. There's fame and fortune waiting for us."

On the run down the coast they held a council of war. Pat was to continue on to Seattle and arrest the fugitive, while Jack and Peggy hastened to Olympia to secure the Governor's recognition of their credentials and his warrant for the deliverance of Andrews to the representatives of the State of New York.

The Governor, a short, fat man, with a black beard, proved unexpectedly tractable, and not only issued the warrant, but invited them both to lunch. It developed that he had graduated from Jack's college. Oh, yes, he knew Andrews! Not a bad sort at all. One of those fellows that under pressure of circumstances had technically violated the law, but a perfect gentleman. Of course he had to honor their requisition, but he was really sorry to see such a decent fellow as Andrews placed under arrest. He was sure that Sam would take the affair in the proper spirit and return with them voluntarily. You must not be too hard on people! Everybody committed crime—inadvertently. There were so many statutes that you never knew when you were stepping over the line. He frankly sympathized with the fugitive, although obliged officially to assist them. You could not help feeling that way about a man you always dined with at the club. Well, the law was the law. He hoped they would have a pleasant trip back. He must return himself to the Council Chamber to a blasted hearing—a delegation of confounded Chinese merchants.

They took the train for Seattle, highly elated. They found McGinnis, together with the prisoner and his lawyer, awaiting them at The Ranier-Grand. Andrews proved to be another stout man, with a brown beard and a pair of genial gray eyes. As the Governor had stated, it was clear that he was a perfect gentleman. He apologized for bringing his lawyer. It was only, they would understand, to make sure that his arrest was entirely legal. He had no intention of attempting to retard or thwart their purpose in any way. Of course, the whole thing was unfortunate in many respects, but that he should be desired in New York to unravel the complicated affairs of the bank was only natural. Everything could be easily explained, and, in the meantime, the only thing to do was to return with them as quickly as possible. Altogether he was very charming and entirely convincing. He hoped they would not consider him presuming if he suggested that a few days in Seattle would prove interesting to them; there was so much that was beautiful in the way of scenery of easy access; and in the meantime he could get his affairs in shape a little.

Peggy thought that was a splendid idea. It would be mean to take Mr. Andrews away without giving him a chance to say good-by to his friends, and she wanted to see Victoria and Esquimault, and Tacoma. While Mr. Andrews (in charge of McGinnis) was arranging his business matters, she and Jack could do the sights. In the meantime they could all live together at the hotel, and no one need know that Mr. Andrews was under arrest at all. Jack saw no harm in this, and neither did McGinnis. Andrews was politely grateful. It was most kind of them to treat him with such courtesy. He hastened to assure them they would not have any reason to regret so doing.

Two days passed. The Dockbridges wearied themselves with sight-seeing, while Andrews busied himself with arrangements to depart. The favorable impression made by the prisoner upon his captors had steadily increased, and in a short time they found

147

themselves regarding him in the light of a most agreeable companion whom fate had thrown in their way.

"And now for New York!" exclaimed Jack, lighting his cigar, as they sat around the dinner-table on the evening of the third day after their arrival in Seattle. "How shall we go—Northern Pacific, Union, or The Short Line and across on The Rock Island?"

"Divel a bit do I care," answered Pat comfortably from behind an enormous Manuel Garcia Extravaganza, tendered him by Mr. Andrews. "Th' longer th' better, suits me. 'Tis the county pays me, an' I loike ridin' in the cars down to th' ground."

"What is the prettiest way, Mr. Andrews?" inquired Peggy, "You know the country. Where would we see the most mountains?"

Had it not been for the thick clouds of cigar smoke, they would have noticed the flash of Andrews' gray eyes which so quickly died away. He hesitated a moment, as if giving the matter the consideration it deserved.

"There's practically no choice," he replied at length, knocking the ash from his cigar. "They're all lovely at this time of year. The Rock Island route is longer, but perhaps it is the more interesting." He paused doubtfully, then resumed his cigar.

But Peggy, who at the thought of the trip had become all eagerness, had observed his manner.

"You were going to add something, Mr. Andrews; what was it?"

Andrews smiled. "Oh, nothing! I was about to say that if it wasn't such a tough journey you might go back by the Northern Montana and connect with the Soo. It's a magnificent trip in summer, but I dare say pretty cold in winter. Wonderful scenery, though."

"Let's go!" exclaimed Peggy. "That's what we are after—scenery! I don't care if it is cold. I've got my furs. Montana, you say? And the Soo? That sounds like Indians. What do you say, Jack?"

"Oh, I don't mind!" answered her husband. "Andrews knows best. He's been that way. Sure, if you say so."

Andrews hid a smile by lighting another cigar.

III

All day long the snow had been falling steadily in big, fluffy flakes. The heavy train ploughed through dense pine-clad ravines, beside torrents buried far below the snow, under sheds into whose inky blackness the engine plunged as into the bowels of the earth, across vibrating trestles, and up grades that seemed never-ending, where the driving-wheels slipped and ground ineffectually, then clutched the sanded rails and slowly forged onward. For two days it had been thus, and from the windows only the gently falling, ever-falling snow met the eye. Heavy clouds shrouded the shoulders of the mountains, and the gorges between them were choked with mist. And onward, upward, always upward groaned the train.

Inside Jack's compartment in the first Pullman sat the four members of our party playing cards, now on the best of terms. They had long since given up condoling upon the weather, and had settled down to making the best of it with cards, chess-board, and books. Between McGinnis and the prisoner flowed an unending stream of anecdotes and adventures. It could not be denied that the erstwhile bank president was a man of much culture and wide reading. He had studied for the bar, and from time to time astounded Dockbridge by the acuteness of his mental processes. This was the afternoon of the second day, and they were just completing their thirteenth rubber of whist.

The snow fell thicker as the light waned; soon the lamps were lighted and the shades were drawn. The through passengers on the train were few, and the good-natured conductor had adopted the party for the trip.

"We're 'most at the top o' the pass," he remarked, as he paused to inspect Jack's hand over his shoulder. "Should ha' made it an hour ago but for this blank snow. I never saw it so thick. Too bad you've missed the whole range, and to-morrow morning we'll be at Souris, and then nothin' but prairie all across Dakota. When you wake up, the mountains'll be two hundred miles west of you. Hard luck!"

"My trick," said Andrews. "What's that, conductor? Souris to-morrow morning? Any stops to-night?"

"Nope; clear down-hill track all the way. There's a flag station an hour beyond the divide—Ferguson's Gulch, and sometimes we stop for water at Red River. There's no regular station there, and Jim wants to make up time, so I reckon we'll make the run without stoppin'. Are you folks ready for dinner?"

The strain on the wheels suddenly relaxed, and it seemed as though the whole train sighed with relief. Ahead, the engine gave a succession of quick snorts, as if rejoicing at once more reaching a level. The train gathered head-way.

"She's over the divide," announced the conductor, taking a

149

bite from the plug of tobacco carefully wrapped in his red silk handkerchief. "Now Jim can let her run."

"What do you call the divide?" asked Peggy.

"The Lower Kootenay," he answered. "Oh, it's great here in summer! Finest thing in Canada, in my opinion."

"In Canada!" exclaimed Dockbridge, with a start. "What do you mean? Are we in Canada?"

"You've been in Canada since three o'clock," was the reply. "We cross the lower left-hand corner of Alberta—look on the map there in the folder. After makin' the divide we drop right back into Montana. They couldn't cross the Rockies at this point without leavin' the States for a few miles."

The conductor arose and unfolded the map.

"Ye see, here's where we leave Clarke Fork, then we skirt this range, turn north, followin' that river there, the north branch of the Flathead, and so over the line; then we turn and jam right through the range. Two hours from now you'll be back in the old U.S."

Dockbridge had started to his feet and was staring intently at the map. It was only too true. They were in Canada. In Canada! And they were holding their prisoner without due process of law! The warrant of the Governors of New York and Washington were valueless in his Majesty's Dominion. Did Andrews know? Jack pretended to study the map before him and glanced furtively across the table. Pat was scowling ferociously at the cards before him, and Andrews was lighting a cigarette. Apparently he had heard nothing—or had paid no attention to what the conductor was saying. With his brain in a whirl Dockbridge folded up the time-table and handed it back.

"Well, I'm getting ravenous," he remarked.

Just then the porter appeared from the direction of the buffet carrying their evening meal.

"Same here," echoed Andrews.

For an hour or more they lingered over the table, Andrews seeming in unusually good spirits. Dockbridge ceased to feel any uneasiness. He realized how easily he might have been trapped, but no harm was done in the present instance, for the minute section of Alberta which they traversed offered no opportunities for the securing of any legal process by which their prisoner could be released. Again, Andrews had not urged the route upon them; that had been Peggy's doing. And, moreover, was he not returning with them of his own free-will? No, it was absurd to have been so upset at such a trifling matter.

"What do you say to some more whist? You and I'll be partners this time, Andrews."

The things were cleared from the table and they began again. The speed of the train seemed to have increased, and the cars swayed from side to side as they sped down the grade. Peggy raised the shade and looked out. The pane was plastered with an ever-changing, kaleidoscopic crust of flakes that spat against it, dropped, clogged against the others, and sagged downward in a dense mass toward the sash. At the top of the glass the storm could be seen whirling down its myriads outside.

"What a night!" she ejaculated, as she pulled down the shade.

At that moment came a prolonged wail from the engine, followed by the quick clutch of the brakes. The wheels groaned and creaked, and the passengers tossed forward in their seats. Again the whistle shrieked. The train, carried onward by its momentum, ground its wheels against the brakes which strove to hold them back. Gradually they came to a stand-still.

The conductor rushed toward the door, and a brakeman hurried through with a lantern.

"Ferguson's Gulch!" he shouted as he ran by. "Must ha' signalled us!"

Dockbridge's heart dropped a beat, and he glanced apprehensively toward Andrews. The latter was smiling, but the hand that held his cigar trembled a very little.

"You're young yet, Dockbridge," he remarked, with slightly tremulous sarcasm. "There are one or two things still for you to learn. One of them is that a United States warrant is useless in Canada. You hadn't thought of that, eh?"

"Warrant is it? Shure this is all the warrant I want," replied Pat, snapping a shining Colt from his pocket. "Plaze don't git excited, me frind. P'r'aps ye don't know it all, yerself. Wan move, an' I'll put six holes in yer carcus!"

Dockbridge grasped Peggy by the arm and drew her breathless to her feet. "What is it? What is it?" she gasped, clinging to him in the aisle. Jack reached over and released the shade. Outside in the darkness red lights swung to and fro. A blast of icy air poured into the car from the open door. He hurried out into the vestibule. The storm was sweeping by swiftly and silently, and absurdly the motto of his old bicycle club flashed into his mind, "Volociter et silenter." The lamp above his head threw a yellow circle against the vast night. He stumbled down the steps and clung to the rail, putting his head into the sleet. It stung his face like the tentacles of a sea-monster. In the foreground stood the conductor, already white with the snow, his lantern swinging to leeward in the wind, shouting to a man on horseback. Four other mounted figures, their steeds facing the blast,

151

marked the point where the light ended and the night began again. Three train hands, each with a lantern, paced to and fro beside the car. Ahead could be heard the coughing of the engine. The man on horseback waved his hand in the direction of the train, flung himself heavily to the ground, tossed the reins to one of the others, and strode toward the car.

"Jones and Wilkes, hold the horses; Frazer and White, come along with me," he directed over his shoulder. He pushed by Dockbridge and climbed into the car. The conductor followed.

"Where is the officer and his prisoner?" he demanded in a harsh voice.

"Inside, your Honor," answered the conductor, shaking the snow from his coat. "This is Mr. Dockbridge, the District Attorney from New York."

"Umph!" grunted the stranger. He was an immense man with a heavy jet-black beard and hair in thick curls all over his head. A broad-brimmed sombrero cast a deep shadow over his features, heightening their natural unpleasantness. Two of the others now jumped upon the platform and entered the car, and Dockbridge saw that they wore some kind of uniform and that the lining of their overcoats was red. Peggy cowered to one side as the three strangers forced their way by her and paused at the door of the compartment.

"Is Mr. Andrews here?" inquired the one whom the others addressed as Judge.

"I am Mr. Andrews. This is the officer who holds me in custody."

The Judge turned to one of his followers.

"Serve him!" he growled.

The one addressed took from beneath his coat a bundle of papers, and selecting one, handed it to McGinnis, who let it fall to the floor without a word.

"Put up that pistol!" continued the Judge.

At this moment Dockbridge, who had listened as if dazed to the colloquy, now mastered sufficient courage to assert himself.

"Here! what's all this?" he exclaimed in as determined a manner as he could manage to assume. "What are you doing in my compartment with your wet feet? Who the devil are you, anyway?" He squeezed by his huge antagonist and took his stand by McGinnis.

The conductor and the majority of the train hands had crowded into the passageway and filled the door with their dripping and astonished faces. The officer handed another paper to Dockbridge.

"This is Judge Peters, sir; and this paper is a writ of habeas corpus returnable forthwith, sir," said the man.

Dockbridge glanced at the paper and saw that the officer's statement was correct. The paper was a writ ordering him to produce the body of Samuel Andrews before the Honorable Elijah Peters, Judge of the Supreme Court of Alberta, forthwith, and show cause why said Andrews should not be set at liberty. He was trapped. It could not be denied.

"Is this Judge Peters?" he inquired politely of the man with the black beard, who had taken off his hat and seated himself upon the sofa.

"I am," returned the other curtly. "And I now pronounce this car a court, and direct you to release your prisoner as detained by you without lawful authority."

He leaned forward and shook his finger threateningly at McGinnis. "Put up that pistol!"

McGinnis looked at Dockbridge.

"Put it up, Pat," directed the latter. "There's no occasion for pistols." He winked at Peggy. "Pardon my lack of courtesy in addressing you, Judge Peters, when you first entered. I was unaware, of course, to whom it was that I spoke."

The Judge shrugged his shoulders deprecatingly.

"I'm naturally taken somewhat by surprise, and hardly feel that I can do justice to my own position in the matter at such short notice. However, as the court is now in session, I can only ask the privilege of arguing the matter before your Honor. If I might be permitted to do so, I would suggest that the hearing take place in some larger space than this compartment, in which my wife desires speedily to retire." He looked inquiringly toward the Court.

"That's right, Jedge," spoke up the conductor. "Don't keep the lady out of her room. You can hold court in the baggage-car."

The black-bearded man grumblingly arose to his feet, leaving a large pool of water in the middle of the floor.

"As you choose. Bring along the prisoner, and be quick about it. I've got to ride fifteen miles to-night."

The crowd streamed down the aisle and into the baggage-car in front. McGinnis followed with Andrews.

"Shall I come along, Jack?" whispered his wife.

"No, stay here. I'm afraid we're beaten. I shall only spar for time, and try to invent some way out of it."

Peggy sadly watched his disappearing form. What a disgusting anticlimax! She reviled herself for being the one who had forced the selection of the Montana route. It was all her fault. When a man's

153

married his troubles begin! Jack would lose his job, and then where would they be? She had gotten him into the fix, and now she would do her best to get him out of it. She threw on his fur coat and cap and followed into the baggage-car. The Judge had seated himself on a trunk. Jack stood at his right with the warrant in his hand. A single lantern cast a fitful glare over the two, around whom crowded the passengers and train hands. Peggy heard her husband's somewhat immature voice stating the circumstances of the wreck of the Boodle Bank. The Judge seemed not uninterested. The crowd was getting larger every moment. Passengers kept coming in in every kind of dishabille, and last of all the engineer and fireman entered by the forward door. Outside, the huge engine hissed and throbbed as if impatient of the delay. Peggy slipped unseen behind a pile of trunks, snapped the big padlock through the staples of the door, then, hurrying back to the compartment, rummaged until she found Jack's box of cigars. Arming herself with these and with her copy of "Moore on Extradition," she made her way back to the baggage-car.

"Yes, yes, I know all that!" the Judge was saying. "But that's all immaterial. It ain't what he did. It's what right you've got to hold him in the Dominion of Canada on a warrant from a governor of one of the United States. Show me that, or I'll discharge the prisoner here and now."

"Excuse me, please," exclaimed Peggy, forcing her way through the throng into the open space under the lamp, "I thought you might like to smoke. Lawyers all like to smoke."

There was an immediate response from the Court.

"Well, I don't care if I do," remarked the Judge more genially. "Confounded cold out there in the snow waiting for the train. Thank y'."

He handed back the box, and Peggy passed it to the engineer and told him to "send it along." Then she whispered in her husband's ear:

"Read him that chapter on 'International Relations.' Keep it going for ten minutes, and we'll win out, yet. I've got a scheme."

Dockbridge took the book, opened it deliberately, and lighted a cigar for himself. Peggy pushed back through the spectators to the sleeping-car. Only a solitary brakeman remained outside in the snow, stamping and swinging his arms.

"Halloo, Mr. Sanders," said Peggy, "you ought to go in and hear the argument. They're having a regular smoke talk. It's so thick I can't breathe. They're giving away cigars. I should think you would freeze."

154

"Well, I'm froze already," answered Sanders. "I reckon I'll go in and hear the fun. Is that straight about the cigars?"

"Of course it is," laughed Peggy, while Sanders climbed on board. The snow swept by in clouds as Peggy gave one glance at the retreating form of the brakeman, and jumped down into the night.

IV

The Judge threw back his burly form against the side of the car and exhaled a thick cloud of smoke.

"Now, young feller, if you have any legal right to detain your prisoner, let's hear it. This court's goin' to adjourn in just ten minutes by the watch, and I reckon when it adjourns it'll take the prisoner with it."

The spectators, who had seated themselves as best they could, looked expectantly toward the New Yorker.

Jack arose, holding the book impressively before him. The gusts from the storm outside penetrated the cracks of the loosely hung sliding baggage-door and made the feeble lantern swing and flicker. The smoke from twenty cigars swirled round the ceiling. The conductor placed his own lantern on a trunk by Jack's side.

"If the Court please," began Dockbridge, "while it's entirely true that no warrant issued out of a court of the United States or by a governor of one of the United States gives any jurisdiction over the person of a fugitive who is held in custody in the Dominion of Canada, it is nevertheless a fact that under the principle of comity between friendly nations the government of one will not interfere with an officer of another who is performing an official act under color of authority." "Sounds well," said Jack to himself, "but don't mean a blame thing." "This principle is as old as the law itself, and is sustained by a long series of decisions in our international tribunals. The doctrine is clearly set forth by Grotius" "that ought to nail him!" "when he says: 'No nation will voluntarily interfere with a duly authorized officer of another nation in the performance of his duty, whose act does not interfere with the functions of government of the other.'" He pronounced this balderdash with much solemnity and with great effect upon the assembled train hands. "Now, your Honor, I am a duly authorized officer of the State of New York, the same being at peace with the Dominion of Canada."

"Bosh!" interrupted the Judge. "You're talkin' nonsense. I

155

won't be made a fool of any longer. Prisoner discharged. This court stands adjourned, and, as I said, it is goin' to take the prisoner with——"

A jerk of the train prevented the conclusion of his sentence. There came another pull from the engine, followed by a succession of violent puffs. The train started.

"My God! The engine!" shouted the fireman, making a spring for the door.

"Locked! Locked!" he yelled, and threw himself upon it. The conductor dived for the platform. The Judge started to his feet.

"This is an infernal trick!" he cried. "Stop this train! D'ye hear? Stop this train at once!"

But the train was gathering head-way every moment, and was fast dropping down the grade. A triumphant whistle shrilled through the night with a succession of short toots.

"For God's sake, open the door!" gasped the engineer. "Get a crow-bar, somebody! We'll be going a hundred miles an hour inside of a minute!" But no crow-bar was to be found, and the door resisted all their efforts. On rushed the train, thundering down the pass, swaying around curves until the frightened occupants of the baggage-car clung to one another to retain their foothold, and every moment adding to its speed. The baggage-man threw open the side door. The night dashed by in a solid wall of white.

"Damme! This is a crime!" roared the Judge. "I'm being kidnapped. Your Government shall be notified—if we're not all killed. Can't somebody stop this train? Do you hear? Stop it, I say!"

For an instant Dockbridge had been as startled as the others. Then it came to him in one inspired moment. Peggy was on the engine! A series of whistles came across the tender.

"Toot—toot—toot! Toot—toot—toot! Toot—toot—toot! Toot—toot!"—the old Harvard cheer that Peggy had heard echoing across the foot-ball field a hundred times.

Of course! She was going to fetch them out of Canada, and then to thunder with all the judges of the Dominion! He began to laugh hysterically. On and on, faster and faster, rushed the train. The pallid faces of the passengers and crew stared strangely out of the blue haze. Breathless, each man struggled to keep his footing, momentarily expecting to be dashed into eternity. The minutes dragged as hours, until at last, from somewhere in the rear of the train, the fireman returned with a wrench, and throwing his whole weight upon the padlock, quickly snapped its staples. The door burst open, sending him flying headlong. Through the car poured a

156

furious gust of wind and snow, blinding, suffocating, and into the midst of this jumped the engineer, and, clambering desperately upon the tender, disappeared.

Perhaps it was the dimness of the light, but Andrews had suddenly begun to look white and old.

At the same moment a red light flashed by alongside the track and the train roared across a suspension bridge without slackening speed.

"Red River!" gasped the fireman, clambering to his feet.

The blood leaped in Jack's veins. Red River! Then they were across the line. Peggy had won! God bless her! With a triumphant glance at the cowering Andrews, he turned upon the frightened crowd.

"You can't beat the Yankee girl!" he shouted. "Judge, you're right. We've adjourned court, and are taking the prisoner with us— into the United States!"